DEATH COMES O'ER THESE MOUNTAINS

A Saga of the Killing Rock Murders

TRAVIS SHORT

Publish Authority

A SPECIAL TRIBUTE
TO FRANK EASTLAND

As this novel goes to press, we are missing, from our midst, the person most responsible for it coming to fruition. Frank Walton Eastland, CEO and founder of Publish Authority was taken from us earlier this year. I will be eternally grateful to him for giving me the opportunity to bring my creative efforts before the public. His generosity, patience, encouragement, and counsel were inspirational, giving me faith in my ability as a writer. I will miss him.

Editor: Janet Silburn
Cover Design Lead: Raeghan Rebstock
Interior Design: Teresa Evans

ISBN 978-1-967213-13-9 (Paperback)
ISBN 978-1-967213-12-2 (eBook)

Published 2026 by Publish Authority,
www.publishAuthority.com
Printed in the United States of America

CONTENTS

All I am or ever hope to be I owe to my mother.

Abraham Lincoln

DEDICATION

To my grandparents, William Jefferson and Dency Hollyfield, and Monroe and Cindy Short, and my parents, James Ivory and Thurza Ann Short, all of whom persevered through adversity and hardship in the hills of Virginia and Kentucky, endowing me with persistence and the will to keep going when the winds of life blew against me. And to my daughter, Jennifer, who brought the Killing Rock Murders to my attention.

PREFACE

U.S. Highway 23 runs from Jacksonville, Florida, to Mackinaw, the most northern city on Michigan's lower peninsula. Route 23 was once known as the Dixie Highway; that nickname came about because after World War II, it carried southerners, especially the Appalachian diaspora from the coal fields of Virginia, Kentucky, and West Virginia, to Ohio, Indiana, Michigan, and other states, seeking better lives in the industrial north. Today, it is still a heavily travelled highway for newcomers to the north and the southerners who relocated but hold deep allegiance to their former homes, where they often return for visits.

As evidenced by each successive census, most coalmining towns lose population every year. Many young people leave for better opportunities as soon as they finish high school or drop out of school at the age of sixteen. Businesses have closed, leaving empty storefronts all along the major streets. Houses, once maintained by coal companies, are falling in, and citizens of all ages, especially the young, have become addicted to pharmaceuticals and other drugs, which are trafficked along Highway 23. This painful truth has given rise to the term *Heroin Highway* for the much-travelled route. Many local and state police task forces have joined in efforts to bring the drug activity of the *Heroin Highway* under control.

Troubles are not new to the route now occupied by U.S. 23. They were occurring in many places even before the turn of the twentieth century—none more so than a small section of that highway known as Pound Gap, which lies at the peak of Pine Mountain in Southwestern Virginia and Southeastern Kentucky. It is a passageway once crossed by Daniel Boone. It was the locale for the battle of Pound Gap in 1862, where General James Garfield led a force of eight hundred Federalists against a lesser army of Confederates, led by Major J. B. Thompson. There is a memorial near Pound Gap commemorating the battle. General James Garfield went on to be elected the twentieth president of the United States, only to be assassinated a few months after taking office in 1881.

That section of U. S. 23 connecting Virginia and Kentucky was inaugurated by the Governors Byrd of Virginia and Thompson of Kentucky on November 9th, 1927. A raised platform was constructed on the Virginia side of the gap. One week later, the same platform was the site of the last recorded lynching in Virginia's history. Governor Byrd ushered an antilynching bill through the legislature in 1883,

Not far from the site of the hanging is the Red Fox Trail, a loop walking path, named for Doctor Marshall Benton Taylor, whom you will meet in this story. And about five hundred feet back down the Virginia side of the highway is a stone monument, describing the murder of five people, four men and one woman, at Killing Rock on May 14, 1892. The graves of these victims can be found about four miles down the

Kentucky side of Pine Mountain, in a cemetery known as Murdered Man's Cemetery. This dire appellation resulted from the burial of at least twenty-five men and women who were murdered in Wise County, Virginia, or Letcher County and Pike County, Kentucky, from the beginning of the Civil War until the end of the nineteenth century.

Today, the serenity of the mountains and valleys from the vistas and overlooks on both the Virginia and Kentucky sides of Pine Mountain, in the vicinity of the Gap, belie the industrialization of the area, beginning at the turn of the twentieth century. The coal-rich mountains supplied nearly 800 million tons of coal between 1900 and 1965, delivered across our nation and shipped to other nations around the world. The views will not reveal how essential that coal was to the World War II effort. Nor will they tell of the founding and construction of a new city, Jenkins, Kentucky, lying at the foot of Pine Mountain, commencing in 1911 by Consolidation Coal Company.

More than 500 million tons of coal were dug from beneath the mountains near Jenkins and the surrounding communities of Letcher County during that time. Not only will the views fail to reveal these momentous coal operations, but they will not hint at the struggles and turmoil of the families who scratched out their livings from the soil before the industrialization of that Appalachian area in Southwestern Virginia and Southeastern Kentucky. The people of these areas welcomed the large coal conglomerates, which provided meager but steady incomes and company housing. Unfortunately, the end of World War II brought with it a reduced demand for coal from the area; this reduction, combined with diminished coal reserves, prompted the major coal companies to abandon their operations, leaving the people of the area with few employment opportunities. Many impoverished coal miners and their families left for jobs in the north, traveling the Heroin Highway, U.S. Route 23.

Poverty and lack of industry are not new to residents of Southwestern Virginia and Southeastern Kentucky. These conditions existed before and after the Civil War, but that conflict fomented new alienations, including animosities, grudges, and internecine feuds. Virginia was, unquestionably, a Confederate state, but along the "Trail of the Lonesome Pine" and Pound Gap, allegiances were mixed and confused. The same was true in the state of Kentucky, which had soldiers fighting in both the Union and Confederate armies. As a result, after the War officially ended, animosities continued, even between family members and close neighbors. The area had its share of lawless men and gunslingers, making life there in the 1880s and 1890s as dangerous as any part of the Wild West. Fortunately, a few stalwart lawmen and deputized civilians were as bold and bad as the men they pursued and captured or killed.

On the Virginia side, at the foot of Pine Mountain, lies the once-flourishing little town of Pound (The Pound), the oldest in the county of Wise. It was the natural watering hole and stopping-off point for people traveling through the Gap to and from the Kentucky side of the mountain and further into Wise County. Muddy wagon trails deepened each spring with the increase in traffic through the gap. Small restaurants, flop houses, and houses of ill repute sprang up along the trail, accommodating men traveling on business or simply looking for diversions from otherwise mundane existences. Since Letcher County, Kentucky, prohibited the sale or consumption of legal whiskey, thriving moonshining and bootlegging businesses were rampant in that county.

Moonshiners in Virginia sold small quantities of alcohol in Kentucky, but were not competitive against the illegal operations in Letcher County. As our story unfolds, Kentucky moonshiners were bringing their wares through Pound Gap to sell in the various cities of Wise County. This situation raised the probability of conflicts that would rock Wise and Letcher County and lead to murder. That murder, even today, engenders arguments and theories as to the guilt or innocence of the alleged parties to a memorable massacre at Pound Gap in 1892.

I have taken some liberties with facts to create this account of that murder, one of the most notorious in Virginia's history. Even so, I have remained true to the central issues leading to the slaughter of one family, the hunt and capture of the accused murderers, the trials that followed, and the uncertainty of the guilt of those who paid the ultimate price for the crime. I trust this story will stir interest in the history of the mountains where I was born and grew up as a coal miner's son. As a youngster, I passed through Pound Gap numerous times, unaware of the events that took place only a few hundred feet away from the Gap. Now, the reader and I can explore, together, the terrible events of May 14, 1892, and understand that the people who died on that day had hopes, aspirations, friends, and family who loved them. They should be remembered as more than names on a marker at Killing Rock and headstones in Murdered Man's Cemetery in Jenkins, Kentucky.

PROLOGUE

E arly in the morning, on October 27, 1893, a crowd gathered around the courthouse in Gladeville, Virginia, the county seat of Wise County. They came from the mountains and valleys of surrounding areas, some from as far away as the adjoining settlements of southeastern Kentucky. They came in wagons, on horseback, and on foot, some having begun their journey the day before. Women dressed in their finery, many carrying babies or holding the hands of small children, and men wearing dungarees and high-top boots, made their way along narrow muddy roads, hoping to arrive in time to witness an event that was fraught with doubt and uncertainty. Some people believed an innocent man was about to be hanged; others were certain of his guilt and eager to see that justice waited at the end of the hangman's rope.

A light rain fell most of the morning but dissipated as the sun broke through about nine-thirty. By 10:00 a.m. the rain stopped altogether, and a light fog that crawled along the valley floor evaporated. The weather had failed to dampen the celebratory spirits of the swarm of humanity, nearly five thousand in all, gradually settling in front of the courthouse and on higher ground, as close to the upcoming scene as possible. People watched from housetops, upper-story windows, and limbs of tall trees. The air was abuzz with excitement. But their loud clamor diminished to murmurs when the nearly one hundred armed men encircling the courthouse were addressed by the captain of the guard in a booming, authoritative voice.

"Keep to your posts, men, and don't let anyone pass through unless I say so."

He was addressing the Wise County Vigilante volunteers, mostly young boys still in their teens. They raised their guns to their chests and shifted nervously from one foot to another. The crowd pressed forward, inch by inch, toward the courthouse door. The guardsmen moved backward, not wishing to fire upon their own people, many of whom they recognized as neighbors and even kin.

A shot into the air stilled the crowd. And the voice of the captain of the vigilantes rang out again. "Hold your ground, men."

The surge toward the courthouse halted, and the discordant rumblings of the crowd ceased momentarily. The celebratory atmosphere faded into a morose silence. After a minute or two, the crowd regained its muted voice, as the participants attempted to make known their reasons for gathering on the muddy bank of the courthouse. Arms reached, pointing toward a second-story window. The impatience of the crowd grew louder once again, manifested in the rumblings that washed across the ever-increasing number of gawkers who had come to witness something none of them fully understood. The armed men shifted nervously in their stances, raising and lowering their guns just enough to display their readiness to fire upon their own people if it became necessary.

A hundred feet away at the corner of the courthouse, close to the adjacent jail, was a wooden gallows with steps, steep and without a handrail, leading to the boxed platform on which a hangman by the name of Charles Renfro stood. His arms were folded across his chest, his face, mostly hidden by a bushy black beard, was expressionless except for two dark eyes that focused on something in the distance, allowing him to escape eye contact with any of the people gathering around him, ten feet below. If he feared any retribution from the onlookers, he gave no indication in his outward appearance but stood stoically with the hangman's noose dangling just above his shoulder, moving gently in the breeze.

A tall man in bibbed overalls, who had just joined the crowd, spat a stream of tobacco juice onto the ground near his feet. He twisted his mouth as if to hide the fact that he was speaking. His words came in a whisper, aimed at a bonneted lady a few inches away. "What's happened to him? Thought it was time."

She didn't answer.

"Maybe they done kilt him already," the man said.

"They wouldn't dare." Her eyes widened at the thought of that possibility.

"Might be a blessin'."

The woman's indignation raised her voice above the noise of the crowd. "Ain't ever a blessin' to kill an innocent man."

"True," the man said. "If he's innocent, it would be a mortal sin."

"He's innocent enough."

"How might that be, Ma'am? How would you know?"

"I'm his wife."

The man looked away, avoiding the soulful look he saw in her eyes. After a moment, he was inclined to say, "I'm sorry for you, Ma'am." But when he turned back to where she stood, the woman had walked away. He watched as she moved closer to the courthouse. The guardsmen stepped aside and let her pass. She stood looking up forlornly at the second-story window, which slid open at that exact moment. A man, clothed entirely in white linen, an open Bible in his hand, appeared. His red beard, streaked with grey, left no doubt as to the man's identity. For more than thirty years, he had ministered to their spiritual needs, delivered their babies, tended to their sick, and protected them as a member of the law. Holding the Bible, he raised his arms above his head and began to speak, his firm voice audible, even to those in the back of the crowd.

"My friends, and even my enemies, you have come here today to witness an injustice, for I am truly an innocent man. You have come to see me hanged right before your eyes. You wonder if I will kneel before you and admit to a crime, an unholy crime, that I did not commit. If this is your reason for standing in the chill of this day, you might be disappointed.

I have no illusions. I know that the sheriff and the hangman will carry out the sentence passed upon me by the judge and jury. They will do their duties as required by law. I feel no animosity toward them, only pity, for I would not want the guilt on my conscience that will surely come to them in the end, for hanging an innocent man. Like all sinners, they will pay the price for breaking God's dictum: Thou shalt not kill.

"I will die today. But don't worry none. Don't pity me, for all is well with my soul. I have made my peace with God.

Jesus Christ, my brother, stands with me before you right now. If any man was ever ready to die, he was never more so than I am, and never in better company than Jesus Christ, an innocent man who rose up from the dead on the third day. So, shall I. After three days, I will leave that wooden coffin you see on the ground by the gallows. I will walk these hills and dales and valleys again to minister to my flock, to ease their minds, save their souls, and cure their ills as I have done all these many years.

Oh, for sure, I am not without sin, and neither is any man. But let me swear upon my life that murder is not one of the sins I have committed. Even if it was, my father in heaven would forgive me. No, no, I am not without sin, but I come to the gallows today purified, saved, and unafraid to meet my maker.

Having testified to my innocence, I now declare myself dead, and I will now preach my funeral. My sermon is taken from Revelation. Please bear with me as I relate my life and death to the passages that I have chose from that prescient text.

> The Revelation of Jesus Christ, which God gave
> unto him, to shew unto his servants things
> which must shortly come to pass; and he
> sent and signified it by his angel unto his
> servant John:
> Who bare record of the word of God, and of the
> testimony of Jesus Christ, and of all things
> that he saw.
> Blessed is he that reads, and they that hear the
> words of this prophecy, and keep those

things which are written therein: for the
time is at hand...
"I am Alpha and Omega, the beginning, and the
ending," saith the Lord, "which is, and
which was, and which is to come, the
Almighty..."
And when I saw him, I fell at his feet as dead.
And he laid his right hand upon me, saying
unto me, "Fear not; I am the first and the
last.
"I am he that liveth, and was dead; and behold,
I am alive for evermore, Amen; and have the
keys of hell and of death." (Holy Bible, King
James Version)

The condemned man read further through the Book of
Revelation, paused, and wiped away tears, then regained his
powerful voice through the remaining few verses. "Friends,
the events witnessed by John and spoke to him by God and
His angels are meant for me as much as for Jesus Christ, for
we are one and the same."

The preacher's blasphemy brought audible gasps from the
onlookers, but none spoke loud enough to be heard by those
standing behind the open second-story window.

The Bible reading lasted for thirty minutes more,
interspersed with comparisons of Jesus and John to the man
in white linen. He concluded his reading from the Bible with
"Amen and amen."

"My friends, and I know I have friends among you, many
who know of my goodness and my innocence. My enemies,
and I have enemies among you who have come to see my life
put to an end. But the life, my life that has been sanctified and

blessed by Jesus Christ, will not die today even though my body be dead for a short period of time."

The man's voice faltered, evidencing a pitiful moan that he subdued, heard only by those surrounding him near the window and a few in the front of the crowd. He turned away from the window, apparently asking for a chair that the sheriff brought to him. He seated himself and opened the Bible, leafing through it as if searching for a passage. After a moment, he handed the Bible to the sheriff, stood, and began preaching again.

"It is always sad to speak at a funeral, which I have done many times, but the event is made sadder when a truly good man is laid to rest. And sadness might be called for today if not for the blessed assurance that the man of which we speak was confident of his resurrection. Yea, though I walk through the valley of the shadow of death, I will fear no evil, for He is with me."

He continued speaking of the good deeds he had performed for those now about to witness his hanging, and the injustice of the sentence of death passed on him by the judge of Wise County. He lapsed for moments when he appeared to grasp for words, quoting various disconnected verses from the Bible. At last, he appeared exhausted and concluded his funeral with these final words to the onlookers.

"I am he that is dead and will live again. Like Jesus Christ, I will live forevermore, walking the fair hills of my Virginia home, waiting for the end time, praising my God for his goodness. I am appointed by God to be his messenger. I have been anointed to preach these words, to tell of the past, of events in our lives today, and of many wonders yet to come. I now bid you farewell, but I will return in a few days to walk among you."

The man, now flanked by the sheriff and a deputy, turned away from the window. After several minutes, the figure, dressed in a white linen suit made by his wife, Nancy, for the occasion, climbed the steps to the gallows box. When he reached the platform, he placed his hands behind his back; the sheriff tied them with a white handkerchief. The man knelt for a few moments, uttering a prayer that only he, the sheriff, two other men in the gallows box, and God could hear. The hangman slipped a white linen hood, matching the suit, over the head of the condemned man. He adjusted the noose about his neck so that the knot would sever the second vertebrae when the trapdoor fell.

The hangman descended the steps and stood beneath the trap door, which was supported by two large beams. At execution, they would be knocked loose, leaving the trapdoor on which the condemned man stood, supported by a single rope. Alongside him, the sheriff stood, holding a hatchet. The hangman had transferred below the gallows, waiting for the order to knock loose the two supporting beams.

The sheriff whispered words of apology to the figure in white, then uttered the fatal words, "Ready." The hangman landed a deafening hammer blow against one of the beams and then the other. The beams fell away, and the trapdoor shuttered but stayed in place. The condemned man fell to the floor of the gallows, thinking his end had come.

The sheriff lifted him to his feet and steadied him with the noose hanging about his neck. After a moment and another whisper to the condemned, the sheriff exclaimed, "Ready," loud and clear. He raised the axe and struck a blow against the rope. He cried out in a trembling voice, "May God have mercy on this poor man's soul."

The body in white linen shot down through the opening,

coming to an abrupt stop, then twisting round and round in one direction until the rope was tight. The direction reversed, and the body twisted in the opposite direction. This continued for more than a minute until the body hung motionless at the end of the rope. The sheriff ran from the gallows and vomited by the corner of the courthouse.

After nineteen minutes, two men emerged from the crowd of onlookers. One removed a knife from his pocket and severed the rope. The body crumpled into a lifeless heap on the ground. They knelt over him. One placed a stethoscope over the heart of the man.

"They're doctors." The loud whispers moved in waves across the crowd, taken up and passed on by others until there was silence again.

"Maybe he's still alive, like he promised," someone said after a moment.

"He ain't Jesus," another man proffered.

"Amen and amen," someone else responded.

The doctors stood and talked in whispers to each other. Then one turned to face the crowd. His voice broke, the timbre becoming bass, like the sound of a funeral dirge, as he announced. "This man is dead. Who will claim the body?"

A pale woman, plainly dressed, a sun bonnet covering her head—the woman who had peered up at the window during the sermon and then stood near the gallows as the timbers were knocked away from the trapdoor—came to the body and bent to touch his face. She stood, facing the onlookers, viewing them with something akin to pity. "He's my husband," she said. "I'm taking him home."

PART 1

CALEB'S STORY

1

WAR COMES TO THE MOUNTAINS

Caleb Wilkens, the eldest of three children, was born in 1845 in a settlement that was later named Whitesburg in Letcher County, Kentucky. When he was twelve, his father, Martin, died in a logging accident. Following her husband's death, Caleb's mother moved her children and their few belongings to live with her widowed brother-in-law, Eli, in Virginia on the South Fork of the Pound River. Caleb worked the fields for his uncle, cut firewood and dug coal for the fireplace, and helped with farming chores. He milked two cows daily and, in the spring, plowed fields behind an almost-blind mule named Codger.

The school was held in the Old Regular Baptist Church, where the only textbook was the Holy Bible, the King James version. It sufficed to teach a class of twelve children, ranging in age from seven years old to fifteen. Reading was augmented by simple math, known as factoring. Since the teacher was a self-taught man, math consisted of basic addition and subtraction. Caleb and his siblings attended school when the weather permitted. And work in the field in the spring did not take priority over school. He was eager to learn and could quote many Bible verses by the time he was fourteen. He particularly liked the Psalms, especially Psalm 121, *"I will lift up mine eyes unto the hills from whence cometh my help…"*

Life with his uncle was not easy for Caleb, but he was content to know his mother and younger brother and sister were safe with a warm bed at night and sufficient food every day. He was grateful to his uncle and felt obliged to work as hard as possible to please the man who saved his family from destitution.

By the end of three years, Caleb had grown to more than six feet tall. With his brawny physique and deep blue eyes, he cut a figure that would surely have been thought handsome to most of the young women he would meet. But there was only one girl, close to his age, who lived within walking distance of his uncle's farm. Her name was Polly Maggard, a pretty auburn-haired young woman of seventeen, almost a year older than Caleb. He first laid eyes on her at the Old Regular Baptist Church, where he attended school and church services sporadically. One Sunday morning, their eyes met when they grew restless of the interminable sermon being preached and began to look around from pew to pew for diversion. Their eyes met in mutual attraction, and they held their gaze until the moment grew awkward. Caleb hoped for an opportunity to speak with her, but Polly's mother led her away after the service was over.

Caleb was unable to get the beautiful girl off his mind. He could think of nothing else all the next day. That evening, after chores were done, he rode the old mule to the Maggard farm, two miles away. The farmhouse was much like that of his uncle, three rooms with a single fireplace in one of the bedrooms that also served as a sitting room, with cane-bottom chairs encircling the hearth. Caleb and Polly sat before the fire for the next hour, but Polly's mother frequently entered the room, ensuring nothing untoward happened. After four or five weekly visits to the Maggard farm, Caleb and Polly were left alone long enough to allow them to embrace and kiss. He knew then that this was the girl he would marry. He began to think about his future and how he might be able to get some land for himself and build a house. He hoped he could do so by the time he turned twenty. But events were about to happen that would put his dreams on hold for a long time. And he would worry that Polly might find someone else.

Fort Sumter in the harbor of Charleston, South Carolina, was attacked by rebel forces and civilians in April 1861, the month Caleb turned sixteen. The news of the attack reached Caleb and his few neighbors in July of that year. The reason for the attack had little meaning to the inhabitants of southwestern Virginia. To Caleb's knowledge, slavery did not exist, and the two or three negroes near Pound, Virginia, lived lives like his own; they all were poor, living off the land and bartering with each other. The issue of state rights, the other purported reason for the Rebel attack, was foreign to Caleb, and he received no satisfactory explanation when he sought answers from his uncle. He knew armies were being raised to fight for the Confederate cause, but he did not understand why. At sixteen, he thought himself too young to join the army. Besides, the Bible taught him that it was wrong to kill.

Caleb's ideas changed in January 1862 when news of the

atrocities committed by Union Forces in Northern Virginia and Kentucky reached the inhabitants of Southwestern Virginia and Southeastern Kentucky. They learned that the Yankees had burned the courthouse in Paintsville, Kentucky, and laid waste to other small towns. They were already nearing Pikeville. Any man in their path who was suspected of supporting the South was conscripted into the Union army. The devils in blue would soon be at Pound Gap and attack the Confederate garrison encamped there. Only a few residents of the communities on both sides of Pine Mountain supported the Northern invasion; everyone else would be at the mercy of the Yankees unless they were stopped at Pine Gap.

Caleb and his family were made aware of a threat to their home when an army lieutenant, dressed in a Confederate grey overcoat with yellow trim and a red sash, rode up on horseback. He described the brutality of Union forces and the burning and looting of homes and businesses in northern Kentucky and Virginia. The lieutenant was alerting every family near Pound of a probable invasion from the Kentucky side of the mountain. He was seeking volunteers to join the garrison at Pound Gap.

"It is imperative that we stop the barbarians before they come into Wise County and burn every home and business in our county. Every man able to fire a gun is needed to man the Confederate fort at the top of the mountain."

After a troublesome night with little sleep, Caleb made a decision that would change his life. He would volunteer to serve with Major J.B. Thomson to defend the Gap against General James Garfield and his overwhelming forces. Caleb was joined by John Wright, who, at twenty, had a reputation as a gun-for-hire, always on the side of the law. They underwent one week of drilling and rifle training before marching up Pine Mountain to join Major Thompson at the garrison.

Snow on the mountainside had collected in drifts of seven feet or more, and the trek up the mountain was made through continuous four-foot drifts. By the time the small platoon of sixteen men reached the garrison, their feet were almost frozen. Each man was issued a muzzle-loading rifle and a small amount of powder and caps. They were all cautioned about the scarcity of gunpowder and supplies.

Major Thompson gathered his men, numbering nearly four hundred. He addressed them in a loud baritone voice, giving Caleb assurances of the rightness of the cause for which he had volunteered. He was confident that his fellow soldiers were equally inspired.

"Men," the Major said, "I don't need to tell you we are facing a dangerous enemy who is invading our land, burning our homes, and taking advantage of our women in our absence. We learned this morning that General Garfield's Union soldiers have reached Little Elkhorn Creek. Snow is hampering their progress, but we expect to be engaged in battle by the day after tomorrow. I know that each of you will do your duty and stand your ground. You must use your ammunition accurately and sparingly. You can be sure that I will stand with you through the impending ordeal that must surely come. Be brave. Be prayerful. May God be with you."

The soldiers, led by Sergeant Major Samuel Hall, shouted "Hear! Hear! God save Major Thompson."

The Major turned and disappeared into the small hut behind him that served as his command headquarters.

The sergeant called the men to order, then issued the command, "Dismissed."

Before the troops could disperse, a scout on horseback rode up to the gate, which was opened to allow the horse and its rider to pass through. The man, dressed in civilian clothes, dismounted and ran into the Major's headquarters. The sergeant followed him.

The soldiers anxiously waited, wondering what news the scout was bringing to the Major. They learned shortly when Sergeant Hall called them all to attention.

"Soldiers," he said. "Gird yourself for battle. Our scouts have learned that the Yankees have already passed through Pikeville, burning and looting. They are encamped near Little Elkhorn Creek, four miles from here. The snow is letting up, and General Garfield's army can be on our doorstep by tomorrow morning. Remember your training and your instructions. May God help us and our righteous cause."

Muster was called the next morning at five a.m., and the men were all reminded again of their duties. They were instructed to check their weapons, making certain they were ready for firing.

Because John Wright was an expert marksman, he was assigned to the most forward rifle pit, more than a dozen of which surrounded the compound housing barracks, offices, and supply cabins. Caleb was assigned with John and was instructed to keep the rifles loaded while John picked off the Union soldiers as they advanced.

A quiet settled over the mountain as the Confederate soldiers waited in position for all hell to break loose. The battle was announced with sporadic rifle shots in the distance; the exchange of fire between the two cavalry. The rifle fire increased in intensity and was more rapid as the Union forces began to appear between the trees down the Kentucky side of the mountain. Soon, Union Cavalry burst through the brush, wielding swords and pistols. When the Confederate snipers began hitting their targets, the Union Cavalry fell back into the woods. After a short lull in fighting, a massive force of Union ground troops rushed forward. Twenty minutes later, after heavy losses, Major Thompson ordered a retreat; the Confederate forces abandoned the garrison and rushed down the Virginia side of the mountain towards Pound, leaving seventeen dead and wounded. Caleb and John Wright climbed from the rifle pit and ran back toward the garrison main gate, looking for a hiding place. Two Union soldiers on horseback cut off their escape path and ordered their surrender. They dropped their rifles and raised their hands, now at the mercy of the Yankees.

General Garfield's standing order was that no prisoners were to be taken. Caleb and John Wright were shackled and blindfolded and held in a small hut while Union soldiers inspected the sixty log huts that served as barracks, commissary, hospital, and headquarters. Gunfire told Caleb that the wounded rebels were being shot. He guessed that he and John would be next. A lieutenant came into the hut. He removed the blindfolds and spoke to Caleb and John.

"You look like a sensible young man, and my guess is that you don't wish to die. My orders are that I should take no prisoners because we don't have enough men to guard them. But I am authorized to make the two of you a bargain."

Neither Caleb nor John spoke.

The lieutenant continued. "This army will soon be on the way to Lynchburg, Virginia. If you are willing to join us and fight for the Union, you won't be executed. I have no choice."

The lieutenant left the hut, leaving the two prisoners to ponder their predicament.

"Hellfire and damnation, John said, "I ain't ready to meet my maker; how 'bout you, Caleb?"

"Me neither, I guess, but I don't feel real good about it."

Moments later, the lieutenant returned to the hut. "How 'bout it, boys; you with us, or not?"

Neither man spoke.

The lieutenant stooped and removed the shackles from Caleb and John.

General Garfield was a candidate from Ohio for the office of U.S. Representative and had previously requested a transfer to Washington, D.C. He was directed to proceed towards Lynchburg, Virginia, to meet up with Colonel Samuel Downing and Lieutenant Colonel John Patrick. The march took 23 days with minor skirmishes with small groups of Confederates along the way. Caleb and John Wright arrived nearly naked and worn out. They were issued replacement uniforms, removed from dead soldiers, still stained with traces of blood.

After two days of drilling, the Ohio Fifth Infantry divisions were ordered to proceed to Washington, D.C. Caleb was happy to be transported by train, his first such ride ever. Despite the constant noise and jostling, he slept better than he had done since before he left home. The 5th Regiment divisions engaged in skirmishes and battles in the countryside around Washington for 2 months. During the Battle of Bull Run, they guarded the trains. On September sixth, 1862, they marched through Frederick, Maryland,

Middletown, and Boonville to Antietam. One hundred eighty men of the Ohio 5th moved onto the battlefield under the command of Major John Collins because Colonel Patrick was ill. The Regiment received fire from rebels who were in earthworks about fifty yards away. They returned fire and were soon engaged in hand-to-hand combat.

The battle raged for most of an hour, during which Caleb stayed as close to John Wright as possible, knowing him to be an excellent marksman and fearless. It soon became apparent that it was every man for himself, with both men losing the ability to differentiate enemy from friendly troops. John and Caleb stumbled across a field of bodies, continuing in the direction of a farmhouse close to a corn field where a battle had raged earlier in the day. As Caleb attempted to step over a bloody soldier, a hand from below grasped his ankle and held tight.

"Help me." The young man managed a whisper that told Caleb he was dying.

Caleb bent close to his face attempting to understand what the fallen soldier was attempting to say.

"You from Ohio?"

"No," Caleb said, "Virginny."

The soldier coughed blood onto his face and attempted to wipe it away from his mouth with the back of his hand. He handed a small, blood-stained tobacco pouch to Caleb.

"Take this," he said. "My little brother sent them to me for my last birthday."

"What are they?"

"Marbles."

"What do you want me to do with them?"

The soldier did not respond. His eyes became fixed.

"What do you want me to do with them?"

John placed his hand on Caleb's shoulder. "He's dead, Caleb."

Caleb remembered Psalm 121 as he closed the soldier's eyelids. "May God be merciful." He placed the soldier's uniform cap over his face.

The two men bent low to the ground and scurried across the field to a small shed behind the farmhouse. They sat on the ground, hidden by weeds growing close to the house, and waited for nightfall. Caleb took the small pouch from his pocket. He loosened the drawstring and poured six glass marbles onto his open hand. The futility of the War washed over him. He sobbed.

John grasped his shoulder. "Don't cry, Caleb. Men don't cry."

Caleb would always remember that John Wesley Wright knew himself well and was a man to be reckoned with. He was happy to have him as a companion even though the two of them had very little in common.

News of the defeat of Confederate forces at Pound Gap reached Caleb's mother and uncle a few days after the disastrous retreat of Major Thompson's forces. Caleb and John Wright were reported as casualties by the Confederate Commander in Mineral City, Virginia. As soon as the snow melted, permitting travel through the footpaths, Caleb's mother walked the two-mile trail to the home of Polly Maggard and gave her the sad news of Caleb's probable death. Polly fell to her knees and prayed for the safe return of the boy she loved; she refused to believe he was dead.

"He'll come back to me," she said. "I know he will."

From their hiding place, Caleb and John waited for darkness, knowing that both armies would be exhausted from a day of intense fighting. It had grown too dark for either army to retrieve their dead and wounded. Even the sentries would be exhausted and not very alert. It was a good time for the two men to put distance between themselves and the army they were deserting. They stayed shoulder to shoulder as they crossed a wide trench filled with dead and dying soldiers; the same trench they had crossed earlier in the day when they first decided to make their escape.

John bent over a dead soldier and began removing his boots.

"What are you doin', John?" Caleb asked.

"Gettin' me a good pair of shoes. Mine are worn out and won't make it back home."

"Mine are worn out too, but I don't want a dead man's shoes."

John stepped across another body and, after a moment, raised a pair of boots near his chest. "Take these, Caleb. You're goin' to need them soon."

Caleb stepped out of the trench and walked on ahead of John, bending low as he moved toward the woods.

John tied both pairs of shoes together and placed them across his shoulders. He followed behind Caleb.

When John caught up with him, Caleb asked, "Where are we headin'?"

"South," John responded curtly.

"What's wrong with you?"

"Nothin', Caleb, 'cept you got to pull your own weight."

John handed him the boots. "Carry your own damn boots. You will be glad you did, 'fore we get back to Wise County."

Caleb took the boots. The two men walked deeper into the

woods, feeling their way through the undergrowth and from tree to tree.

John grumbled, "What I wouldn't give for a crescent moon; problem is, the Yanks would have the same moon. We'll just keep goin' like we are now."

"Where are we goin'?" Caleb asked. "If I am goin' to follow you, I should know where we're goin'."

"South," John responded without explanation.

"Where south?"

"Just south for now, Caleb. I know if we head south, we will run into Harper's Ferry, and from there, we will figure out how to avoid the Yankees and get ourselves down to Charlottesville. There ought to be Confederates in Charlottesville or close by. So, we can get food and outfits and even a horse."

For the moment, the direction they walked was not important. Their main concern was getting distance between them and Antietam and avoiding sentries or advance cavalry, which regularly patrolled in the vicinity of encampments of both armies.

"How far do you reckon we are from home, Caleb?" John looked for confirmation of his own assessment of the trip that lay before them.

"I guess three hundred miles or so. At least that is about what I figured we walked to get to Antietam, not countin' that train ride we had."

"The way I figure it is that we walked in a lot of circles, probably nearby four hundred miles altogether."

"Four hundred miles? Dang, John, I didn't think it was that far."

"No, we'll go in a much straighter line if the Yankees don't get in our way."

"I think we better stay away from Harpers Ferry. What if the Rebs ain't there?"

"Maybe," John said. "We just need to get close enough to get our bearin's."

The two men walked on in silence, except for the rustling of leaves and brush made by their own feet. After three hours of walking, they fell, exhausted, onto the ground. A horse whinnied in the distance. Caleb and John scurried to find shelter under a growth of vines and shrubs. After three or four minutes, the horse and rider broke through the brush and galloped past the men, not more than six feet away.

Both men fell to the ground and crawled back to their hiding place.

"That was too close." John shivered at the thought of being captured and returned to the Union command. He and Caleb would be shot for desertion, especially since their lives were spared at Pound Gap.

After resting for a moment, Caleb sat up. "I think we ought to move on. I bet the Yanks bivouacked for the night. We should be makin' distance between us and them."

"Guess you're right. The way I figure, Harpers Ferry is southwest of us, maybe twenty miles. We need to get to the west of the Potomac."

"Which way is west?" Caleb looked skyward for a glimpse of the moon but saw only the night sky through the tree branches.

"The way we'll be goin'." John sat on the ground and removed his boots. He slipped the boots of the dead soldier onto his feet. "Better get you some walkin' shoes on, Caleb. It's a long way to Pound Gap."

They picked their way through the woods until sunrise.

Considering it unsafe to walk farther until nightfall again, they walked deep into a thicket and lay back against a tree.

"Hear that?" Caleb sat up straight.

"Shhh." John put his forefinger to his lips. "Listen, sounds like someone's hurtin'."

He crawled twenty feet toward the sound, then turned and motioned for Caleb to join him. He pointed towards a dark heap on the ground, listening for sounds coming from that direction, moans of someone in great pain. He crawled across the ground with Caleb following closely behind. After a moment, he recognized the uniform of a Union cavalry officer lying under a dead horse, probably the same officer who passed close to them during the night.

The officer spoke in hushed tones, obviously laboring to make a sound. "I am glad to see you boys. Glad you're not Rebs."

John and Caleb got closer but said nothing, fearing the Union officer might have his pistol at the ready. It was a good time to be wearing a Yankee uniform, even if it was tattered and dirty after 4 months of continuous wear.

"Nothing to worry about, boys. I need help," the officer grunted.

"What happened?" Caleb asked.

"My horse stumbled over a downed tree and broke his neck. I tried crawling from beneath him, but my leg is in too much pain." His command of English reflected his West Point training.

"We'll see what we can do." John moved closer.

"What outfit are you with, boys?"

Neither John nor Caleb answered. They set about the task of freeing the lieutenant. They broke two limbs from the tree that lay across the path and used them as levers to partially raise the dead horse off the cavalryman's leg. Anguish was evident on his face as he slid backward away from the horse.

"I owe you boys my life. If you're on the run, I won't turn you in."

"Guess we are," John said. We're headin' back to pound Gap."

"Where's Pound Gap?"

"Virginny, Pine Mountain." John was reluctant to reveal more than he had already said.

"You Rebs?"

"We ain't Yanks." John reached alongside the horse's saddle and lifted a rifle out of its holster, making certain the officer had no advantage should he decide to take them into custody.

"You won't need that," the lieutenant said. "I owe you boys my life. Where'd you get Union outfits?"

"We got captured. We don't hate nobody. We just want to git back home," Caleb assured him.

The officer pulled a small map from his pocket and unfolded it. "See here. If you're going to get there by way of Harpers Ferry, you might not make it. We just took control of the ferry last week and have soldiers patrolling for at least ten miles in all directions. You should head due west to Shepherdstown. You'll cross the Potomac there, then turn southwest to reach Kearneysville and head south for Winchester, Virginia." He tapped the page with his forefinger to emphasize where Shepherdstown was located.

"We're goin' 'round Harpers Ferry for sure." John gave the officer his arm and helped him to his feet.

Caleb broke off a piece of the tree limb and handed it to the injured man. "A crutch," he said.

"Three to four days, you ought to be in Virginia." The

officer tapped the map again for emphasis, pointing at a spot on the map across from Kearneysville, West Virginia. "Virginia's no more than 20 miles south of here."

"Where you goin', Sir?" Caleb asked.

"Harpers Ferry."

"Are you walkin'?"

"No," the lieutenant said. "They'll be sending a search party out from Harpers Ferry soon. I should have been there four hours ago. You boys better get moving before they find me."

"If you got a compass on you, you won't be needin' it anytime soon."

"I do have one." Reaching into his pocket, he said, "I hope it survived my fall." He pulled out a tarnished brass locket and flipped open the cover. "Still works," he said.

Caleb accepted the compass as he smiled at the lieutenant with modest gratitude. He picked up his gun. From the ground

John stood stiffly and saluted the lieutenant. "You got anythin' to eat in your saddlebag, Sir? We ain't et in two days."

"Some hardtack and a few pieces of jerked beef. You're welcome to it." He slipped a water pouch from his belt and handed it to John. "You'll need water too."

John bent over the dead horse and put his hand inside the leather bag. He pulled out a packet wrapped in corn shucks, unwrapped the hardtack, and held it up for Caleb to see, then turned to the lieutenant. "Thank you, Sir."

"Before we part, do you mind telling me your names. Boys?"

John responded. "I'm John Wesley Wright, and this here is

Caleb Wilkens. We hail from Pound, Virginia, and your name, Sir?"

"Lieutenant Joshua Cummins, Mobile, Alabama."

"Alabama? Why are you fightin' for the Yanks, Sir?"

"Gentlemen, a man is only as good as his word. And I took an oath at West Point to defend the United States against all enemies, foreign and domestic. The states that joined South Carolina in rebellion are enemies of my nation. That does not mean that I have no compassion for my fellow countrymen who live in the South and fight for her."

John saluted again. "You are a true gentleman, Lieutenant Joshua Cummins."

The officer leaned on his crutch and returned the salute. "Good luck to you. If we never meet again on earth, I will see you in heaven. God save the Union."

"God save Virginny," John said.

When they had travelled about a mile, Caleb asked, "Do you think we can trust that Yank, John?"

"I think so, Caleb. I'm a good judge of horseflesh, and he seemed trustworthy to me."

"Maybe," Caleb said, "but we need to put a lot of distance 'tween us and him."

They hastened their pace, traveling in daylight, fearing to stop and wait for nightfall, but understanding that they needed to walk further into West Virginia, as far away from Harpers Ferry as possible.

By the end of the second day, the hardtack and jerked beef had been eaten, and their water pouch was almost empty. They reached the Potomac River and filled the pouch. Even though the water might be unsafe to drink, they had no other source. They walked along the river's edge and found a small skiff tied up to a piling. Fearing they might be seen, Caleb and John waited in the growth alongside the river until the sun began to set. Only one oar was in the boat, making rowing against a quartering current a difficult task. An hour later, they were across the river, on the outskirts of Shepherdstown. They rested in the tall grass for a while before continuing their journey.

"I think Shepherdstown is off to our right," John said. "Maybe we should head southwest now, find a place to bed down for a few hours."

"I'm gittin' mighty peckish, "Caleb said. "We need to find somethin' to eat soon."

"Let's git some rest first. We can catch a chicken 'round those barns later after they come to roost." He pointed to two barns or outbuildings in the distance.

"What good's a chicken, John? We ain' got no matches, and we ain't got no fahr."

"You got a flint on that gun. I'll make a fahr."

Traveling mostly by night, six days later, the two men found themselves standing on a road east of Winchester, Virginia. They moved off through the woods to a back road that led to a farmhouse south of the city. A clothesline was bent low to the ground with washing out for drying. John watched while Caleb made his way across an open field. He reached the clothesline and began removing a shirt.

"Hold it right there, Yank," the woman's shrill voice

commanded. "You blue devils ain't stealin' nothin' else from me."

Caleb dropped to his knees with his arms raised above his head. "I ain't no Yank, ma'am, honest I ain't."

The woman moved closer, her rifle pointed at Caleb's head. "You devils done kilt my man and took my boy off to fight up north. You done burnt half this city, and you stole my chickens and runned off my cow. You ain't takin' nothin' else from me."

"Ma'am," Caleb said, "Them Yanks captured me too and took me and John up to Antietam to fight. We escaped a few days ago and are tryin' to get back home to The Pound."

As Caleb pleaded for his life, John stealthily moved in a wide circle, allowing him to get behind the woman. He crept slowly behind her and clasped his arms around her waist. The rifle fell to the ground. The woman slipped from his grasp and dropped to her knees beside Caleb, her hands raised in prayer.

"We ain't goin' to hurt you, ma'am. We just need some hep. John reached his hand to her and helped the woman to her feet. We just got to git out of these garbs 'fore we git shot by our own people."

The woman got up slowly, her hands trembling. "Don't harm me," she said. "I ain't got much left, but I'll share."

"We're sorry to ask, but we ain't et in two days, 'cept some acorns and hickory nuts. If we can git a bite to eat, we'll be on our way."

"Come on in the house. I got a pot of beans on the stove. They ain't much, but they'll go good on an empty stomach."

The woman set a bowl of pinto beans, a sliced onion, and a cornpone on the table. "You boys be seated," she said. "It ain't much, but I'm thankful to the Lord fer it."

"'Scuse me, ma'am, but do you think we can wash up 'fore we eat. It's been a while since I had clean hands, and I shor don't want to sit down at your table without washin'."

The woman pointed to a small table against the wall. Caleb poured water from a tin bucket and washed his hands with a piece of lye soap. After he finished, he walked to the kitchen door, opened it, and emptied the pan on the ground outside. He handed the wash basin to John, then pulled back a chair and sat. "If you don't mind, ma'am, can I ask your name?"

"Lucinda Gray. My husband, bless his sweet soul, was Samuel Gray. The Yanks kilt him a month ago."

"We're mighty sorry, ma'am," John said.

"And your names?" Lucinda asked.

"I'm John Wright, John Wesley Wright, and this here is Caleb Wilkens. We got captured by General Garfield at Pound Gap some months ago. "To be honest, ma'am, I can't remember; fact is, I don't even know what month it is."

"September," she said, "almost October."

"We're goin' to be havin' some cold nights soon. You wouldn't happen to have some old coats we can git, do you, ma'am? Somethin' we can wear over these uniform coats?" Caleb opened his jacket to show it was worn thin.

"I think so," Lucinda said. "After dinner, I'll look for something for both of you."

They took their seats at the table. Lucinda bent her head in prayer. "Thank you, Lord, for this food. We are grateful to have it in the midst of troubles for our blessed state of Virginia. We trust, Lord, that you will continue to provide for us. Kindly bless Caleb and John and make their burdens light as they continue on their journey home. Please bless our soldiers and their great leader, Robert E. Lee. Amen."

"Amen," Caleb and John said in unison.

After dinner, Caleb got up from his chair and walked out to a woodshed across the yard from the kitchen. He began chopping wood for the woodstove. After a few minutes, John joined him. They stacked the chopped wood under the shed.

While they worked outside, Lucinda searched through old clothes that belonged to her deceased husband, Samuel. She found two winter coats, old but serviceable. She tied the coats in separate bundles, each with a worn quilt.

"I wish we could pay you, ma'am," John said, but we ain't got a penny 'tween us."

"You don't owe me, boys. If you fight for Virginia, I owe you."

"Thank you." John turned for the door, followed by Caleb.

"Wait," Lucinda said. "There's something else I want to give you."

She pushed the kitchen table aside and pulled back a small woven rug. Underneath was a wooden cover, which she removed. Seeing the surprise on the two men's faces, she explained, "A hidden tater hole; Samuel built it last year when the war started."

She disappeared down a ladder into the cellar. When she returned, she held up four jars of green beans. "I don't want to give you more than you can carry."

The men gratefully accepted the jars of beans and put one jar in each pocket of the coats Lucinda had just given them.

"I hate to ask after all you've done for us, ma'am," John said, "but you don't have any matches to spare, do you?"

"None to spare, but I'll give you a few. Do you have water?"

"Yes, ma'am." Caleb held up his water pouch. "We filled these up from your well. Thank you for everything."

"God bless you, boys. I hope we can meet again after we run all the Yankees out of our land."

The sun was setting when Caleb and John slipped across the yard, beyond the sheds where the woods thickened. By then, a chill was in the air. They removed their Union coats and turned them inside out. They would still provide warmth while concealing their Union army origin. With the sun setting to their right, the two men headed south, facing a trip of two hundred fifty miles to their homes in the hills of southwest Virginia.

2

COMING HOME

Snow was falling in mid-November when a haggard and weary young man staggered from the forest and knocked on the door of Joseph Martin, a farmer in Guest Station, Virginia. He carried a weak, barely conscious soldier on his back. When the door opened, John Wright bent forward and eased Caleb onto the kitchen floor, his feet protruding onto the threshold.

"He's awful sick," John said before the robust farmer could speak. "I been carryin' him on my back for the past two nights."

"Lord, help us," the farmer exclaimed. "Bring him on in."

John pushed Caleb's feet aside and closed the door. "Sorry to impose on you, but we just about can't go no further without some hep."

"Where you comin' from?"

"Antietam, up in Maryland. We been travelin' for the past two months about, avoidin' the Yanks all the while."

"Bring that boy next to the fire." The farmer shooed a cat

from a rocking chair in front of the fireplace and motioned for John to set Caleb in front of the warmth. "How long's he been sick?"

"A week or more. I think he's got the Croup. He's had an awful high fever and has been out of his head for the past two days."

The farmer put his hand to Caleb's forehead. "This boy is burnin' up. He may have lung fever. We better git Doc Taylor to see him."

"Where would he be?" John inquired.

"Gladeville, if he ain't out on a visit to hep somebody else. He lives in Scott County but spends pert nigh most of his time in Gladeville with his uncle, who is teachin' him medicine."

"I don't think Caleb can stand too much jostlin' 'round. He's 'bout gone to meet his maker."

"No, we'll get Doc Taylor to come here if we can."

John's usual controlled demeanor wavered, and tears filled his eyes. "Be a shame if he don't make it home after all we been through."

"I want to hep boys, but I don't even know your names or if you ain't part of a Yankee outfit."

"I'm John Wright, and this is Caleb Wilkins. We're both from The Pound." John thought of adding that he also lived in Letcher County, Kentucky, but decided he did not need to explain anymore at that moment. "And your name, sir."

"I'm Joseph Martin. My wife, Dency, is down at the church heppin' some widows and mothers who lost their husbands and sons at Munfordville. We just learned of that awful battle that took place in September. Been a while gettin' word of our loved ones back here."

"Where's Munfordville?"

"Kentucky; don't know 'zactly where it is."

"It's good of your missus to hep others."

"We lost our son, James, at Manassas. He was just eighteen. Dency feels like she owes him somethin', and this is her way of payin' it."

"How do we git holt of this Doc Taylor?"

"I'll have to ride over." Mr. Martin took a heavy Mackinaw coat off a hook on the wall. "You come hep me git my wagon hitched up. I may have to bring the doc back with me if he don't ride his own horse."

"Do you want me to come with you?"

"No, I'm goin' to stop by the church and bring Dency home 'fore I go so she can hep care for the boy until the doc can git over here."

Dency Martin was a pretty woman, not more than thirty-eight years old. Her head was covered by a scarf, which she removed as soon as she entered the house, revealing her dark hair, pulled into a bun. The brisk weather she had just passed through had added a rosy color to her cheeks. She removed her coat and hung it on a hook on the wall where her husband had earlier removed his Mackinaw. She extended her hand to John, "I'm Dency Martin."

"John Wright, ma'am; glad to make your acquaintance."

"Likewise," she said, then turned to the young man who appeared to be sleeping in the rocking chair before the fire. "And this boy must be Caleb. My husband says he is mighty sick."

"Yes, ma'am, we think he's got lung fever; been that way for more than a week."

"Let's get him into bed and get something on his chest. Doc Taylor may not be here for at least two to three hours if he's coming at all."

"Ma'am, he ain't had a bath in at least six months; no tellin' what he smells like under them clothes he's wearin'."

"It's alright," she said, "I can wash the bedclothes after he's gone."

John helped Caleb to his feet and held him upright while they walked together to a room adjoining the kitchen. Dency turned down the bed covers while John slipped off Caleb's coat and shirt.

John sat by Caleb's bed as Dency prepared a linseed poultice. She placed a wool baby blanket on Caleb's chest and applied the poultice.

"I wish I had some opium or Dover's powder to ease his pain. There's some chicken broth on the stove. I'll warm it up. Maybe you can get him to drink some. Alcohol might help, but we don't keep any here. I hear tell there's plenty of moonshine to be had in Wise County, though."

She left the room, then returned with a cup of broth. "Maybe you can get him to drink this."

John lifted Caleb's head off his pillow and held the cup to his mouth. Caleb slowly responded, taking several sips before he motioned "no more." He lay back on the pillow, breathing easier than John had seen in several days. After a few minutes, he appeared to fall asleep.

John and Dency sat before the fire, waiting for Joseph to return with Doc Taylor. The flames flickered. John stirred the fire with a poker and placed two large lumps of coal on top.

When he sat, Dency said, "I understand you boys are from

Pound. It's unfortunate you couldn't have made it home without being delayed any further."

"Well, ma'am, I couldn't be delayed by better company than you and Mr. Martin."

"That's nice of you to say, John, but I know you are eager to get home. Your friend could stay with us if you want to go on ahead tomorrow."

"No, I couldn't do that. We been together since the Battle of Pound Gap. I ain't leavin' him 'til he can go with me. I'll be glad to sleep in the barn while he stays here if that's better for you."

"We wouldn't hear of it," she said. "And I know Caleb is happy to have such a good friend."

"Ma'am," John said, "if you don't mind me sayin' so, you shor talk awful nice, like those officers from West Point. I hope to learn to speak that way one day."

"You will, John, if you really want to. I teach school at our little church. If you ever want to join us, you can."

"Thank you, ma'am. I'll shor give that ample thought."

———

Doc Taylor was a young man, not yet thirty. He was ambitious and driven by a desire to learn about the world and make a name for himself. He admired his uncle, Doctor Daniel Hollyfield, who served with the Confederate Army until he lost a leg and an arm in the battle of Greenbrier River. The battle occurred before West Virginia broke away from the state of Virginia. A citation from the commanding officer, General Henry Jackson, described Doctor Hollyfield's bravery as he assisted with the amputation of his own leg. He returned to Gladeville, Virginia, after his injuries, but no longer practiced medicine extensively because he was unable to travel to see the sick who needed his services. Instead, he devoted much of his time educating his young nephew, Marshall Benton Taylor, in the art of medicine.

For three hours, Dency and John watched over Caleb as they waited for Joseph to return with Doc Taylor. Twice more, Dency applied the warm linseed poultice to the small wool blanket on Caleb's chest. He drank a few more sips of the chicken broth she brought to his bedside, an indication that he was gaining some strength.

Three hours had passed when the horse-drawn wagon could be heard from inside the house as it traversed the gravelled road leading from the main road to the house. The wagon stopped for a few minutes, then could be heard moving toward the barn.

Dency left the bedroom, anticipating her husband and the doctor. A knock on the door was followed by the entrance of a tall, red-bearded man with bushy hair, matching the color of his beard. Mrs. Martin, I presume; and I am Doc Taylor." He removed a glove and extended his hand. "My pleasure," he said. "Where's the patient?"

"He's in here." Dency motioned for the doctor to follow.

"Oh, yes," Doc Taylor said, "your husband is putting the horse away. Said he'd be up shortly. Because it's so late, I'll be spending the night. I hope you don't mind."

"We'll be happy to accommodate you, Doctor Taylor."

As Dency and John looked on, the doctor placed a stethoscope on Caleb's chest. "Doesn't sound good. How long has he been like this?"

"A week or more," John said.

"Why'd you wait so long to get some help for him?"

"We been on the run from the Yanks, Doc."

"Why didn't you stay and fight?"

"We was on the wrong side. We got captured at Pound Gap and took north with General Garfield. Then we was sent to fight at Antietam with an Ohio regiment. We escaped nigh on to two months ago and headed south."

"Sounds like you're lucky to be alive," the doctor said.

"Yes," John responded, "and we owe a lot to a woman up near Winchester who hepped us with food and clothes. And, if Caleb survives, we owe these good folks here more than we can ever repay."

"I'm happy you boys have almost made it back home." The doctor turned to Dency. "What have you been treating him with?"

"He's got a linseed poultice on his chest, and he drank a little chicken broth. I don't have anything else to give him."

"I have some opium powder. That might ease his pain and let him rest easier." He opened his valise and pulled out a red-colored tin, then lifted a small jar with clear liquid from the bag. "Alcohol and opium, not too much, I always say, but a little does wonders to ease aches and pains. I use it myself on occasion."

Joseph Martin could be heard when he entered the kitchen. He came to the bedroom and stood alongside his wife. "How's he comin', Doc?"

"I guess we'll know more in the morning. Rest is what he needs now."

After Caleb was sleeping soundly, Joseph Martin, Dency, and Doc Taylor stood by the bedside as John Wright sat on a chair close to his friend. "Come and sit by the fire," Dency said. "I'll make all of us some hot cocoa. I think we could all use something warm to drink right now, don't you, Joe?"

Her husband nodded. "Yes, that would be good."

"If you folks don't mind, I'll just stay beside Caleb." John moved his chair closer to the bed. "I'm awful tired. I aint't slept for at least two days."

Dency crossed the room and pulled back a curtain. She removed two quilts and a pillow. "You can make yourself a pallet on the floor if you want to stay with Caleb. I wish I could do something more, but we only have one other spare bed, and the doctor will sleep there."

"That's fine," John said. "I want to be right here if Caleb needs me. We've took care of each other a long time, and I don't want to leave him now. Besides, I ain't slept in a bed since last March. A pallet will feel real good."

The next morning, Doc Taylor checked on his patient early while Joe Martin performed his chores at the barn. The doctor applied a linseed poultice to Caleb's chest and gave him a small drink of moonshine, containing opium powder. Fifteen minutes later, Caleb was sleeping.

"Best thing he can do right now," the doctor said.

John stood, "If you don't mind, ma'am, I will excuse myself, and when I come back, if I can bother you for a pan of warm water to wash up with, I will shorly appreciate it."

On his way to the outhouse, he met Joe, returning from the barn with a milk pail. "All that from one cow?" he asked.

"She's a good 'un, best Jersey I ever had."

"My folks have got a Jersey. She's a good one, too. I can't wait to get back home and milk her like I used to do."

"Where do they live?"

"Our land and house are in Whitesburg, a few miles from Little Elkhorn Creek. After the war started, I took my Ma to

South Fork in Pound to be near my brother. I s'pose she's still there."

"Know exactly where that is. Bought me some good Kentucky moonshine when I was there a few months ago."

"I bet I know who you bought it from, Jason Blevins."

"How would you know?"

"'Cause he makes the best shine around, and he don't care who knows he makes it. I understand that before the war, the Feds hunted all over his property for a still, but ain't ever found one."

"I heard that too, but you can't never tell what's true."

"Pity for sure," John said. "Ain't nothin' wrong with a smidgen of moonshine on occasions, 'specially on a cold mornin'; that is if you don't let it take hold of you."

Joe picked up the bucket. "A God-fearin' man won't let the devil take control just 'cause he takes a little nip ever so often." He turned back to the footpath without denying or confirming where he bought the moonshine. "See you inside."

When John returned to the house, he filled a wash pan with warm water and took it outside to wash his face and hands. He returned to find that Dency had prepared a breakfast of fried eggs, pork, and cornmeal gravy. She set the table for four. Dency bowed her head. "Thank you, Lord, for bringing us safely together on this day. We are blessed in this house to have the good company of Doctor Taylor, John, and Caleb. We pray for a speedy recovery by Caleb. We are appreciative of all you give. Please keep our brave soldiers in your good grace. Bless this food, Lord. We are truly thankful. Save our great state of Virginia from the northern invaders. Amen."

After breakfast, Joe and Doc Taylor went to the barn to

hook up the wagon for the trip back to Gladeville. John sat by Caleb's bedside, watching his good friend sleep. He continued his vigil while Joe drove the doctor to Gladeville in the horse-drawn wagon. Dency rode with them to the Old Regular Baptist Church to teach her twelve students.

In the early afternoon, as John dozed in the chair beside Caleb's bed, he heard someone call his name. Startled from sleep, he thought it was Joe Martin returning from Gladeville.

Caleb stirred and sat up in bed. "John, where are we?"

"We are in Guest Station."

"Whose home is this?"

"Joe and Dency Martin. They have let us stay here since yesterday."

"Where are they now?"

"Mr. Martin is takin' Doc Marshall Taylor back to Gladeville, and Dency is at her church, teachin' school. The doctor got here yesterday evenin' and took care of you."

"My chest hurts awful." Caleb rubbed his palms across the compress on his chest. "What happened to me?"

"Doc says you have lung fever. You are lucky to be alive."

"But I want to get home, John, and I know you do too."

"As soon as you're better. When you can walk, we'll get Mr. Martin to take us home."

"I want to see Polly. I hope she didn't give me up for dead and marry somebody else."

The wheels creaked and screeched as the horse-drawn wagon made its way along the twelve-mile rocky terrain from Guest Station to Gladeville. An intermittent light snow with wisps of wind accompanied the driver and his two passengers for the first hour of the trip. By the time they reached Gladeville, snow stopped, and the sun broke through. An hour later, the horse pulled his burden up a narrow road leading to John Wright's small one-room cabin in a hollow near Pound. He had brought his mother there from Whitesburg when the war started. The cabin was close to John's older brother, Clayton, who promised to look after her while John was away. There was no sign of life or indication that the house was occupied.

"Guess they're not expectin' me." John let go a deprecating laugh. "My ma probably went to my brother's house since she ain't heard from me in so long; prob'ly give me up for dead."

"Can I give you a ride someplace else?" Joe Martin asked.

John pointed up the hill to where the winding road continued. "No, it ain't far up there. You better just git Caleb on home 'fore the weather turns."

They shook hands, and Joe turned the wagon, heading back down the road with Caleb, his hair down onto his shoulders, looking gaunt and unkempt, sitting next to him. Two miles further up the main road, Caleb directed Joe to a large log home surrounded by a rail fence. As the horse-drawn buggy neared the front porch a bearded man appeared at the door, his gun in hand. "Who goes there?" he called out to the driver, then stepped onto the porch, his gun raised at the ready.

Aware that internecine differences caused people of the area to suspect everyone, friends and strangers alike, Joe Martin stood, raised his hands, and responded loudly. "Joe Martin Guest Station."

By then, a woman, about forty, appeared on the porch alongside the man.

"What can we do for you?" The man yelled.

Joe shouted, "I have your son, Caleb, with me."

The woman ran down the steps toward the wagon, shouting to the top of her lungs. "Glory be. Thank ye, Jesus."

Caleb stood. "It's me, Ma. I've come home." He jumped from the wagon and enclosed her in his arms.

A LONG WAY

No words were spoken for minutes as mother and son clung to each other, their sobs penetrating the air above the sounds of the joy of family members who came running to embrace Caleb. Caleb's mother fell to her knees, her hands raised in prayer. "Thank you, dear God, for answerin' my humble prayer and returnin' my good son to me."

Caleb's Uncle Eli walked down the steps to the wagon and offered his hand to Joseph Martin. "Sir, thank you for bringin' our boy home. I don't know where you found him, but we shor are happy you did."

"Oh, I didn't find him; he found me. He and his friend John Wright staggered into our house five days ago, and we took care of him and his buddy."

"I'm Eli Wilkins." He pointed to Caleb's mother, who was clinging to her son. "And this is my wife, Ginny. Won't you come in the house and rest a spell?"

"I shor wouldn't mind a few minutes before a fire. It ain't been a bad trip, but after more than two hours of airish weather, I'm 'bout ready for a soft seat." He rubbed his behind and laughed.

"Could you eat a bite 'fore you git started back home?"

"No, thank you, "Joseph said, "just some hot coffee will be fine."

Ginny had saved a small portion of a pound of coffee she purchased several months earlier. "I can give you some coffee mixed with chicory if that's alright."

"That'll do just fine, ma'am." She carefully spooned enough into a pot to make three cups of hot drink, which she served in her best cups. Joseph clasped his drink with both hands and sipped the hot brew, making sounds of satisfaction between sips. "That'll warm the cockles of a man's heart. Thank you, Mrs. Wilkins."

"Ginny, please," she said.

Caleb was too weak to do much talking, but around the fireplace, in a subdued voice, he related his experiences after getting captured at Pound Gap. "Mr. Martin and his wife, Dency, took real good care of me. And Doctor Taylor came to Guest Station from Gladeville to git me on the mend. I been blessed by these folk, shor 'nuff."

After an hour, Joseph Martin got up from his chair. "Thank you, folks, for your kind hospitality. I got to get movin'; still nearly two hours back to Guest Station. Let me know when this boy is well. Dency and I will be prayin' for his recovery."

Caleb stood and threw his arms around Mr. Martin. "Thank you, sir, for all you done for me. Please tell Mrs. Martin I am grateful for her care. When I am good enough to travel, I'll ride your way and pay my respects."

"You'll be most welcome, son," Joseph replied.

Eli walked with Joseph to the porch and watched while he

climbed aboard his wagon, drove down the small trail onto the main road, and disappeared into the woods.

"What a nice man," Ginny said after Eli returned to sit before the fire.

Caleb pondered why Uncle Eli introduced Ginny as his wife, but he was hesitant to ask. His mother sensed his uncertainty. "Uncle Eli and me was married while you was gone, Caleb. We hope you don't mind."

"It's alright, Ma, I love Uncle Eli like I did Pa." He stood and gently touched his mother's face. "He's done us all like we was his own."

"It's biblical," she said. "It's right there in the Bible, Deuteronomy."

"I'm glad, Ma. Honest."

She hugged him. Thank you, Son."

Then they were quiet, both content that their conversation had taken place. After a moment, Caleb spoke. "Ma, I got to git a bath. I ain't washed nothin' but my hands and face since I last saw you. And I got to go see Polly."

"Not this evenin', son," Ginny said. "You need to git some rest. I'll heat some water and pour you a tub, and I'll git you some clean clothes. We'll take you to see Polly tomorrow, early."

Caleb was too weak to offer much resistance, but he had thought of seeing Polly almost every minute since meeting attractive Dency Martin. The encounter heightened his recollections of pretty Polly and how sweet she smelled. The idea that she was now only two miles away caused an uneasiness he needed to resolve. "I guess she don't even know I'm still alive, and maybe she got herself a new sweetheart."

"No, Caleb," his mother said, "we see her at church, and

she always wants to know if we have heard from you. She told me she won't ever give up believin' you'll come back to her."

"I need to go to her now, Ma."

"Not this evenin'. Eli will ride over to her house and let her know you've come back to us, but that you ain't in any shape to ride over there tonight." She went to the kitchen and added coal to the cook stove, then placed a large pot of water on the stove.

"You can bathe here in the kitchen," she said.

Caleb was awake before dawn the next morning. He was gaunt and still very weak after two weeks of the debilitating illness that almost took his life. But he was determined to ride to the Maggard farm, two miles away. He saddled his uncle's best horse, Major, hoisted his foot into the stirrup, and swung his leg across the saddle.

Ginny came onto the porch just in time to see him ride up the rock-strewn road, along the rail fence, on his way to see Polly, the girl she knew her son would marry one day. Tears filled her eyes at the thought of losing Caleb again, this time for good. She had prayed repeatedly for his safe return home, and now she would pray for his happiness, wherever he might be. She turned back into the house, seated herself in a rocker before the fire, and rocked back and forth contentedly. She silently thanked the Lord again for Caleb's safe return.

Giving no thought to the brisk wind on his face, Caleb brought Major to a fast trot. Eight months earlier, he'd bid Polly goodbye, believing that a skirmish at the top of Pine Mountain would send General Garfield and his troops back to northern Kentucky. Instead, that army marched toward Antietam in victory with him and John Wright as captives. He was not proud of taking up arms against the Confederates and would never speak of it again unless he was forced to explain his reasons for doing so. Thoughts now were of Polly. He believed General Lee and his army would soon be victorious, and Virginians could live in peace once again. He and Polly would be married, raise a family, and live in tranquility in the hills of southwestern Virginia. He urged Major on as the Maggard homestead came into his view.

As Caleb dismounted, Polly burst through the doorway, calling his name. "Caleb! Caleb!"

He bounded up the steps and wrapped the young girl in his arms. "I'm never leaving you again."

They kissed, locked in an embrace. Caleb held her close while her tears of joy wetted his shoulder, and her subdued sobs told him of her joy at his return.

She pulled away and stepped back. "Let me look at you. You ain't well," she said.

"I've been down with lung fever, but I'm doin' much better. Seein' you is what I needed most of all."

"You're still the most handsome boy I know." She smiled broadly and placed her hand gently on the side of his face.

"And you're purtier than ever. I weren't about to die and leave you to marry somebody else."

"If somethin' happened to you, I would just be an old spinster. Come inside," she said, "and git out of the cold."

"Soon as I tie up Major, I don't want him to go runnin' off."

Back on the porch, he kissed her again. "You goin' to marry me, Polly?"

"If you want me to, I will for sure."

Caleb swooped her up in his arms and carried her across the threshold. They sat before a lively fire, holding hands. Shortly, they were joined by Polly's younger brothers and sisters, sitting on the floor, asking Caleb to tell them about his adventures.

"Ain't much to tell," he said. "I got captured at Pound Gap and taken to Maryland. Me and John Wright walked home. "How far?" They wanted to know.

"A long way," Caleb said wistfully. "It was a long way."

4

A BEGINNING

Caleb slowly regained strength at home with his mother, Ginny, tending him. He insisted that he was well enough to be up helping his uncle Eli with the farming chores, but Ginny wouldn't hear of it. His confinement was made bearable by the daily visits of Polly to his bedside. During these visits, Caleb and Polly made plans to marry after her twentieth birthday in August, four months after Caleb would turn nineteen, giving him time to acquire some land and build their own cabin. Knowing that Polly would be his wife, Caleb's spirits were buoyed, and he was given renewed incentive to fully recover from his ailments.

They realized their plans were tenuous at best, aware that a civil war was raging across the country with both Union and Confederate troops frequently passing through Pound Gap on their way to join battles in Kentucky or Virginia. With their homes on South Fork only a few miles from the gap, their families were constantly vigilant, fearing that Union raiders might venture off the much-travelled trail. They also had to fear wandering Confederate deserters who roamed the mountains to avoid capture by the Yankees or their own troops. And there was always the possibility that Caleb, who was eligible for conscription by the Confederates, might be discovered living at home. Conscription was not likely because he was officially listed and assumed dead, resulting from his capture at the Battle of Pound Gap a year earlier. Eli and Caleb kept their rifles loaded, ready to fire if anyone from either army approached in a threatening manner.

News of the war was sparse and usually weeks late in reaching the remote hills and valleys of Wise County. Anyone sending and receiving mail made the trip to the post office in The Pound by foot, wagon, or horseback, traveling over frozen, cragged roads and snow drifts in winter and muddy wagon ruts in summer. Occasional copies of the *Richmond Inquirer* or *Lynchburg Times Dispatch* reached a few prominent addresses in Pound, and the news they contained slowly made its way by word of mouth to the ears of residents who absorbed the tardy news with relative equanimity, believing their fates were in the hands of the Lord.

The Old Regular Baptist Church not only condemned sinners by name at each Sunday meeting but lifted their voices in prayer for Robert E Lee and the Army of the Potomac. Whatever news the elders of the church had been made aware of was passed on to the congregation. But mostly, the folks of the mountains knew little about the war other than the ominous word-of-mouth news of sporadic skirmishes, occurring along the Trail of the Lonesome Pine and the state line at Pound Gap. Past Christmases had been celebrated with mountain music, bonfires, and the firing of guns on January 5th, the Eve of the Epiphany. Now, it was instead marked with prayers and quiet reflection by the people of Pound and surrounding communities. Nothing was done in celebration to attract the attention of Yankee scouts or deserting soldiers who may be roaming the woods.

An unusual warm spell blew through the valleys near the end of January, melting snow on the hills and turning the roads into mud and mire. Caleb was fully recovered and able to do his usual chores. He was eager to investigate land available for claiming on Bold Camp, ten miles from South Fork, but the trip would be too much for old Major, struggling through mud and deep troughs in the roadway. There was always a danger of debilitating injuries to a horse traversing such muddy conditions. He hoped for several days of warm weather to dry the roadway, or wintry weather to freeze it firm again. Near the end of January, he got his wish when snow came down in torrents for three days, leaving drifts of three to four feet. Caleb reconciled himself to the thought that his plans for getting started building a cabin would be on hold until spring. But his thoughts changed with good news brought to him by John Wright, during the worst weather all winter.

Eli saw the tall rider on a black stallion approaching, plodding slowly through the deep snow, his face covered with a red bandanna to break the chill of the cold February day. He stepped onto the porch, his gun raised to the ready, and called Caleb over his shoulder. "Come here, Son." He pointed with his weapon to the dark figure. "You know who that might be."

"Can't say, Uncle, right off."

"Git your gun, Caleb."

"Yes, sir." Caleb left the porch and returned in a moment with his rifle raised to his shoulder. He had no desire to shoot anyone but would do so if his family were threatened.

They stood with their guns ready to fire as the horse and

rider continued forward, apparently undaunted by the guns pointed in his direction. When the horse reached the gate, the rider dismounted, removed his face-covering, and called out Caleb's name. "It's me, Caleb; it's John Wright."

Caleb propped his gun against the porch rail and ran down the steps and through knee-deep snow to the gate, where John was standing. He unchained the gate and threw his arms around John. "You're a sight," he said, "a blessin' for shor."

"It's good to see you well again, Caleb. I been worryin' 'bout you but had too much goin' on to get up here to see you."

"What brings you out here now in this weather?"

"I got good news for you, and it couldn't wait."

"Must be mighty important."

"It is, Caleb. I'm on my way to Culpepper; goin' with Riley Mullins…"

"The old man? He's older than my Uncle Eli." He turned his head towards his uncle, watching from the porch.

"No, his son, Riley, my age. He's puttin' together a company of cavalry soldiers, men who can ride and shoot on horseback. They'll be part of the Virginia Cavalry when they get to Culpepper."

"And you're goin'?"

"Yeah, I got to go."

"Why? You already done your bit, just like me."

"No, Caleb, we're 'bout to lose this war if we don't start winnin' soon. They got a crazy general by the name of Tecumseh Sherman and a drunk named Useless Grant layin' waste to Vicksburg, Mississippi. For all I know, they done took that city and are marchin' right over to Virginny."

"How'd you know that?"

"I rode over to Guest Station last week to git some books from Dency Martin, and I seen a copy of the *Richmond Gazette*, told the story."

"What do you think you can do 'bout that?"

"I owe them Yanks for makin' me fight against Virginny. Bet you feel the same way."

"No," Caleb said, "I seen enough killin' already, and I couldn't kill nobody."

"You did at Sharpsburg when you had to."

"No, John, I never did aim my gun in anger." He put his hand into his pocket and pulled out six marbles. "You remember that poor Yankee boy from Ohio that gived me these?" He held out his hand for John to see. "I can't ever forget that boy. I bet he wasn't as old as me."

"Don't change my mind none. That young feller woulda kilt me and you if he weren't kilt first. You got too big a heart, Caleb."

They stood for a moment, quiet as their emotions settled, then Caleb spoke, "Come on up and meet my Uncle Eli." He walked towards the porch, beckoning John to follow. On the porch, John and Eli shook hands.

"Come in the house and warm yourself," Eli said.

They sat on chairs near the open fireplace.

"Might do that for a spell," John replied, "then I gotta git goin'. I just come to give Caleb some good news, which I ain't told him yet." He laughed. "'Cause he ain't let me ketch my breath."

"Pa," Caleb said, "this is John Wright, the feller who saved my life. He carried me on his back for at least ten miles, I was told."

"Praise the Lord," Ginny said from the kitchen. She came into the front room, carrying a coffee pot and cups. "Guess you can use somethin' warm, Mr. Wright, after ridin' through such awful weather. We can't git any more coffee, so it is mostly chicory but drinkable."

"This is my ma, John," Caleb said.

John stood and tipped his hat. "Why, yes, ma'am, I rightly could stand a mite of somethin' hot. I'll take it black if you don't mind."

Ginny filled three cups and then returned to the kitchen.

Caleb raised his cup towards John. "I shor am ready for some good news. Since getting' back to health, this weather has kept me housebound, except for the few times I got down to see Polly."

"Well, you know I told you young Riley Mullins was pullin' out soon, headin' up to Culpepper."

"Yeah." Caleb leaned forward in his chair, eager to hear the rest of what John had to say.

"Old man Riley has got hundreds of acres staked out up in Bold Camp. Guess he's got at least twenty acres of bottomland cleared, and he plants it each year. I understand he's got a ten-acre piece with a cabin built on it, not much bottom land, but enough to raise a small garden."

"How much does he want for it?"

"That's the good news, Caleb. A dollar an acre, but he just wants someone to help him plantin' and hoein' when spring comes each year."

"He don't want no money?"

"Since young Riley is off to war, the old man just wants someone to hep him plant and tend his crop, maybe clear some more land."

"You think he might be willin' for me to git the place."

"I done put in a good word for you with young Riley. Just

git up to Bold Camp as soon as you can, and the old man will make a deal with you, I'm sure."

Caleb and John walked to the gate post where John's horse was tied. "When do you leave?"

"Two days. We should be in Culpepper in a week if we don't run into any Yanks on the way. Then we headin' up north to join up with General Longstreet."

"I'm gittin' married this summer. Hope you can be here."

"I don't know, Caleb, I reckon I'll be back when the war is over." John stepped into the stirrup and threw his leg across the saddle."

"You be careful, John," Caleb chuckled. "You won't have me there to look out for you."

"That would be good, Caleb, but you ain't bad enough, not nearly as bad as John Wright." He turned his horse and dropped a strap across the horse's flank. "Git up, Charger."

The deep snow melted during the second week of February, and the roads became passable for horses, sleds, and buggies. Caleb hitched the old mule to a sled that would traverse the muddy ruts easier than a wheeled buggy. He and Polly packed a lunch of biscuits and bacon and wrapped warmly for the ten-mile trip, which would require at least three hours each way with the old mule pulling the sled. Major could have pulled the sled faster, but Caleb believed Codger would be more sure-footed on the muddy road up Bold Camp.

Caleb's heart was in his throat when he pulled back on the reins and stopped the mule in Riley Mullins's yard, beneath a barren oak tree. Before Caleb had time to climb down from the seat on the sled, Riley Mullins, a gray beard to his chest, was standing on the front porch with a rifle in his hand. He spat a stream of tobacco juice onto the ground.

"Who might you be?" Riley called as Caleb's feet touched the ground.

"Caleb Wilkens, Mr. Mullins." He walked towards the porch while Polly remained on the sled.

"What's your business up here, Son?"

"John Wright said you might need some help with all your chores around here."

"That's right," Riley said. "You think you might want to work for me?"

"Yes, sir. I think I might."

"Well, you and your missus come on in the house, and maybe we can talk about it."

Caleb helped Polly down from the sled, and they followed Riley, who stood at least two inches taller than Caleb, into his house, where a fire blazed in the fireplace.

"There isn't anything like a good oak fire." Riley rubbed his hands together, then held his palms upright in front of the flames. He motioned for Polly and Caleb to be seated.

"This is Polly Maggard, Mr. Mullins." Caleb volunteered. "She ain't my wife yet, but she's fixin' to be."

Riley spoke without turning his head to look at the couple. "When's the wedding?"

"In August, when Polly is twenty."

"Why aren't you off fighting in the war?" Riley spoke without accusation or condemnation in his voice. It was obvious that the old man was attempting to gauge the younger man's character.

Riley's manner of speech was much like that of Dency Martin, giving Caleb pause about his own way of speaking. After a few seconds, he responded. "'Cause I been there, up in Antietam, Sharpsburg. Me and John Wright almost lost our lives. That was after we was captured by the Yanks at Pound Gap last year. I just got back last month, been gittin' over lung fever."

"Lots of young fellows your age gone off to join with General Lee, just like my son."

"To tell you the truth, Mr. Mullins, I don't know which side I'm on."

"If you're goin' to work for me, you got to be on my side and I'm on the side of Virginny."

"I will be on your side; I promise you that."

Riley stood. "You want to bring your young lady? If not, she can stay here. I'm sorry, but my wife is bedridden, and can't be up for long. I'm sure she would enjoy Polly's company for an hour or so while we take a look at the property and cabin."

Polly nodded. I would be pleased to visit with Mrs. Mullins while Caleb goes with you."

***

Caleb followed Riley to the barn. They saddled two horses, mounted them, and rode towards an open field that began its expanse just beyond the barn. After twenty minutes, they entered the woods. Riley got down from this horse, and Caleb followed. He stood next to the taller man, pointing across a shallow ravine to a small log cabin sitting on a knoll a few hundred feet above the open field.

"That's the ten acres I'm looking to sell. There's no bottom land, maybe two acres. The rest has good timber."

"I ain't got no money, Mr. Mullins, but I'm willin' to work for you to pay for the property."

"I know you don't have money, but you look strong and fit. You give me three summers, and the property is yours. If you have to work more than ten hours a day or on Sundays, I'll pay you something extra, whatever I think it's worth to me.

Caleb extended his hand.

"Not yet, Son. I want you to see what you're getting in the bargain." Riley turned away and mounted his horse. "Let's ride up to the cabin and take a look at the rest of the property before we do any dealing."

Caleb got on the other horse, and the two men rode in the direction of the ravine. A trail had been worn near the bottom where the ravine flattened out. Riley pointed back towards his field. "You can forge a road along my field and make a trail from here up to the cabin. There's a seam of coal just above us and a spring that runs all year long with good water. You won't need to dig a well."

They rode on to the cabin, where they both dismounted and went inside. With the door open, there was barely enough light to see around the one room. Riley opened the shutters covering the single window, giving more light.

"I built this two years ago, expecting my son, Riley, to build onto it, but he's not interested in farming or logging. Guess he's going to be a soldier if he doesn't get himself killed."

"Let's pray not, Mr. Mullins."

"Praying hasn't a lot to do with it. Though keeping his head down can't hurt." He laughed just for a second, then stared pensively into the distance.

Caleb understood the old man was masking his true feelings and concern for his son's safe return after the war. "I'll pray anyway. It might hep."

After a moment of silence, Riley spoke. "What do you think, Son? Can you make a home out of this place?"

Caleb looked around. He could envision a door on the back wall leading to a bedroom. He would build it large enough for Polly and the children that were sure to come. He could see them all gathered around the fireplace he would add to the outside wall. All he wanted now was enough to build a home for the girl he loved and the children he was sure they would have. "I shor can, Mr. Mullins. I'll add a room before Polly and me git married."

Riley extended his hand. "We got a deal, young man?"

"We do, Mr. Mullins."

5
____

ROUGH GOING

From the middle of February until the same time in March, Caleb worked on the cabin, subsisting on hardtack, jerked beef, and squirrels and rabbits that he killed. He slept on a small feather-filled pallet inside the cabin. Outside, he erected a lean-to of slender pine saplings and shrubs to shield Codger from inclement weather, and he built a stone firepit for cooking. Often, Riley Mullins brought milk, soup-beans, cornbread, and other food left over from supper. Uncle Eli made two trips to Bold Camp during that period, bringing biscuits, canned beans, and salt-bacon sent by Caleb's mother.

Eli sketched a simple plan for building the addition to the cabin. He helped Caleb cut and notch the logs to match the layout he had drawn. By the middle of March, 70 pine logs, with bark removed, were ready for building. But commencement of that work would have to wait until Caleb plowed and harrowed twenty acres of bottom land, preparing for the planting season that began in late March and early

April after the last heavy frost. Tending crops and harvesting them would entail continuous work until the end of September.

Caleb spent Sundays and a few hours each evening splitting cedar logs for roof shingles and wedges for plugging holes that would not be filled by the mud and clay chinking between the logs. The stream that flowed from his freshwater spring provided a source of clay and sand for the mixture required for the chinking. By the end of March, all materials were in place for building the addition that would be home to Caleb, Polly, and the children who were sure to come. He would need help lifting logs into place after the structure was built to waist height.

When planting began, Caleb, Riley, and Talton Hall, a hired hand from Letcher County, Kentucky, worked the field together. At night, Talt, as he preferred to be called, stayed with an uncle who lived at the mouth of Bold Camp. He was fourteen, big for his age, and eager to earn money, he said, to buy a gun. Even though the hours were long, and pay was only one dollar daily, Talt usually worked diligently alongside Caleb and Riley. However, when Riley left to do his other chores, Talt would sit, while Caleb continued to work.

"Come on, Talt," Caleb said. "Don't take advantage of the old man's blind trust."

"I don't git paid no more no matter how much I work."

"But he believes we will git our work done even if he ain't out here to watch us."

"Then I reckon you shouldn't be leanin' on your hoe, talkin'. Seems to me you need to get back to work."

"If Riley finds out, you will git run off. You know that. don't you?"

"I hope you don't tell him, Caleb." There was a threat in his voice even though Caleb was taller and brawnier than Talt."

"I won't unless he asks," Caleb said.

"You better hope he don't ask." Talt walked over to a horse-apple tree in the field where his jacket lay on the ground. "Guess you don't know who I am, do you?"

"Just what you and Riley told me."

"And what did Riley say?"

"I ain't sayin', but I know about you and your pa."

"Yeah, he done kilt three men, and they call him bad Dave Hall. I'm gonna be badder than him. They'll call me Bad Talt Hall by the time I'm your age, Caleb." He brandished a long-barreled Navy pistol. "Take a look at this and you'll know I mean what I say."

"You can put that away, Talt. I done faced bigger guns than that, and I didn't run. I ain't scared of you."

"If you're so brave, whynt you up north with young Riley fightin' them Yanks?" '

"'Cause I already done my bit, and I ain't ready to kill no one, not even a Yank."

"I shor would like to kill me a Yank, or a Yank lover. And we got a-plenty of them here in Gladeville and Letcher County."

Caleb began to cover the seed corn at his feet. Riley had deposited them in groups of three kernels along each row, at one-foot intervals. There were many more kernels to cover before he would reach the end of the row. And many more rows remaining before the two-acre field would be covered and ready for germination.

Caleb got to the end of his row and looked back at Talt,

still sitting on the ground. He motioned for him to get to work. He hoed back along Talt's row, meeting him halfway. They turned together and walked to the far side of the field and began covering two more rows of seed corn. They did not speak again until the field was completely covered, but Caleb wondered how a boy of Talt's age could have become so imbued with hate and a desire to become famous by killing. The thought gave him a foreboding, a fear that Talt might shoot him or Riley Mullins, or anyone else who might rankle him.

As they walked toward Riley's barn, Talt asked, "How much money do you think that old man is worth?"

"Which old man?"

"You know who I'm talkin' 'bout even if you play ignorant—old man Riley, that's who."

"I don't have an idee in the world."

"I was just thinkin'." Talt pulled a twist of tobacco from his pocket, took a chew, and offered the twist to Caleb."

"Thank you, but I don't chew."

"Like I was sayin', Caleb, ain't nobody up here in this holler but that old man and me and you, and his old woman is sick in bed."

"That's enough, Talt. I don't want to hear no more."

"Who knows how much money that old miser has got hid in that big house?"

Caleb stopped walking and took a firm hold on Talt's arm. "I don't believe in killin', but if somethin' bad happens to Mr. Mullins, I'll come after you. That's fer shor."

"Dang," Talt said, "You know I wuz jist puttin' you on, don't you, Caleb?"

"No matter, Talt, but don't bring that gun with you when

you come back to work tomorrow mornin'. If you do, I'm tellin' Riley about our talk today."

Back at the barn, Riley finished milking his cows. He set two buckets on a table as Caleb and Talt put away their tools. "You boys got all that corn covered?"

"Yeah, we shor did." Talt spoke up. "I wonder if I can git paid today."

"I don't see why not, Riley said. "I'll have to run in the house to fetch your money. Let's see, you worked five days. So, I owe you five dollars."

Riley and the boys walked to the back door. Riley took the milk buckets into the house and returned after a few minutes. He counted out five dollars for Talt, then handed two dollars to Caleb.

"You don't owe me that, Mr. Mullins."

"Take it, Caleb. You do a whole lot more than you have to. I'm not blind, young man."

Talt looked at the bills in his hand. "These is Yankee money. I want to be paid in Virginny money."

"You count your blessings that I still got real money. Virginny money isn't worth much right now, and from the way things look, it's not getting any better."

Caleb reached to shake Riley's hand. "Thank you, Mr. Mullins. I appreciate your kindness."

"It's nothing you didn't earn, boy."

Talt threw his jacket across his shoulder, giving Caleb a disgusted look, and walked to the corner of the house. "I got to git if I'm goin' to make it home 'fore dark."

Riley called out to Talt, "Hey, boy, I don't think I'll be needing you anymore."

Talt kept walking without looking back or responding to Riley's dismissal.

"I don't trust that boy," Riley said.

Caleb bid him good evening, then walked up the hill towards his cabin. He had a troubling thought that he and Riley had not seen the last of Talt Hall.

Before sunset, he unbundled a bail of corn fodder and laid some in the feed box for Codger, then carried water from the spring to fill a wooden trough Uncle Eli brought from South Fork. He fell asleep inside the cabin with the door and window open. Sometime during the night, an uneasiness came over him. He got up and closed the door, then loaded his rifle. Standing by the open window, he listened for unfamiliar sounds. He heard only the tree frogs and crickets and the occasional barking of one of Riley's hounds coming from the vicinity of the barn. The barking stopped. Caleb listened again but heard nothing amiss. He lay down on his pallet, staring up at the ceiling with Talt's words weighing on his mind. After a while, his eyelids grew heavy, and he fell asleep, awaking at the first shreds of dawn coming through the window the next morning.

Caleb turned nineteen on April 17th. He was halfway down a row of tobacco beds when he remembered. It was just another day for him, but his passing thought was that time was getting ever closer to August when Polly would be twenty and the two of them would be married. The addition to the cabin was moving slowly. He would have to change his work schedule to finish their home before her birthday.

Since Talt had been terminated, Caleb realized he needed help with the twenty acres of crops that required tending and eventual harvesting. He also needed assistance in raising the side logs for the new room of the cabin. His mind was devoid of workable solutions to that problem.

Riley worked alongside Caleb most days, but his chores, milking the cows and feeding other livestock and chickens, kept him busy much of the time. He also cared for his wife, morning, noon, and evening, preparing meals and bathing her. Caleb could see that these things were taking a toll on Mr. Mullins. He was grateful for the money Riley paid him almost every week, even though their agreement did not require anything more than the cabin and ten acres of land, but he concluded that the two of them could not continue to meet the demands the farm placed on them. He reluctantly decided that he must discuss these things with Riley.

The evening of his birthday, Caleb approached Riley while he was milking one of the cows, "I tell you, Mr. Mullins, I don't know how you keep doin' all the things you do each day. I'm forty years younger than you, and I can't keep up with you."

"I think you do a pretty good job of keeping up, and you're getting strong as an ox."

"It ain't easy, Mr. Mullins…"

"Odd, you mention that today, Caleb. I'm not a fool, and I can see that this place is getting the best of both of us. I used to hire four boys each summer and kept them all busy, but they all went off to the war."

"I don't want to cost you money, but I need hep. In the fields. You don't have to give me extra any longer, just pay it to someone else."

"You don't get anything from me you don't earn; nobody does. I been thinking a lot about it myself. Tomorrow, I'm riding up to Rob Vanover's place. He's got four younguns running his sawmill and grinding mill. He doesn't need all of them. I'll hire two or three of the Vanover boys to work the summer for us; we need them if they're willing. How's that sound?"

"Maybe I can git some hep raisin' my cabin."

"Probably so," Riley said. He picked up the milk pail and started towards the house.

"Mr. Mullins," I been thinkin' about somthin' else. Your missus can use some hep too."

"What you got in mind?"

"Well, Polly, my sweetheart, she ain't doin' nothin' for the summer. She can come up here and stay if you have some place for her to sleep."

"What would she charge?"

"Nothin', just her board, and she can hep me too."

"I'll give that some thought, Caleb." Riley resumed walking away from the barn. After a moment, he turned and faced Caleb. "You know my wife has got consumption. It can be passed on to other folks."

"Polly will be careful."

"We'll talk about it again tomorrow," Riley said.

―――――

Caleb drove the sled home the next weekend and returned in a wagon with Polly. On Monday, two Vanover boys, Charlie, eighteen, and Kermit, seventeen, were at the field working when Caleb arrived at Riley Mullins's place about noon. As soon as Polly was settled, Caleb joined the Vanover boys and worked until late afternoon. Afterwards, the three of them set the notched logs into place for the addition to Caleb's cabin.

"What do I owe you fellers?" Caleb asked.

"Nothin'," Charlie said. "Just name your firstborn after me."

"What if it's a girl?"

"Name her Violet, after my ma. That would please her."

"I shor will," Caleb replied. "I like that name too, 'bout as good as Polly."

They laughed as they headed back down the hill towards the barn. "We got to git goin'," Kermit said. "We got a two-mile walk to home 'fore dark."

After the boys left, Caleb and Polly sat on the back porch, basking in their first solitary time together in almost two months. Polly's twentieth birthday and their wedding date were fast approaching. Much work remained to complete the additional room to the cabin and make the entire structure ready by August. A fireplace and chimney had to be built and roof shingles installed before the interior could be started. Polly's presence allowed them to make plans and to work together in the evenings and on Sundays. By the end of April, the shingles were in place, and stones were gathered for building the fireplace, hearth, and chimney. With help from the Vanover boys, they were installed.

Progress made on the cabin was reason to celebrate, but the month of June was not without its disappointments. News of the war spread slowly through the hills and valleys of Wise County. For those who revered General Lee and anticipated his vanquishing the northern invaders post-haste, disillusionment and disappointment set in. News of battle casualties, especially young men from the local counties, appeared to portend doom for the Confederate cause. The Confederate dollar, issued by the state of Virginia and other states, was almost worthless. Deserters from both armies roamed the hills and hollows, foraging and stealing to survive. The inhabitants of these remote places found ways to cope with a life that had been one of drudgery before the war, now gradually growing more dire.

While Polly and Caleb planned for marriage, Riley prepared to lose his wife to the dreadful disease that ravaged her body. She grew weaker each day, with swollen joints and incessant coughing. Near the end of July, she was spitting blood with each cough. Polly stayed close to Lizzy's bedside despite the possibility of becoming infected with consumption. Desperate to save his wife from a disease for which there was no possibility of recovery, Riley rode his horse to Gladeville to get advice from old Doctor Daniel Hollyfield.

"There's not much I can do for her," the doctor said. He took a tin off a shelf and opened the lid. "Here's some opium. Give her a good-sized pinch in some shine a couple of times each day. It won't cure her, but it will ease her way out of this world."

Lizzy died the first week in August, with Riley, Polly, and Caleb watching over her. Riley built a wood casket, lined with black satin. Doctor Marshall Taylor preached at Lizzy's funeral under a spreading oak tree before the pallbearers carried her up the hill to her final resting place in the family cemetery.

News of General Grant's capture of Vicksburg and the unspeakable defeat of Lee's Army of Northern Virginia at Gettysburg reached The Pound and Wise County. Riley Mullins waited with dread for news of his son, who rode with General Longstreet, Lee's immediate subordinate at Gettysburg. Three weeks passed before a letter reached Pound Post Office. The letter was from Lieutenant Riley Mullins, who, in a few short words, summed up his harrowing experience to his father. "We've tucked tail and are heading south," the letter read.

The futility of the war weighed heavily on the minds of Caleb and Polly as they rode their wagon towards South Fork, where they were to be married by Uncle Mac Cantrell. Regardless of what was unfolding all around them, they, like all the other resilient people of the hills, had no choice but to go on with their lives.

6

———

POLLY

"My brother, John, has run into bad times. He's coming from Whitesburg, in Letcher County, to stay a while." Riley explained his brother's problems to Caleb two days before a wagon load of "younguns," ranging in age from one to seventeen, came to a stop under the barren oak tree in Riley's front yard. The children, dressed in hand-me-downs and rag-tag coats, sat quietly in the wagon. The father, John, and mother, Patsy, whose dress was only marginally better than the children's, climbed down from the buckboard and were greeted by Riley as he descended the steps to meet them.

There were six children, four girls and two boys. Oma, the eldest, a pretty girl with dark hair and eyes, sat in the back of the wagon, her head bowed, obviously ill at ease with her family's dire situation. The girl was shabbily dressed, her hair in need of brushing. She glanced at Caleb, who returned a smile. He thought that she was attractive with her dark hair and eyes, but not as pretty as his Polly.

Ira, the youngest boy at seven, jumped down from the

wagon and ran to his uncle and threw his arms about the tall man's legs, and looked up at the bearded man. "Thank you, Uncle Riley."

"You're welcome, young man. What would be your name?"

"I'm Ira," the precocious young boy said. "Someday, I will be famous."

"Famous?" Riley teased.

"Yeah, and rich like you."

They all laughed heartily.

"He's a talker," John said as he embraced his brother. "We are all grateful; that's for shor. And we don't plan to be a bother to you for too long."

Caleb stood aside, careful not to interject himself into what he gathered was a reunion of two brothers who had not seen each other for a long time. But Riley had other ideas. He called Caleb's name and motioned for him to join the group.

"John and Patsy, this is Caleb Wilkens, the young man who has worked for me all summer. He and his new wife, Polly, moved into the little cabin up there." He pointed towards the knoll where the small house was barely visible through the oaks and pines. "It was a blessing to have Polly caring for Lizzy during her last days. I couldn't have made it without her. And Caleb, here, I trust him like I would young Riley."

"Where is he?" John asked.

"Off to war with General Longstreet."

"At least, we know what side he is on. You can't never tell in Kentucky. Some are for the Yanks; others are for General Lee. I hear tell some people even voted for Mr. Lincoln last election. Me, I jist want this damned war to be over." He pointed at Ira. "From the looks of things, it'll still be goin' on when that boy there, gits grown, big enough to go off to war hisself."

"I doubt that, Johnny," Riley said. "From what I hear, it won't be going on much longer."

"You hear sometin' bad from Riley?"

"Not much. He doesn't say, but Lee just got beat bad at a place called Gettysburg in Pennsylvania and had to head back to Virginny."

Caleb listened to the brothers talk and remained silent at first. He wondered if there was news of his friend John Wright. Last he heard was when John left Pound to ride with Riley. "General Longstreet's cavalry make it alright?"

"Yes, Caleb, I think so. The only thing Riley wrote to me was that they were heading south."

Caleb took the news to Polly, careful not to make the Confederate cause appear hopeless. After a dinner of shucky beans, canned tomatoes, and corn bread, they knelt by their bed and prayed for the Army of Northern Virginia, especially for Caleb's good friend, John Wesley Wright, the bravest man Caleb would meet during his lifetime.

In November, Polly discovered that she was going to have a baby, a pregnancy that troubled her through the next seven months, when a baby girl was born. Polly was tended by her mother and an elderly midwife, Sadie Hubbard. By Polly's count, the baby was not due for another six weeks, but her pains became unbearable one early morning in May. At the time, Caleb was preparing for a day in the field, working with the two Vanover boys, hoeing corn. Instead, he hitched the wagon to Codger and rode as fast as possible to South Fork, ten miles away, to fetch Polly's mother. On their return trip, he stopped at a run-down cabin near the mouth of Bold Camp and beseeched Sadie Hubbard to come with him to assist with the birth of their first baby.

He paced outside the cabin, waiting for news from Polly's mother. He could hear Polly's muffled sounds of agony, and wished it were him in pain, and not his Polly. A little girl was born late that afternoon, frail and jaundiced. There was no way of weighing her, but Sadie guessed her to be just over five pounds. She sadly speculated that the baby would not survive more than a week, but Polly was determined to save her baby girl. When Caleb was allowed into the room, he rushed to Polly's side, bent, and hugged her.

"I'm sorry," he said. "I know it was awful for you."

"No," she assured him, "We have a baby girl, and it was worth the pain."

"That's wonderful. We'll name her Violet, just like I promised Charlie Vanover."

"I'll give you a son next time, sweetheart, I promise."

"There won't be anymore," Caleb said, "You can't go through that again."

"Yes, I can, and you will have your son."

"I'll love my daughter as much as a son. I promise."

And Caleb's promise was solemn. He showed his love for Violet in every way possible, carefully watching her during her fitful periods after Polly was exhausted from a full day of caring for her child. His hopes for her normal progression from crawling and sitting to taking her first steps were not realized. Violet did not turn over without assistance until she was nine months old. She sat up at fourteen months and finally took her first halting steps at eighteen months to the delight of Polly and Caleb. There were times when Violet appeared robust and healthy, but she frequently lapsed into periods of high fevers and vomiting. Twice, Caleb and Polly rode with her to Gladeville for an examination by Doctor Marshall Taylor, who prescribed quinine, but Violet's symptoms periodically returned.

Quinine was difficult to come by because of the northern embargoes of southern ports. Polly used the small amount provided by Doctor Taylor sparingly. When the quinine was exhausted, she prepared sassafras tea for Violet. During these anxious times for the young parents, news of the war did not seem to matter, and did not reach the little cabin on the knoll above Riley Mullin's house. It was about the time Violet began to walk that news of General Sherman's capture of Atlanta, Georgia, reached the hills of southwestern Virginia. The news came with the arrival of young Riley, worn and weary after two years of harrowing battles and narrow escapes from death.

"General Sherman, a crazy man, burned Atlanta two months ago, and I suspect, made it all the way to Savannah, burning everything in his path. If he cuts the South in two, the Confederate cause is lost."

"John Wright with you?" Caleb asked, as young Riley handed the reins of his horse to his father.

"No, he stayed with Colonel Halford, General Longstreet's cavalry commander. Last I saw of him, he was riding off towards Petersburg and Richmond with Halford and seven or eight other soldiers. Petersburg was under assault by General Grant, and John wanted to be in that mix. Seven of us rode out in advance of Longstreet's main cavalry and got cut off. We couldn't get back to our main unit, so we kept riding south. I couldn't see much use in running north, right into the enemy's hands."

"Where'd the others go?

"Home," young Riley said, "to what's left of it upstate. If Petersburg and Richmond fall, that will be the end of the Confederacy."

"What'll happen to John Wright and the others?"

"No telling'; there's just no telling."

***

Winter came early with the first heavy snowfall at the end of November, covering the mountains and valleys with a four-inch blanket of snow that did not melt until a warm spell late in January, when Polly broke her blessed news to Caleb.

"I'm with child, honey, and I know in my bones it will be a boy."

"I don't want you to go through all the pain you done with Violet."

"Don't worry," she said. "God knows what he's doin', and He wants you to have your son."

Caleb got up from his chair before the fireplace and walked to where Polly was sitting, holding Violet. He bent and embraced her. "I love you so much, Polly."

"I know," she said, "and I thank God for it."

"When are you due?"

"By my count, next August, and I've already thought of his name. I want to call him Caleb, like you."

"No. I have thought about what I would name my first son—I want to name him Gabriel. If that is all right with you."

"Gabriel?"

"Yes, Gabriel, the guardian angel. The name means "God is my strength". He'll need to be strong to survive on this little patch of earth we live on. You know it will be ours after harvest next year, and his after we're gone."

"It is a wonderful name, Gabriel Wilkens. And I'm sure you will teach him everything he needs to know to make it in this world. Let's pray to God we will have our healthy Gabriel by this fall."

"I pray so." He bent and kissed Polly's cheek, keeping to himself thoughts about the ordeal Polly experienced, giving birth to Violet, and the fear they both harbored concerning their little girl's tenuous health.

———

The first signs of spring came in early March, reminding Caleb that the fields would need plowing before the end of the month. That was when he would begin his last year of indenture to Riley Mullins. He would also prepare an acre for his own garden.

While the weather was fair, he hitched up his mule and made the ten-mile trip to South Fork to visit his mother and Uncle Eli. Unbeknownst to Caleb and his family, the Confederate capital, Richmond, and Petersburg were being evacuated by General Lee and his Army of Northern Virginia. But rumors of the final collapse of the Confederacy had already reached the ears of The Pound's merchants and officials.

A sign, "No Confederate Money Accepted," was nailed to the wall behind the counter, a clear reckoning with the pending defeat of the southern armies. Mr. Johnson was a tall, balding man with rimless glasses. He wore a white apron, showing evidence that the proprietor had wiped his hands on it many times. Caleb went to the back of the store, where he picked up a ten-pound bag of flour and carried it to the counter.

"Do you have coffee and sugar, Mr. Johnson?"

"A little sugar," the man replied. "Do you have money?" He turned his head and pointed to the sign behind him. "Don't think you can afford coffee these days. It would cost me near about fifteen dollars a pound if I could find anybody to sell it to at my price of twenty dollars."

"How about chicory?"

"I got chicory, a dollar a pound."

"How much is the flour?"

"Eight dollars a pound, that bag here…" he placed his hand on the bag of flour Caleb had lifted onto the counter, "… is eighty dollars." He pursed his lips apologetically. "Things'll probably git worse fer a long spell."

"I'll jist take the chicory and sugar then." Caleb returned the flour to the back of the store and came back to the counter. "How much do I owe you, Mr. Johnson?"

"Well, son, it ought to be a dollar ten cents, but I got to charge you two dollars cause sugar is might' scarce here in Wise County, and I can git that price for it all day.

Caleb smiled and took three dollars from his coat pocket. He peeled off two dollars and gave them to the proprietor. "I guess we done lost the war, Mr. Johnson."

"I 'spect so." He put the sugar and chicory into a bag and pushed it across the counter towards Caleb. "Thank you. The only thing we can do now is pray to the Almighty."

"I 'spect so," said Caleb.

The town post office was two hundred feet down the muddy street in the back of the only barber shop in town. Caleb entered. A small, bearded man appeared at the window. He was barely tall enough to reach the opening in the steel screen that separated the postmaster from the public. "You have any mail for Eli Wilkens?"

The postmaster muttered to himself, checking into the alphabetically arranged cubby holes. Without looking at Caleb, he spoke. "Nothin' for Eli Wilkins, but somethin' here for Caleb Wilkins."

"That'll be me," Caleb said. "Who's it from?"

The postmaster held the letter above his head, squinted his eyes, and read, "Says from Corporal John W. Wright, CSA." He reached the letter through the window. Caleb took it hurriedly. Outside, he tore open the envelope and held it up in the light to read the roughly scribbled words of his friend.

Richmond, Virginia, February 2nd, 1865

My dear friend, Caleb,

I hope this letter gits to you and I hope it finds you well. I have been sittin on my horse all day, waitin for orders to move out, but to tell you the truth, we don't know which way to go. We can go south, but Grant, that drunk, will jist follow us, beatin us all to hell. You know how I hate to lose, but I bout had my fill, and will be glad when 'tis over. Still, I will fight as long as we have any hope.

I spect we will be leavin Richmond any day now if God don't help us more than He is helpin now. If General Lee pulls his army out, there ain't no reason for me to stay. I done made plans to head for England after the war cause none of us in the south will be safe, specially Reb soldiers, except the backwoodsmen and their families in southwest Virginia and eastern Kentucky. So, you stay jist where you are.

Me and a friend will be joinin up with a Wild West show in London. I spect I'll be famous fore I come home.

I hope you and Polly are happy with a bunch of little ones.

Your friend always,
John Wesley Wright (Bad John Wright)

On his return trip to Bold Camp, Caleb said a prayer for John Wright, and despite John's professed bravado, Caleb knew that John would be praying too.

The fields were ploughed in March, and planting began in April. Polly tolerated her pregnancy without difficulty while caring for Violet through her frequent episodes of high fevers and nausea. Caleb worked alongside the Vanover boys without the direction or help of Riley, who suffered from self-diagnosed chronic rheumatism and lumbago. The numerous tasks that Caleb performed now included milking two cows and feeding the horses each day. He happily assumed the additional responsibilities, knowing that when winter came, he would own his ten acres and cabin unencumbered. He felt obliged to help Riley Mullins because Riley had made it possible for him and Polly to have a home of their own. It wasn't much, but more than many young men just turning twenty could claim as their own.

News of Lee's surrender at Appomattox and the murder of Abraham Lincoln spread quickly through the mountains and valleys about the first of May. Like most southerners, the hill people were wary of their future, not knowing what President Johnson's plans were for bringing the southern states back into the Union. Although some in the South had despised President Lincoln and viewed John Wilkes Booth as a hero, many thought Lincoln a kind man and believed he would have been lenient during Reconstruction. They also felt akin to his humble beginnings, having been born in a small cabin in Kentucky.

Much of the South was destitute, without crops or industries. But life in the hill country of Virginia and Kentucky changed little during and after the war. The hill people had been self-sufficient, subsisting on crops they planted and cultivated or bartered for with their neighbors from the time of the early settlements. Their remoteness from large cities or densely populated areas made them less susceptible to vindictive policies that the South endured after the war. Life in the hills went on, free from intimidation except for internecine feuds, caused by lingering differences from the war, pitting brother against brother, father against son, and neighbor against neighbor. These mountain feuds and animosities would eventually be exacerbated by moonshiner territorial conflicts.

After hearing of the ending of the war, John Mullins hitched his horse to a wagon and packed his family into it, preparing for a trip across Pine Mountain into Letcher County. "We done lived off you long enough, Brother, and it's time we be gittin' back home, if we still got one."

Riley assured his brother that he and his family were welcome to stay as long as they wished. "It's been good having you, John. If you go, we might never see each other again."

"True enough, I reckon, Riley, but we been livin' off you long enough. We need to git back to our house and make it right for livin' in again. Since this war has been lost, I think we will be better off in Kentucky than here in Virginny. Them blue devils may come ridin' through here, burnin' and stealin' and killin'. I think we'll fare better 'cross the mountain where there's as many Yanks as there is Rebs."

"Those Yanks won't be comin' up these hollers where they suspect one of us hill folk is hidin' behind ever tree," Riley said.

Oma spoke. "Pa, I'm stayin' to take care of Uncle Riley. He needs someone here to look after him." She shifted her eyes towards Caleb, who stood quietly aside, watching John

"I'm stayin' too Pa," eight-year-old Ira said.

"No, no," his father insisted. "Oma can stay, but you'll just be in the way, Ira."

They loaded the wagon with jars of beans and tomatoes, and with potatoes and apples that had been banked for winter. John ran down four hens and a rooster, which he placed inside a small cage and attached to the back of the wagon. With his wife, Patsy, and five of his children, he turned his horse toward Pound and Pound Gap. After they set out on their journey, no one in the wagon spoke for the longest time. Patsy broke the silence.

"I'm worried 'bout Oma."

"Why," John asked.

"'Cause I think she's stuck on that boy, Caleb."

"Why do you think that?"

"A mother knows."

"Won't do her no good. That boy, Caleb, loves that purty wife of his like nobody I ever seed."

"I just hope she don't cause him no trouble."

"I wouldn't worry 'bout that, I would worry 'bout Ira more than Oma. That boy thinks he's already growed up."

"Ira?" Patsy sounded surprised. "You ain't ever goin' to have to worry about Ira. That boy will do fine all his life; you just wait and see."

"That's probable true, but for now, I want him close around where I can keep my eye on him."

The Mullins family rode on muddy roads through Pound. It had been four hours since leaving Riley's place when the wagon topped Pine Mountain, crossed through the Gap, and started down the other side. Two soldiers in blue stepped from the woods, one on each side of the narrow trail. They brandished their rifles. John brought the wagon to a halt.

"Where you bound?" A sergeant asked, stepping closer to the wagon.

"Whitesburg, a few miles beyond Little Elkhorn Creek," John responded. "You know where that is?"

"What are you carryin'?" The corporal on the other side of the wagon walked to the rear of the wagon.

"Hey, Sarge," the corporal called out. "We can use the chickens, can't we?" He set down his rifle and began to undo the ropes securing the cage.

John stood. "You can't have my chicks." He directed his words at the corporal.

"What do you mean? We'll take what we want."

The corporal appeared to have difficulty undoing the knots John had tied. "Hey, Sarge. Give me a hand here."

John watched as the sergeant rested his rifle against a pine tree. When he saw that both soldiers were busying themselves, attempting to undo the knots, he lashed a whip across the horse's back. "Git goin', Thunder."

The horse lunged forward, quickly picking up the slack in the rig, setting the wagon into motion. It sped down the trail, careening dangerously around the steep curves and between the trees.

"Get down," John commanded his children. He held the arm of his wife as she slipped beneath the buckboard.

Shots rang out, then silenced. John knew the soldiers were reloading, which gave him time to put distance between himself and his pursuers. A half hour later, they were safely off the mountain and moving slowly through the valley that would soon turn toward Whitesburg.

"That's what I'm affeared of. If we run into any more soldiers, all of you git down, cause I ain't stopping 'less they kill me, and we're shootin' first by God."

"We should've stayed with your brother."

"No," John said, "I am goin' to be my own man, by damn. And we're goin' home to Whitesburg."

Patsy's hands went to her face. She bent her head and sobbed. "They'll kill us afore we get there, John."

"No," he said, turning for a moment to look at his sixteen-year-old son, Enos. "Load them two guns, and you keep one at the ready. Give me the other. We're goin' home, come hell or high water."

"Give me a gun, too," Ira stood beside Enos.

"Sit down, Son," John spoke to Ira without looking back. "Your time for killin' will come soon enough." He slapped Thunder across his flank. "Git up." The horse went into a gallop.

After leaving Little Elkhorn Creek behind, John slowed the horse into a gaited trot. With Whitesburg coming into view, a lone soldier in tattered Confederate Gray stepped into the wagon's path and reached for Thunder's halter. "Whoa," he said, "not so fast."

Enos raised his rifle, pointing it at the soldier. "Git back, Reb, or I'm goin' to blow you to kingdom come. Don't you know the war is over?"

"Over? Did we win?" the soldier yelled, letting go of the halter and stepping back into the brush alongside the trail.

"No, you lost," Enos responded.

The soldier's voice faded as the wagon rushed onward. "Lost? The damned Yankees won?"

"Nobody won," John's voice boomed back over his shoulder. "We all lost."

He lashed Thunder. "Git up, boy." The horse moved in a rush. John did not bring Thunder to a halt until they reached a run-down cabin in a valley near Whitesburg.

A healthy baby boy was born on August 23, 1865, in a little cabin on the hill above the home of Riley Mullins. Polly was attended by both prospective grandmothers: Caleb's mother, Ginny, and Polly's own mother. Outside the cabin, Caleb paced, waiting to hear the news and praying that the baby would be healthy. At 3a.m., Ginny called from the door of the cabin, "Caleb, you have a healthy baby son. Come see."

Caleb ran to Polly's bedside and embraced her. "Thank you, honey. Are you all right?"

"I'm fine, my husband, and you have your son, just as I promised."

Ginny handed the baby boy, wrapped in a knitted blanket, to his father.

"Hello, Gabriel," he said. "I know you will make me proud someday." He stood in silence, tears filling his eyes as he looked into the baby's face. After a few moments, he returned him to Polly, bent over her bed, and kissed her face. Outside the cabin, he sat on a bench, his face in his hands, giving thanks to God that Polly had delivered their new son without difficulty. His thoughts turned to his young daughter, Violet, who was just learning to walk at eighteen months of age. His many prayers for improvements in her health had not been answered. She still experienced periods of very high fevers and painful bouts that frequently lasted for hours. His visits to Doctor Taylor with her had not helped, and the prescribed quinine was no longer available in Pound or Gladeville. While he grieved for his daughter's poor health, he was hopeful his new son would not suffer as Violet had done since birth.

Gabriel walked at ten months, and by his second birthday, was taller than Violet. Polly and Gabriel had accepted the probability that she would never develop into a healthy child. Despite their efforts to shield her from exposure to the prevalent childhood diseases in the mountains, she developed a condition affecting her breathing, with extreme swelling around her face and nostrils. Caleb and Polly rode to South Fork for Ginny's help. She suspected diphtheria and sent Eli to Gladeville to bring back Doctor Taylor. They both returned to South Fork three hours later, but by then, Violet had passed away; it was two months before her fourth birthday.

Caleb built the little casket of pine wood and lined it with a pink blanket Polly's mother had knitted for her granddaughter. A sorrowful crowd walked up the hill above the cabin and placed the casket into the ground. There was no funeral service except the reciting of the Lord's Prayer and the Twenty-third Psalm, led by Caleb. "May Violet find the peace and good health in Heaven that she never had here on earth."

"Amen and amen," the few mourners lamented.

After the funeral, Caleb turned his attention to the tasks of fall harvesting, bundling fodder, and preparing for the coming winter. He relished the idea that by the time for planting next spring arrived, his debt to Riley Mullins would be completely paid and that he would earn a dollar each day for his labor starting next spring. Despite the tasks that kept his attention, his thoughts often turned to his little girl, who had lived such a desperate life. He knew that Polly also mourned Violet months after her passing, and he comforted her with Bible readings and assurances that both would see Violet in Heaven.

Their sorrow was lifted a year later, when Polly discovered she was pregnant with her third child. Their daily visits to the little grave above their cabin were made easier with the belief that God was sending them a new baby girl to ease the pain of losing Violet.

In her sixth month of pregnancy, Polly developed a sporadic cough that grew more incessant within weeks. It persisted, accompanied by high fevers, and several days later, she began coughing up small traces of blood. Caleb recalled that Lizzy, Riley's wife, exhibited such symptoms before her painful death by consumption. The thought that his Polly might suffer the same consequences shook his soul. He blamed himself for allowing her to stay by Lizzy's bedside when she was dying of the dreaded disease of the lungs. He sat alongside Polly's bed, holding her hand, praying silently that God would send a cure. He thought of his mother. She always had a solution for every problem he ever had. He would send for her to come and help Polly.

The next morning, young Riley rode to South Fork during a light snow to inform Ginny about Polly. She arrived that afternoon, having ridden alongside young Riley through the snow and falling temperatures.

After a fitful night's sleep for Polly, Caleb left her in his mother's care while he performed his morning chores. By noon, Polly's coughing spells had increased in frequency and intensity with bloody expectoration.

"Where is Caleb?" she asked as she sat up in bed.

"Outside, dear," Ginny replied. "Do you want me to get him?"

"No, not now. I have to git back on my feet so I can be useful to my husband." Polly stood, then suddenly bent in pain. "My baby is coming." She dropped back onto the bed, grimacing in pain. "Call Caleb," she said. "I need him now." Ginny rushed outside, cupped her hands to her mouth, and called Caleb's name. Minutes passed before he arrived.

"What's wrong, Ma?"

"Polly's got complications. You'll need to fetch Sadie Hubbard. She'll know what to do."

Three interminable hours for Polly passed before Caleb brought the wagon to a halt by the cabin door and helped Sadie to the ground. They rushed inside to see Polly sitting on the side of the bed. She held out her arms toward Caleb. "I love you, husband," she said.

Caleb bent and held her close to his chest. "I have loved you since the first day I laid eyes on you, Polly. I won't ever stop lovin' you."

As her head rested against his shoulder, she whispered, "I'm dyin', Caleb."

"No," Caleb said. "No." He lowered his wife back onto the bed. "I won't let you go."

As he stood, he saw blood on Polly's lips and recognized the inevitability awaiting his wife. He turned his face away so Polly couldn't see the tears in his eyes. He put a heavy coat on Gabriel, took him by his hand, and led him outside. They walked to Riley Mullins's back door, and Caleb knocked.

Oma cracked open the door.

"Will you keep Gabriel tonight?" Caleb asked.

"Is something wrong with his mother?"

Caleb nodded, his lips pursed in anguish. "She's dying," he whispered.

Oma led the child into the house, then returned to the door where Caleb was waiting.

"I don't want Gabriel to hear his mother's agony."

"He can stay with us as long as he needs to," Oma reassured Caleb. "I am so sorry about Polly. She is such a sweet girl."

"Yes, she is." Caleb wanted to say, "and so are you," but thought better of it. He turned away without saying more.

Thoughts of all the things he might have done differently to make Polly's life easier coursed through his mind as he trudged through the snow up the small hill to his cabin. He stood by the door, summoning the courage he would need to watch his wife's life come to an end. Moments later, he knelt by her bedside. Taking her hand in his, he brought it to his lips. "Please, Caleb, save our baby," Polly said in a whispered plea.

"We'll save you both," Sadie assured her. "Do you think you can stand?"

"Maybe, for a little spell." She slowly sat up on the side of the bed.

Assisted by Ginny and Sadie, Polly got to her feet and took steps about the small room.

"You need to walk," Sadie said. "It'll help the baby to come."

It was getting darker in the cabin. Ginny lit a second

candle in the bedroom and a kerosene lamp in the kitchen. By nightfall, Sadie and Ginny were exhausted but continued to encourage Polly to exert every effort to birth her baby. Sadie took a small bag from her satchel. "She's running a high fever; maybe this will help some." She held out a handful of small, dried leaves and petals."

"What is it?" Ginny asked.

"Feverfew; I'll give her some more shortly. Maybe it will bring down her fever."

Sadie roused Polly and told her to take the feverfew with water." Afterwards, she got Polly to her feet and repeated the walks about the room. The midwife continued her routine throughout the night, helping Polly take measured steps. An exhausted Caleb lay on a pallet in the adjacent room, praying for his wife. Early in the morning, he closed his eyes and fell into a fitful sleep. When Ginny nudged him awake, the sun was breaking through the trees with glimmers of daylight coming through the single kitchen window,

"A baby boy has come, Son," Ginny said, the tenor of her voice telling Caleb all was not well. Caleb stood. "Can I see him now, Ma?"

Ginny touched his face sympathetically. "He was stillborn, Caleb. There's nothin' that can be done for him."

He peered around his mother, looking at the bedroom door. "How's Polly?"

"Not well. We think she has bed fever. She's coughing blood, too."

Caleb hugged his mother as tears ran down his face. "She's dyin', Ma. What will I ever do without her?"

"We will all have to do without her. I don't know how you will get over her, Caleb, but with God's help, you will. You have Gabriel to see grow up and be a good man like you. That is what Polly would want you to do."

Two days later, they buried Polly on the hill above the cabin alongside the small grave of her little daughter, Violet. They both rested in the shadow of a barren oak tree. During the short ceremony, Caleb held four-year-old Gabriel's hand. Young Riley Mullins and Oma stood near the tree as Gabriel, his father, and the two Vanover boys lowered Polly's wood casket into the ground.

"Where is Mommy goin', Pa?" Gabriel asked, looking up at his father for answers to an unfathomable question for a young child.

"Too Heaven, Gabe. She's goin' to Heaven," Caleb said.

Codger hauled his burden behind him along frozen roads. The wagon he pulled carried Caleb and Gabriel towards South Fork and the sanctuary that only Caleb's mother could provide during his time of mourning. He needed to be away from the graves on the hillside while he gained strength and renewed his faith in a God that had allowed such sorrow into his life. He reached South Fork in the afternoon, carried Gabriel into the house, then unhitched Codger. Once inside, he felt safe and unburdened. He was a widower at 27 and uncertain about how he could continue his life without Polly. During the next two months, he assisted his uncle with chores each morning and evening. He often took walks, sometimes holding Gabriel's hand as they trekked through the woods.

There, he felt as if his wife were still with him, saying it was all right for him to be happy, to go on with his life.

As the month of March neared, Caleb prepared for spring planting. He gathered corn, beans, and other seeds that would be planted in April. With the help of the Vanover brothers, he would have to prepare at least ten acres for Riley Mullins as well as his own garden. It was time to return to his and Polly's cabin on the knoll above Riley's house. In mid-March, he hitched up Codger and set out for his cabin in Bold Camp.

His first chore after arriving home was to prepare a grave marker for Polly. The small stone with Violet's name on it had fallen over and had to be righted. He selected a large flat stone on which he carved Polly's name and the dates of her birth and death. Below her name, he added "Son—Martin". He dug a small trench at the head of the grave and set the stone in place, then knelt. "Thank you, Polly, for bein' part of my life, and thank you for lettin' me love you." He sat beside the stone, holding Gabriel on his knee, contemplating thoughts of "goodbye" to the girl he had loved for so long.

As he walked down the hill, he felt that a burden had been lifted from his soul. He thought of the Bible passage, "The Lord giveth and the Lord taketh away."

Thank you, Lord, for giving me Polly for a while. He looked at his four-year-old son and took him by the hand. He realized that in Gabriel, he would always have a part of Polly with him.

OMA

Codger did not show up for his morning feeding. Caleb whistled and waited to hear the old mule bray, but heard only wind rustling through the trees above his cabin. Codger had been slowly growing blind. Caleb thought he might have broken through the fence and wandered into the property of Riley Mullins. He set out on the path that led past the water spring and further uphill to the coal bank, where he often dug coal for the fireplace. He whistled for the mule as he made his way along the narrow sled path. When he was able to peer above the slag and rock pile, he saw Codger, lying immobile, near the mouth of the coal mine. Apparently, the mule had fallen from the bank above the mine and broken his neck.

Caleb, young Riley, and the Vanover boys buried Codger in a grave dug two hundred feet downhill from Caleb's cabin. An old friend was gone from Caleb's life. As he stood looking at the mound of dirt covering the mule, Caleb thought of the hundreds of rows of earth he had plowed with

Codger and all the many times the mule pulled the wagon or sled to South Fork and returned. His eyes grew moist as he thought of the gentle manner of his equine friend.

"Stubborn as a mule." Caleb had often heard it said. But that did not apply to Codger. Perhaps because of his advanced age or just his unusually compliant manner, he had been one of a kind. He would be difficult to replace even if Caleb could afford the price of a new workhorse.

That night, he knelt by his bedside and offered a prayer of thanksgiving for the blessings in his life. He owed much of his good fortune to Riley Mullins for his generosity and would always be grateful to him. He thought of Polly and experienced the loss he felt since her passing. His little daughter, Violet, suffered for the four years of her life, and his youngest son perished while being birthed. Even with his losses, he would always be grateful to God for the love of Polly and having all of them in his life. He gently touched his young son's face, sleeping next to him, and wondering what he would do without Oma's dedication to Gabriel. He fell asleep with those things on his mind. Sometime in the middle of the night, he awoke, thinking of Oma. A pang of guilt crossed his mind, and he apologized to Polly for his indiscretion.

As Caleb performed his daily chores, Gabriel was in the care of Oma. Each morning, she greeted Caleb with a sweet smile and assurances that she was happy to keep Gabriel while his father worked. Caleb realized he was growing fond of the young woman, but in the evening, when he returned with Gabriel to their cabin, the essence of Polly filled his heart, and he chastised himself for the feelings he was having for Oma. He was not ready to move on to someone else, at least not in a romantic way.

One evening, when he approached Riley's back door, Oma was waiting on the small porch, Gabriel by her side and a covered pot in her hand. "Here's something for you and Gabe," she said.

"Thank you. It will be good to eat real home cookin'."

"I hope you like chicken and dumplings."

"It's been a long time."

He took Gabriel by the hand and started up the hill, the image of Oma remaining in his mind. He was sure she was still standing on the porch watching him until he was out of her sight. He didn't understand why he felt guilty, knowing she cared for him. He looked back to see her still standing there. She raised her hand to wave, but, having second thoughts, she lowered it quickly.

That night, as Caleb helped his son dress for bed, Gabriel touched his father's arm to get his attention.

Caleb looked down. Yes, Gabe?"

"I love Oma, Pa."

"That's OK, Son," his father assured him as he turned back the covers. "Let's say your prayers."

They knelt by the bed as Gabriel began. "Now I lay me down to sleep…"

Sleep did not come easy for Gabriel as he searched his conscience. Polly had been gone for less than five months. It did not seem right for him to have thoughts of another woman so soon after losing the one he had loved for so long. He had always known how unselfish Polly was, and she would want him to be happy, not mourn her passing for the rest of his life. And Oma was a good girl, sweet, and caring. She would be good for Gabriel. Caleb eventually fell asleep pondering these thoughts.

The next morning, looking up at Oma as she stood on the

porch, three steps above him, Gabriel at his side, he searched for the words he wanted to say to her. Somehow, "I love you" would not form on his tongue. Those were words he had only said to Polly, and he couldn't say them to anyone else with the same sincerity. He had feelings for Oma that he could not put into words. He helped Gabriel up the steps, then turned to leave for the barn.

"Did you have something you wanted to say to me, Caleb?" Oma asked after him.

He turned back to her. "Yes, Oma. Will you marry me?"

"Do you love me, Caleb?"

"I could learn to," he said.

"How long will that take?"

"I don't know, but I know I could."

She turned for the door, and he stood looking after her. Just before she entered the house, she called to him, "Caleb, I love you, and I will marry you when you have learned to love me." She went inside and closed the door after her.

Caleb stood for a moment, contemplating his loss.

From planting until harvest, Caleb brought Gabriel to Oma's door and took him home each evening. No word of marriage or love was spoken between them. On many mornings, Caleb thought of bounding up the steps onto the porch, taking Oma into his arms, and telling her he loved her, but thoughts of Polly kept his feet on the ground.

One afternoon, when he went to the back porch to get his son, Oma and Gabriel were sitting on the top step. Gabriel was crying.

"What's wrong with him?" Caleb asked.

"I don't want her to go," Gabriel said through his tears.

"Where is she going?"

Now, Oma was crying, too. "I'm going home to Whitesburg.'

"For good?"

"Probably."

"Why? I thought you was happy here."

I was, but I'm not now," she said. "Besides, Cousin Riley is getting married and will bring his wife, Dessie, to live with him and his pa."

"Why can't you stay until after harvest?" That was not what he intended to say to her, but those words came out of his mouth.

A look of disappointment crossed her face. "I can't stand loving you any longer and not being loved in return."

Caleb had not given thought to Oma ever leaving her uncle's home. The idea of her not being there every day was something he had never contemplated. He was not ready to lose another love in his life.

"Don't go," he said.

"Why?"

"Because I love you, Oma,"

"Since when?"

"For a long time. I just didn't know how to tell you."

"Do you still want to marry me?"

"Yes," he said. "I do. Will you marry me, Oma?"

She nodded, reaching out her arms toward him.

Caleb met her on the second step and embraced her. He kissed her for the first time, a long, enduring kiss, and brushed away tears from her face. It was good being in love again.

A three-week-old edition of The *Abingdon Standard* carried a front-page story of a killing in Wise County on Wednesday, April 15, 1872, two days after Caleb and Oma were married. The paper reported that Thomas Talton Hall, known locally as Bad Talt Hall, age 22, of Letcher County, Kentucky, shot Wilbur Stone of Gladeville, Virginia. The story reported that an altercation involving a woman of ill repute occurred in *Ruby's Rest Awhile* tavern in Pound, a place frequented by men traveling to and from Gladeville, Pound, and Letcher County through Pound Gap. According to the report, the fugitive was captured in Whitesburg by John Wright, a deputy marshal for Letcher County, and returned to Gladeville, where he was being held for trial.

Caleb touched Oma's shoulder. "Does it say anything else about John Wright?"

"Let me see," she said, looking down the column. "Yes, it goes on to say, Mr Wright is known in Letcher County as Devil John Wright. He is credited with killing two outlaws in Letcher County and has arrested three other men charged with feuding and murder. All are awaiting trial in the Letcher County jail in Whitesburg. Mr. Talt is expected to go on trial sometime in July this year."

Caleb reached for the paper and read the account again.

As he slowly read over the column, Oma asked, "Isn't John Wright the boy who saved your life after Antietam, the one from South Fork?"

"Yes, and I wonder why he ain't been here to see me."

"Maybe he's just been busy catching bad men."

"Maybe so, but I would like to see him. We might have to visit your folks in Whitesburg and see John while we are there."

"I would like to see Ma and Pa. It has been a long time."

"We'll do it this spring, before Talt Hall's trial," he said. "I want to go to Gladeville to see that when it happens." He stopped for a moment, then spoke again. "I'm glad John caught Talt before he had a chance to shoot him in the back."

"Talt Hall; I've heard you speak of him. Is that the boy that worked one summer for Uncle Riley?"

"Yes," Caleb said. "I think he was just itchin' to kill somebody, ' specially a Yank."

"What do you think will happen to him?"

"Maybe they'll hang him; do the world a lot of good."

Oma reached for Caleb's hand. "Don't say that, Honey. Don't wish death on anybody."

"He's a bad'n," Caleb said. "I know that without a doubt. He don't like Yanks or anyone who ever was friends with one. He would like to kill hisself one, that's for shor. He don't care who, maybe me or John Wright."

"Well, we don't have to worry 'bout that, because we're not Yanks."

Caleb pulled her close to him and hugged her. "You're right, Oma. It's just that I didn't like bein' 'round him when he worked here. He's out to make a bad name for hisself, somebody to be feared of."

That night, Caleb lay awake staring into the darkness, remembering Talt Hall's threats and his brandishing of a long barreled revolver when they were hoeing in the field. "Goin' to kill me a Yank or a Yank lover if I ever cross one." Caleb had sensed the intimidation at the time, almost certain Talt Hall knew he and John Wright were conscripted and forced to fight for the north, and he wondered if Wilber Stone had ever served in the Union Army or supported the Union cause.

Caleb told himself he would never turn his back on Talt Hall if they ever came face-to-face again.

Caleb was returning from the field just as Oma and Gabriel were leaving Riley Mullins's back porch. Oma carried an armload of newspapers and books.

"What have you got here?' Caleb asked as he took the load from her arms.

"Old copies of Harper's Weekly and some books for Gabriel. I'm teaching him to read." She held up two books with colorful covers. "This one is a McGuffey Reader, and the other one is a McGuffey spelling book, things he needs to learn. I want him to be a doctor or lawyer. So, he must learn to read."

"He can read now," Caleb said.

"A few words, but I want him to learn better than you and me."

"I can read the Bible some, but not like you. Did you teach yourself?"

"No, Uncle Riley taught me and gave me all these books and papers, and I just kept reading and reading, over and over. I want Gabriel to grow up to be an important man. If he studies hard, he can become a lawyer. I intend to help him get started now."

Caleb dropped the magazines, books, and newspapers to the ground. He took Oma into his arms and kissed her sweetly. "You are a blessing, Honey. Thank you for loving Gabriel so much."

"I love you, too, Caleb."

They embraced for several seconds until Gabriel tugged at his father's hand. "Let's go home, Pa,"

When they arrived at their cabin, Oma said, "Stoke the fire, and I will cook something for supper."

"No," Caleb replied. "Let's just have milk and cornbread. I want to hear you read something from this book. He held up a weather-beaten copy of a book with the barely readable title, *Practical English.* The author's name was obliterated, but appeared to be *Samuel Johnson.*

"No." She picked through the books and papers on the floor until she found the one she was looking for. "Let Gabe read from this one. I taught him some already." She held up a battered copy of a small black and grey book; the title on the spine read *George & Lucy.* She opened the first page and handed the book to Gabriel. "Light the lamp, Caleb, so you can hear your son read."

Gabriel began haltingly as Oma and Caleb looked on. "George was Lucy's…what's that word there?" He looked up at Oma and pointed his finger at the mysterious letters.

"That word is *brother,* Gabe."

He continued reading.

"I'll get the milk and bread ready," Oma said.

Caleb sat beside his son as he stumbled through the next few words. His heart raced at the thought of how fortunate he and Gabriel were to have Oma in their lives. Knowing that if anything unfortunate happened to him, Oma would love and take care of Gabriel as if she were his natural mother. That gave him hope. God had given him two wonderful young women, and he would be forever thankful for each of them.

Early in June, after Caleb got his spring planting done, he hitched his new plow horse, Tater, to the wagon and lifted Gabriel and Oma onto the buckboard. The road from Bold Camp to Pound was beginning to turn into muddy ruts caused by recent rainstorms, slowing their travel. It was nearly noon when Caleb opened the gate and led Tater into Uncle Eli's front yard. His mother, Ginny, came onto the porch, wiping her hands on her apron. She hurried down the steps as she spoke, hugged Caleb, and then Oma.

"Thank the Lord," she said. "It is so good to see all of you."

"We can't stay long, Ma," Caleb said as he helped Oma and Gabriel down from the wagon. "We just need to rest a spell, and then we're goin' to ride by and see Polly's Ma and Pa before we go on to Whitesburg."

"I don't think Polly's mother is doin' well, Son; just ain't got over losin' Polly. And she might take it hard, knowin' you done got married so soon after, you know?" She took Oma's hand, "Nothin' against you, Oma. I'm so glad about you and Caleb, but losin' a daughter so young and all has been hard on Polly's poor mother."

"I'm sorry for her, too, Ma, but me and Caleb love each other, and Polly's gone forevermore. It isn't like I stole her man. She went to Heaven and left him here, and he doesn't need to be living alone, just him and little Gabe. That's how I see it."

"It's goin' to be fine, Ma." Caleb put his arm around Oma's waist and pulled her close. "Don't worry 'bout that. Gabriel loves Oma just like he would his real ma. Ain't no difference to him or her, and I'm thankful to the Good Lord for that. If Polly's folks are upset about me and Oma, they'll get over it. I know Polly looks down on me and Oma and Gabe and blesses all of us."

After dinner, Caleb fed Tater and gave him water, then loaded Oma and Gabriel onto the wagon. Uncle Eli and Ginny waved goodbye just before they disappeared down the trail into the tall pines and oak trees fronting the property. It was almost 2:00 p.m. when they pulled into the roadway leading to the home of Polly's parents. Oma waited in the wagon while Caleb went inside. A few moments after the door closed behind him, he reappeared, bounded down the steps, and helped Oma and Gabriel down from the buckboard.

"Come on inside," he said, "they want to meet you and see their grandson; ain't seen him since Polly's funeral."

They topped Pine Mountain two hours later and entered Letcher County through Pound Gap. Caleb stopped the wagon to give Tater a few minutes' rest before beginning the downhill trek along the wagon trail. He reached under the buckboard, pulled out his new rifle, loaded it, and set it upright on the driver's side.

"Why are you getting the gun ready?" Oma asked.

Caleb climbed aboard the wagon. "These hills are full of feudin' fools and moonshiners, and I don't want to run up on one without bein' ready."

Oma had never given consideration to the fact that problems between hill folk still lingered. The war had been over for seven years. "Why are they still feuding, Caleb?"

"Still ain't got over their differences, I guess, and they're just protectin' their territory. Anyway, I don't want to git caught in the middle of somethin' and not be ready to protect my family.'

The easy trip down the mountainside took less than an hour before passing Little Elkhorn Creek and turning towards Whitesburg. They traveled along the same trail Oma's family had taken, before folks in the area and roving bands of soldiers knew the war had ended. Traveling along that trail was perilous then but had become safer because of men like Devil John Wright, fearless in pursuing renegades. Caleb kept a steady eye on the path ahead, occasionally touching his rifle stock for comfort. "You never know when you might cross someone who thinks you're a revenuer lookin' for his moonshine still. I'll be ready for that if it happens."

Small log and clapboard homes appeared in clearings along the road, indicating that they were approaching the city. Caleb relaxed and allowed his rifle to slide to the floor of the wagon. A rider on horseback appeared in the distance, at first a small, indescribable man, but he grew larger and ominous as he continued at a gallop in their direction. Caleb pulled up on the reins. "Whoa, Tater."

The horse stopped. Caleb reached down and brought the rifle to his side just as the horseman stopped his bay alongside the buckboard. A holstered rifle hung down the right side of the horse. On his left-hand side, the bearded rider carried a long-barreled pistol. He pointed to Caleb's rifle. "You won't need that. I'm not about to give you trouble. Where you folks headed?"

"Right here, Whitesburg," Caleb replied. "Why you ask?"

"Depends on where you're coming from."

"Pound, since early this mornin', we're kinda weary by now."

The man smiled. "You don't know me, do you, Caleb??"

"John! John Wright?" Caleb jumped from the buckboard to the ground. The two men embraced.

"The one and the same," John said, laughing as he spoke. "Don't take you long to forget an old homely face like mine."

"Ain't so, John. That awful beard scared me from guessin' it was you, and you shore don't talk like the John I know."

"I guess not, Caleb. I learned the King's English while riding with Robinson Circus in London. I'll tell you all about it when we get time. I'm pressed right now, but we'll get together real soon. Do you remember when we thought you might be dying? I told Mrs. Martin I was going to learn to speak the way she did. Well, by God, I've done it."

John stopped talking and looked up at Oma, sitting quietly on the buckboard. He turned his head aside and whispered, "Where's your Polly?"

"Died a year ago from consumption."

Keeping his voice near a whisper, he asked, "This your new wife?"

"Yes. I want you to meet her."

The two men stepped closer to the wagon. "John, this is my wonderful wife, Oma."

John doffed his hat. "Good to meet you, Ma'am. You got yourself a good man here."

Gabriel clung to Oma's arm, obviously fearing the menacing man dressed in all black with the well-worn hat atop his head.

John sensed the boy's anxiety. "Don't worry, Son. I'm only bad to bad people, and I'll bet you're a good boy. What's your name?"

Gabriel stood tall. "Gabriel, Sir."

John laughed. "You just grow up and be as good as your pa, and you'll get along fine in this world."

"Oma will make sure of that," Caleb said. "She's a mighty good wife and mother. How 'bout you? Have you ever found a wife?"

"I got me two," John said, interrupting his words with a broad smile. "Mattie and two boys here in Whitesburg, and a new wife in Gladeville. I'll tell you all about it one of these days when we can visit for a spell."

"Good," Caleb said. "Where are you bound now?"

"Heading to Gladeville. Got several horses for sale there and some takers, I hear tell. I think. I need to be there by morning to make the deal. I have twenty more on my place here in Whitesburg, and I'll be bringing some of them across the mountain soon. Maybe we can get together then."

"For sure. But you better git goin' now, John. Ain't safe to be on these trails after dark."

"You mean it ain't safe for the bastard that crosses my path, don't you, Caleb? I haven't met the man I'm scared of yet. Just don't put me up before those Yankee cannons, and I will have no fears."

"I'll be back on Bold Camp in a couple of days. Why don't you come round and visit a spell with us?"

"I might just do that," John doffed his hat toward Oma and kicked his horse in the flanks. He was gone in a rush, riding toward Little Elkhorn Creek.

Caleb got back aboard the wagon and took the reins in his hands. That's John Wright for you, Oma. He don't fear any man. Git up, Tater."

The horse continued pulling its burden towards the burgeoning city of Whitesburg.

Tater came to a halt in front of a two-room log cabin that rested on a bluff above the city of Whitesburg. As Caleb and Oma climbed down from the buckboard, a fifteen-year-old Ira burst through the front door and bounded down the steps. Standing a head taller than his sister, he enclosed her in his arms, "Oma," he said, "how we've missed you."

"I've missed you, too, little brother." She stepped back and looked him up and down, "No, you're not a little brother anymore. I've missed seeing you grow up, haven't I?"

By then, the family, including John Mullins, Patsy, Mendy, and three other children, had gathered on the front porch. Caleb helped Gabriel to the ground and then spoke to family members standing above him: "We thought it was past time to see you all again."

"That's for shor," John said. "Come on up here." He motioned with an exuberant wave of his arm. "We're jist about to sit down for supper, and I bet you're all hungry."

"We're starved, Ma," Oma said, "we haven't eaten since this morning except for some bread and salt pork."

Gabriel tugged at Oma's dress. "Some cake too."

"Only you." Oma smiled and tousled his hair.

Caleb set a small carpet bag containing extra clothing onto the ground. Ira picked up the bag and carried it up the steps. Caleb, Oma, and Gabriel followed.

On the porch, Oma embraced her mother as tears filled both their eyes. "I didn't think I was ever goin' to see my purty girl," Patsy said.

"Well, here I am, Ma."

"You look so good, Oma. You must be happy,"

"I am good, and I am happy. Happier than I've ever been." She touched Caleb's arm. "Thanks be to this good man."

Patsy turned to Caleb. "I was sorry to hear about your wife, but I'm awful glad that you and Oma got married."

"Me and Gabriel are too, Ma," Caleb said. "Oma has filled a mighty empty spot in our lives, and we are grateful to God for it."

Patsy went to the stove, removed he lids on two large pots, and stirred their contents. "Nothin' fancy here," she said, "Poke salad and pinto beans, cornbread too. We'll butcher a hog this fall, but right now we don't have much meat. Pa would have killed chickens if we knowed you was comin'."

"Thank the Good Lord for poke salad and soup beans", Caleb said. "They've kept us all alive in these hills through a lot of years. We are grateful for what we have."

"Amen," John said. "Let's eat."

———

After supper, Patsy carried a lantern to the front porch and set it on the railing. "It'll be getting' dark soon, and I don't think we're goin' to have much moonlight."

John and Caleb seated themselves in the two cane-bottom rocking chairs while Oma and her mother sat in a swing. They spent the evening in the waning daylight catching up on family happenings. The talk inevitably turned to the maladies the hill people experienced and the prevalence of moonshine in the hill counties, especially Letcher and Pike counties.

"Where'd Ira ride off to?" Oma asked.

"To see that Potter girl, Louranza."

"Louranza?"

"Yes, she's Jerome and Arminny Potter's girl. She's just thirteen, still a baby."

"Ma, you talk like Ira is an old man. He's only fifteen," Oma said.

John interjected, "He thinks he's grown, though; acts more like he's twenty-five."

"I'm worried about Ira," Patsy said. He's taken up with Mr. Jason Blevins, the biggest moonshiner in these parts; comes home with money he's got no business makin'. Why, I bet that boy has already saved fifty dollars."

"Doin' what?" Caleb asked.

John spoke up. "I've talked to Mr. Blevins about it, told him I don't want Ira doin' anythin' illegal. But Jason says there's nothin' to worry about; the Feds ain't goin' to arrest no fifteen-year-old boy."

"What's the boy doin', Pa?" Caleb stood and turned to face his father-in-law.

"Well, I guess he's carryin' whiskey down to the chicken fight arena."

"Where's that?"

"In Blevin's barn. They fight them roosters there about once a week. The Feds have raided the place two or three times, but they ain't never arrested nobody. No, no, I'm wrong. They did arrest Jason Blevins one time, but turned him loose the next day."

"Why'd they let him go?"

"I think he has friends in Frankfort."

"Frankfort? Where's that?"

"The state capitol, I'm told."

"Why don't Jason Blevins deliver the moonshine to the fights hisself?"

"He don't want to git caught. Says he don't make moonshine."

"But I think most people know he makes it."

John laughed. "Everybody 'round here knows, but the Feds can't catch him. They threatened to burn his house down if he don't tell them where his still is."

"Why would they burn his house?"

"'Cause they know the still is somewhere in his house, must be a secret room or somethin'."

Caleb moved across the porch and stood by Oma's chair. "Sounds like that boy of yours may be headed for trouble, and Mr. Blevins ain't doin' him no good."

"Yes, Pa," Oma said, "that makes me worry about him."

"Us, too." Patsy spoke up. "But Ira is bent on makin' enough money to start his own business, and he don't care how he gits it."

"What worries me 'bout the whole thing," John said, "is that Ira knows where the still is hid in Mr. Blevin's house. If them revenuers find out he knows, they'll rough him up until they git it out of him."

"Sounds to me like you need to step in, John, 'fore the boy gits in real trouble," Caleb said.

Oma got up from the rocking chair. "I think it's time for my little brother to come to Bold Camp and spend a few months with us. What do you think, Caleb?"

"I think that would be fine. I can't pay him, but I bet his Uncle Riley will have some chores he can do and get paid for.'

"That's what we'll do, Sister, we'll send him home with you," John sighed deeply and took a chew from his twist of tobacco. "What do you think, Mother."

"That would be a world of relief for me," she said, but I don't think he'll be real happy about leavin' Louranza."

"Yeah," John said, "he runs the legs off that horse of his, goin' over there to see her two or three times a day. "

"And that's another reason why I want him to go stay with you and Caleb a while, Oma," Patsy said. "'Fore he gits in trouble with that girl."

A horse galloped up the roadway towards the house. When it got closer, Caleb could see the white stocking feet of a sleek sorrel; he watched Ira dismount, then called to him. "What's his name?"

"Danny Boy," Ira said. "Want to ride him?"

"Not tonight, maybe tomorrow."

Caleb turned to John and spoke in a hushed tone. "OK, we'll take him with us when we leave tomorrow, but you can be the one to break the news to Ira, Pa, not me."

After breakfast, Caleb and Oma packed their wagon and set out on the road toward Pound Gap. Ira rode ahead, allowing him to stop to visit Louranza before leaving Whitesburg. He caught up with Caleb and Oma in Little Elkhorn Creek for the trip across Pine Mountain. Late that afternoon, they pulled into Riley's front yard. It was covered by horses and buggies.

Caleb pulled up on the reins and disembarked. Young Riley watched from the front porch. He hurried down the steps and met Caleb. He spoke quietly, ensuring that Oma, sitting on the buckboard, could not hear. "Pa's been killed."

Caleb held onto young Riley's shoulder, steadying himself. He wanted to cry out, but kept his outrage and sorrow inside to shield Oma, "Who? When?"

Ira galloped into the yard on Danny Boy. He dismounted before his horse had completely halted. Holding the horse by the reins, he yelled, "What's happened?", the cry in his young voice portending a dreadful answer. He stood quietly and listened to the two men talk.

"We don't know," Riley said, in answer to Caleb's question, but it must've been someone who knew his way around our place."

"How'd they kill him?" Caleb asked.

"Shot him on the back porch when he came in from the barn. Guess they were waiting inside the house."

"Wish I hadn't gone to Kentucky. Maybe I could've stopped it."

"You can't blame yourself, Caleb. My wife and I left him, too. We went to Pound to visit her folks."

"Someone's been watching your and my comin's and goin's."

Riley spoke. "Everyone knew the old man was sick. No doubt, they heard my Pa kept a lot of money, and they came looking for it. Must've been someone that worked around the place for Pa."

"Sheriff been out here to check?"

"Yesterday, but he won't find out anything. We'll just have to do it ourselves."

"And I bet I know where to start." Caleb set his jaw. "I never hated any man, but I vow to find Talt Hall myself and make sure he hangs."

"Talt Hall? Bad Dave Hall's son? I think he's still in jail, awaiting trial for that murder he did in Pound."

"Maybe, but this looks like his handiwork," Caleb said. "He worked with me one summer in the field here when he was fifteen. He bragged about his Pa killen' three men, and he was showin' off a long barreled pistol. I don't put this past him for shor."

"Guess we ought to tell that to the sheriff. If Talt is still in jail, he will start looking for someone else."

"Right now, I got to think about how to tell Oma. She loved her uncle so much. It'll break her heart, I fear."

Ira followed young Riley into the house. Caleb climbed back onto the buckboard.

"What happened?" Oma asked.

Caleb chirped at the horse, then turned the wagon up the trail towards his own cabin.

"What's happened, Caleb?" Oma asked again.

"I'll tell you when we git home."

"Tell me now, Caleb, please."

He could think of no way to soften the words he was about to say. Your uncle's been kilt."

She slumped in her seat, her hands covering her face. "Oh, Lord," Oma cried. "Don't let it be true."

Caleb held her to his shoulder. When her sobs subsided, he helped her down from the wagon. She leaned against him as they walked together into the house. Caleb returned and lifted his son to the ground. "Go stay with your mama while I feed the horse and put the wagon away."

Caleb heard Oma's cries of anguish as he unharnessed Tater and filled his feed trough. He fell to his knees and prayed for Oma, Gabriel, and the soul of Riley Mullins.

The next afternoon, Riley was buried on the hill above his house. He was interred beside his beloved wife, Lizzy. Brother Mac Cantrell delivered a heartfelt and endearing sermon befitting the beloved man of Bold Camp. The preacher's sermon touched Caleb. Overcoming his usual reticence, he asked to say a few words about his friend and benefactor.

He cleared his voice and spoke haltingly. "I am a simple man of few words, but the person we are layin' to rest today is close to my heart. He was like a father to me, doin' more for me than most fathers in these hills can do. All you good people have come to pay your respects to a man so well deservin' respect. I will miss him. I know all of us who knowed him well will miss him as much as I will."

Caleb's voice broke, and tears ran down his face. Oma reached for his hand and kissed his wet cheek. "I am so proud of you, Caleb," she said.

Young Riley and Caleb shifted uneasily on their feet as they stood across the desk from Sheriff Jimmy Pennington. He turned his face aside and spit a stream of tobacco juice that made a hollow ring as it hit the rim of the spittoon beside the sheriff's desk. "I was mighty sorry to hear about your Pa, Riley, and me and my deputies will do everything we can to find out who done it."

"Is Talt Hall still locked up here in Gladeville?"

"To tell you the truth, boys, he broke out two weeks ago. I understand he hightailed it to Letcher County."

"Did you go after him?"

"No, we didn't want nobody else kilt. 'Sides, I don't have no jurisdiction in Kentucky, You boys know that. But I did ride over and talk with Sheriff Stamper in Whitesburg. He's lookin' out for Talt as we speak. He also got Devil John Wright on Talt's tail."

"We don't know for sure, but we suspect he was the one

that killed my Pa," Riley said, "and that makes the capture of Bad Dave Hall's boy important to me."

"If he done it, boys, we'll git him one of these days." The sheriff extended his hand to Riley. "Sorry for your loss, Mr. Mullins."

Outside, as they untied their horses, Caleb said, "I don't hold much hope for the sheriff gettin' his hands on Talt. But the worst thing that could happen to him is havin' Devil John Wright on his tail. If anybody can find him, John Wright can."

The summer passed as most others had. Ira worked the fields with young Riley, Caleb, and the Vanover boys. Less than half the regular fields were planted since most of the crops were for personal use and not for sale.

After harvest in September, Ira was ready to return to Whitesburg and Louranza. "I'm goin' home Saturday," he told his sister during evening supper.

She looked up from her plate. "Not by yourself, Ira. It's not safe on those trails."

"I don't know why not. I'm about to turn seventeen and can ride as well as any man," He stood, looking down on his sister, who was still seated at the table.

"I know, brother, but it isn't safe. Caleb will ride with you."

Caleb got up from his chair at the kitchen table. "Your sister is right, Ira. I'll get Riley to ride with us. We'll go with you to Elkhorn Creek. You won't have any problem from there since you do it all the time."

At the foot of Pine Mountain the next day, Caleb and Riley bid Ira goodbye and turned their horses up the mountain toward Pound Gap. Ira kicked Danny Boy in the flanks and galloped in the direction of Louranza's house.

"It sure is good to be that young and in love," Riley said.

"Yes," Caleb lamented. "The heartaches come later, don't they?"

"We all have our share. Ira will, too, but I hope not for a long time. That boy loves life better than anyone I know."

They topped the mountain on their way home in less than an hour and reached Pound another hour later. As they passed *Ruby's Rest Awhile*, Caleb was reminded that Talt Hall killed a man there and was on the loose. He patted the rifle that was holstered and secured to his saddle. He cringed at the thought of aiming that rifle at Talt and pulling the trigger if necessary.

"What's on your mind, Caleb?" Riley asked.

"Those troubles of life we was talkin' about earlier." He slapped his horse's flank. "Git up, Tater."

In the Fall of 1873, Oma discovered she was pregnant. She carried her baby to full term without complications. Her mother, Patsy, and Ginny assisted with the birth of a seven-pound baby boy that Oma named Creed. The cries of the baby just after coming into the world brought Caleb and six-year-old Gabriel into the small bedroom. Patsy cradled the infant, wrapped in a wool blanket. "He's beautiful," she said, "looks just like his mother."

"No," Oma spoke from her bed. "He looks like his father."

"How's my darlin' wife?"

"She's doin' fine, Caleb, just like she had done it a thousand times," Ginny said.

"She's good at everything she does." Caleb kissed his wife's cheek, then reached for his new son. "I hope he looks like his mother instead of me. He'll stand a better chance in this old world if he does."

He took the baby into his arms and lowered him for Gabriel to see. "Your new brother, Gabe, a present for your eighth birthday."

Gabriel pushed back the blanket from the baby's face. "He's so red. Is he an Indian, Pa?"

"No, Gabe, he's just like you."

After lowering the baby so Gabriel could get a better look, Caleb said, "Let's give him back to his mama so he can get something to eat. Me and you will walk down to tell Uncle Riley and Uncle Ira about your little brother.",

Caleb and Gabriel left the three women with the new baby and walked down the hill to Riley's house to break the news to Ira and Riley. They found them engaged in a fierce game of checkers.

"Who's winnin'?" Caleb asked.

Riley pointed at Ira. "This young rascal is the most competitive man I've ever seen. He doesn't give his opponent a chance in hell."

"I guess that's why we won't ever have to worry about Ira, will we, Riley?'

"Not unless someone kills him for his money. He tell you how much he's set aside already?" And he's only seventeen."

"No," Gabriel said. "I guess I don't want to know. He'll be fine if the revenuers don't catch him sellin' 'shine for Jason Blevins."

Riley nodded. "He told me about that. They make a lot of 'shine over in Letcher County. I guess Ira is just doin' what everybody else does over there to make a livin'."

Ira jumped Riley's last kinged checker and got up from the table. "I'm beginnin' to believe Jason done got those lawmen paid off. If I know where his still is, they should too, and I ain't sayin'. I done put away three hundred dollars in two years. I'm goin' to start me a business just as soon as I marry Louranza."

"Good for you," Caleb said.

"Just think how much I could make if I hauled that stuff over the mountain to The Pound and Gladeville."

"You wouldn't get away with that," Riley said.

"For a while, I could. Long enough to make some real good money. I'll sell mercantile, too."

Caleb put his hand on Ira's shoulder. "It's a boy. We came to tell you."

"How's my sister?" Ira asked. "Are you goin' to give it my namesake?"

"Just fine. She's just fine, and the baby, too. She named him Creed."

Riley laughed. "I'm not sure we could handle two Iras in this family."

His comment brought a chuckle from Caleb.

"Well, anyway," Ira said. "I can take my ma and your ma home tomorrow, and I'll git there in time to see Louranza."

Riley teased, "You've only been gone three days. You afraid she's got another feller?"

"No," Ira replied, "We're gettin' married next year. I miss her when I don't see her." He turned to Caleb. "You know how that is; don't you, brother?"

Caleb clasped his shoulder. "I shor do, Ira."

While Caleb tended his crops and cared for the hogs and chickens, Oma devoted her spare time to educating Gabriel and caring for Creed. She often walked to Riley's home and selected books that she could use to teach Gabriel to read advanced texts.

"Our boy is so smart, Caleb. He can grow up to be a doctor or lawyer, anything he sets his mind to be. I want to help him."

"Me too, Oma, but he needs to learn how to farm and tend to the livestock," Caleb said. "Besides, he's too young to know what he wants to do."

"He is not too young to learn, and that is what I want."

"He might have to farm to make a livin' one of these days."

"He can learn that too, but he's got too good a mind not to do something more. I don't want him to grow up poor, or to sell moonshine like my brother."

Caleb worried that his wife was disappointed with her life. "We don't live fancy, Oma, but we do well enough."

Oma walked over to her husband, tiptoed, and kissed his cheek. "You are the best husband in the world, and we do well only because you have always worked so hard. I want Gabriel and Creed not to live desperate lives; that's all."

Caleb returned her kiss. "Me too, Honey, and I'll do all I can to hep. Maybe I can learn to read better if you'll teach me."

Oma threw her arms about Caleb. "That makes me so happy."

They stood in an embrace until Gabriel tugged at his father's hand, "I want to learn, Pa."

"And you will, Son," Caleb assured him.

After supper, Oma went to a shelf on a kitchen wall. She pulled two worn volumes from the shelf and carried them to the table for Caleb to see. "Riley found these for me. Got them from Doctor D.B. Hollyfield."

"What are they?"

She held up a thick book with a yellow and black cover, *School Days of a Backwoodsman.*

She put it into Gabriel's hand. "Written by Doctor Hollyfield. And he gave this one to me, too." She held up a larger volume, titled, *Commentary on the Law of England."*

"Ain't that hard to read?"

"Yes," Oma said. "It's too hard for me right now, but I will learn to read it, and I will teach Gabriel after I learn. But he can read now from the old copies of *Harper's Weekly* and the *Abingdon Standard.* He's way past the children's books I got from Uncle Riley. Want to hear him read?"

"Shor," Caleb reached across the table and pulled an oil lamp close to Gabriel. "Go ahead, Son, read for us."

Reading lessons became a daily staple for the Caleb Wilkins family for the next year. Oma meticulously pointed out the correct pronunciation of difficult words and emphasized the need to speak plainly, speaking the words as they were spelled, especially those ending with the letters "i, n, g".

"My Uncle Riley had no formal education," Oma said, "but he educated himself, just as Doctor Hollyfield did. The seven years I spent living with him were the best thing that could have happened to me."

Caleb laughed. "Better than living with me?"

"No, of course not, Caleb. You and Gabe, and now Creed, have made my life a wonder. I wouldn't change anything."

Caleb's eyes filled with tears. He clasped Oma's hand. "You have made these last few years of my life worth livin'."

"Living," she emphasized with a smile, bringing a chuckle from Caleb.

"I may be a hopeless case, but I'll try my best."

"That's all we can do, isn't it, Gabe?"

"Yes," Gabriel said, and began to read from a book titled *Little Meg's Children*.

"Thank God for Uncle Riley and Doctor Hollyfield." Oma stood and looked over Gabriel's shoulder as he read. She smiled with satisfaction, glancing from the book to look at Caleb, who was smiling too.

———

Ira and Louranza were married the following September. She was four months pregnant at the time. Riley heard the news while picking up his mail at the Pound post office. Louranza's grandparents on the Potter side of the family carried the news from Whitesburg to The Pound. Five months later, Ira and Louranza were blessed with their first son, whom they named John Harrison after Ira's father.

Caleb came into the cabin from tending his horse and cow. He brought the news of Ira and Louranza with him after learning from Riley. We'll go visit when the weather is better. Your Ma ain't seen Creed since the day he was born. "

"I know," Oma said. "And he's walking and beginning to talk."

"And gittin into all kinds of mischief." Caleb picked up Creed and held him as he spoke. "What is Gabe readin', – I mean reading?"

"Last week's *Abingdon Charter*."

"You know, I been thinking 'bout them folks I met in

Guest Station when me and John Wright was on our way home from up north."

"You mean the Martins, the people you told me about, who saved your life?"

"Yes, Dency and Joe Martin. Dency teaches school. I bet I can git her to keep Gabe for a while and let him attend her school."

Oma clapped. "Yes, and when he's ready, we can let him apprentice with Doctor Marshall Taylor."

"No," Caleb said. "I want him to work for a real doctor. I will talk with Doctor Hollyfield. He ain't doing much doctoring right now, and I bet he will hep Gabriel become a doctor if that's what Gabe wants."

"Alright then. When do we go to see the Martins?"

"As soon as the weather breaks," Caleb said.

The harsh winter delayed a trip to Guest Station with a nine-year-old boy and a toddler. In April, Caleb loaded the wagon with bedding and a large piece of canvas in case of rain. They stopped in South Fork and visited Ginny and Uncle Eli. After an hour, they began their trip to Guest Station, arriving two hours later. Caleb drove the wagon up the gravel road and stopped a few feet from the porch of the Martins' home. As Caleb descended from the wagon, Joe Martin came out of the house carrying a rifle.

"It's me, Mr. Martin," Caleb called out.

"All right," Joseph Martin replied, "but who are you?"

"Caleb Wilkins." Caleb walked to the steps and looked up at Joe Martin. "I guess I have changed a bit in fifteen years, but you still look the same, Mr. Martin."

Joe came down the steps and shook Caleb's hand. "It's so good to see you made it. Dency and me wondered if you survived since we never heard from you."

"I hope I didn't seem ungrateful, but I didn't know how to send a letter, and with the war and all, I just got busy getting married and raising a family."

Caleb walked back to the wagon and helped Oma to the ground. "This is my wife, Oma, and up in the wagon is Gabe. He'll soon be ten, and his little brother, Creed, is almost two."

Joe took Oma's hand. "I am pleased to make your acquaintance, I'm sure," he said.

"And I am so pleased to meet you. Caleb has spoken of you and your wife often. He has told me he owes his life to you two."

"I hope we helped a little, but Doctor Marshall Taylor is the one who really saved his life, got him on the road to recovery."

When Gabe and Creed were off the wagon, Joe led them into the house. He called for Dency, who was in another room. When she came to the kitchen, he said, "Guess who has come to see us."

"Praise the Good Lord," Dency said. "It's Caleb Wilkens, and this must be your pretty wife."

"Yes, Mrs. Martin, this is Oma, and this young man is Gabriel, and the baby is Creed."

"I'll bet you are all starved," Dency said. "Come, take a seat at the table, and I will get something ready for you all to eat."

"We'll be happy to be seated, but we ain't hungry. We et at my Ma's just two hours ago."

"Are you on your way to visit someone? Joe asked.

"No, we come to see you and Miss Dency."

"How can we help you, Caleb?" Dency inquired.

"We've come to ask for your help with our boy, Gabriel. He is so smart, and we want him to be educated properly."

Oma said. She placed a copy of McGuffey's Eclectic Speller and McGuffey's Reader on the table. "He can spell many words from this speller and can read from McGuffey's Reader."

"Can he factor?"

"He reads better than most grownups," Caleb said. "Oma taught him. He ain't so good at factoring, but can do some, much better than me."

Oma took an old edition of Harper's Weekly from a folder and set it on the table before Gabriel. "Read whatever you like,"

Gabriel read an article concerning the re-election of Ulysses S. Grant as president of the United States in 1772. The article was critical of many of the Reconstruction reforms that took place during Grant's first term and decried the avarice of carpetbaggers who were moving to the South from up north.

"The South ain't ever goin' to be the same," Joe Martin said.

Dency retorted, "And that might not be a bad thing after we get through this long period of adjustment."

Joe said, "As you can see, we think a little different about some things, but I know she's right."

Dency looked across the table at Gabriel, "How's your factoring?"

"I can do some adding and subtracting, Ma'am."

"Good," she said, "that's a start," then she spoke to Caleb. "What do you have in mind for the boy?"

"We hate to give him up, but we come to see if you would keep him here with you and teach him for a year. We'll pay you what we can."

"Dency was silent for a moment, turning to look at Joe. Joe stroked his chin and then nodded to Dency.

"We'll do it," she said. "I'm a teacher, and Gabriel seems eager to learn. I want to help."

"Thank you, Mrs. Martin," Oma said, "We can't ever repay you, but we will pay what we can."

"You won't owe us anything. I will do it for my James that I lost in the war. Maybe God brought us all together for this moment."

Oma got up from her chair and walked around the table to hug Dency. I won't ever forget your kindness. And neither will Gabriel. As Caleb said, we will never be able to repay you."

"If Gabriel grows up to be a good doctor or lawyer in our county, that will be repayment enough."

After tearful goodbyes, Caleb headed the wagon back toward Gladeville and onto South Fork. It was supper time when they arrived at Ginny's and Uncle Eli's home, and too late to continue to Bold Camp and their cabin, which was ten miles away. They spent the night at South Fork. After breakfast the next morning, they hitched Tater back to the wagon and set out for home. Their conversations were about their pride in Gabriel and their hopes for an easier life for him and Creed.

"I am so lucky that I found you, Oma," Caleb said. "Gabriel couldn't have a better mother than you."

"He's a special boy, Caleb, and you're a special man. I'm the lucky one."

Caleb drove through Pound and turned onto the Bold Camp road. He spoke to Oma as he pointed to a large cabin in the distance to his right. "That's where Talt Hall's uncle lives.

Talt stayed there when he worked the summer with me at Riley's."

"That awful boy. Do you know his uncle?"

"Never met him, but ain't heard nothing bad 'bout him."

He slapped the reins against Tater's flank. "Git up."

They traveled up the valley with Bold Camp Mountain rising above them. The deciduous trees were almost filled with leaves. The towering Pines and poplars shadowed the road.

"The blackberry and huckleberry bushes will be blooming before long," Oma said. "Spring is such a beautiful time." A shot rang out, and then another. Oma clutched Creed to her chest and slumped forward. Caleb grabbed his gun and aimed it at an onrushing rider. As he pulled the trigger, the horse and rider veered into the woods and disappeared. Caleb could hear the horse galloping through the brush as the sound of its hooves faded away. He halted Tater and put his arm about Oma. "Are you hurt?" he asked, then saw blood spreading down her dress.

"Is Creed OK?" she whispered.

Caleb turned around the wagon and headed back to South Fork. "I've got to get some help for you. Ginny will know what to do." He lashed Tater across the back. "Git moving, boy."

When they exited the woods and drove onto the main road leading into Pound, Caleb stopped the wagon. Oma was still clutching Creed, but she wasn't speaking.

There ain't nothing I can do here, he thought, and brought Tater quickly to a gallop.

Twenty minutes later, he pulled into Uncle Eli's yard, screaming as he arrived. "Help, help, help."

Uncle Eli came rushing out of the house and down the

steps, followed by Ginny as Caleb attempted to lift Oma from the wagon. "What's happened, Caleb?"

"Oma's been shot. Bowl Camp Road."

Ginny fell to the ground and wailed. "Lord, God Almighty, help us."

Eli climbed up on the wagon and removed Creed from the grasp of Oma, who was slumped over in her seat, desperately holding onto her son.

Caleb ripped away the buttons on her dress to examine her wound, which was steadily oozing blood. He tore a piece of his shirt and held it against her stomach to stem the flow of blood. "Hold on, honey," he said, "hold on."

She opened her eyes for a moment. "I love you, Caleb." She whispered.

Eli placed his hand over her heart, then searched her neck for a pulse. "It's too late, Caleb. She's gone to be with God," he said.

8

SIX MARBLES

Caleb and Eli carried Oma's body onto the porch. Eli went to the shed and returned with two boards, which he set on chairs in the kitchen. They laid the body on the boards and set a penny on each eye. Gabriel and Eli left the room while Ginny removed Oma's clothing and dressed her in a gown belonging to Caleb's youngest sister.

Outside, Caleb was inconsolable. Tears ran down his face as he helped Eli fashion a wooden casket and nail it together. Darkness overtook them before they completed their work.

"We'll finish first thing in the mornin'." Eli said as he placed his arm around Caleb's shoulders. "Let's go inside. You probably need to eat somethin'."

"I'm not hungry, Pa. I don't know if I ever will be again."

Caleb and Eli sat with Oma's body while Ginny attempted to quiet Creed and coax him to eat food she had mashed to a soft consistency.

Caleb bowed his head and mouthed a prayer. He repeated the gesture often during the night. In the early morning, he dozed and toppled onto the floor, where he lay until daylight. When he awoke, he stood to see Eli still near the body, watching over her.

"The Lord giveth, and the Lord taketh away," Caleb said. "My heart is broke, but God knows what He is doing."

Eli lined the casket with a blanket that Ginny had completed the previous week.

Together, he and Caleb placed Oma's body inside and tacked the cover loosely. They loaded the casket onto Caleb's wagon and set out for his cabin on Bold Camp at mid-morning. They arrived in Riley Mullins's yard before noon and informed him of Oma's death.

"We'll bury her tomorrow," Caleb said. "Will you ride to Whitesburg and let her Ma and Pa know what's happened?"

While Riley made the trip to Whitesburg, Caleb and Eli dug a grave twelve feet away from Polly's, leaving room for Caleb to be buried between the graves of the two wives.

Oma's mother and father, along with Ira, arrived late that evening. After an all-night wake by her mournful family members, along with Ginny and Eli, Oma was buried on the hill above the little cabin she had loved so dearly. She would always be close to the place she had made into a wonderful home for Caleb, Gabriel, Creed, and herself.

Caleb was too emotional to speak. He sat quietly while Ira comforted his mother and spoke lovingly of his sister. Brother Cantrell read from the Psalms and said kind words about the terrible loss of one so young, and he condemned the violence that still plagued the hills and valleys they all called home.

Caleb listened to the sermon while he silently vowed to find the man who killed his wife. He would start by hunting down Talt Hall. Brother Cantrell uttered the words that held no place in Caleb's heart at that moment: *Vengeance is mine, sayeth the Lord.*

Caleb was not a vengeful man, but he was certain that the bullet that killed his young wife was meant for him, and just as certain that it came from the rifle of Talt Hall. He said to himself, "No, forgive me, Lord, but vengeance is mine, not yours."

After the funeral, Ginny and Eli packed Creed's clothing and a favorite toy, a stuffed sock with an embroidered face that Oma made. "I don't know what I'll do here without his noise," Caleb wondered. "With Oma and Gabe both gone and now Creed, it is going to be lonesome."

Ginny and Eli made a bed for Creed in the front of their wagon. "We'll take care of him as long as we need to," Ginny said.

"I hope it won't be too long, Ma. I've got things I have to do, and I can't do them with a small child to care for all the time."

Patsy and John prepared their wagon for the return trip to Whitesburg. Before leaving, they walked the short distance up the hill and stood over Oma's unmarked grave. Afterward, Patsy put her arms around Caleb. "Thank you for makin' my daughter's life so happy."

"No more than she made mine, Ma."

Caleb reached for John's hand. "Do me a big favor?"

"You know I will if I'm able."

"You know John Wright?"

"I know of him but never met the man."

"When you git to Whitesburg, find him and tell him I need him."

"I will," he said and then prompted his horse to get moving.

Two days later, John Wesley Wright rode up the hill to where Caleb worked in the field. He spotted Caleb across the field, hoeing a row of sprouting corn. Without halting, he turned his steed down the row and stopped a few feet from Caleb. "You need me?"

Before Caleb could speak, John continued. "I heard about your wife. I'm sorry for your loss, Caleb, and I'm here to help all I can."

Caleb looked up at John. His rugged appearance told Caleb he did not ever want to be in the bore sight of Devil John Wright's rifle. "I think Talt Hall killed my wife."

"That isn't like Talt. He isn't one to kill women and children. He's a damn scoundrel, but I wouldn't think that was his work."

"He had no reason to shoot my wife. I think he was aiming at me."

"We'll see, Caleb. I'll round him up and take him in. I know where to find him. When he isn't in Pound at Ruby's or in Gladeville, he's in Pike County or around Little Elkhorn Creek. I'll find him, wherever he is."

"I thought he was running from the law."

"No more. They let him go 'cause witnesses say he shot Wilbur Stone in self-defense."

"You believe that?"

"Not me, Caleb, but I'm not the law."

"You ought to be."

"Maybe I'll run for sheriff of Wise County one of these days. I have land and horses and two wives there." He laughed. "You know, Caleb, every man needs three or four wives and a bunch of kids with each one of them. You just have to keep 'em separated."

"I don't know what I might do with more than one, and I don't hardly know what I will do without the one I just lost."

John got off his horse and led it across the field, walking alongside Caleb.

When they reached the cabin, Caleb asked. "You got time to set a spell?"

"Longer than a spell. We've got much to talk about, my friend. If you can put me up tonight, I'd welcome the invitation to spend the night with you."

"With me here alone, I got plenty of room and a reasonable good bed you can sleep in."

Caleb stirred the fire under the pot of pinto beans and set it to warm. He then set the table and ladled out bowls for each of them. "I hope these ain't soured on me. They been in the pot for almost a week now, the last thing Oma cooked."

After dinner, Caleb built a small fire outside, more for light than warmth. He and John sat on the ground close to the fire. John began his tale of adventures spanning the ten years the two friends were apart.

"You remember the letter I wrote you from Richmond?"

Caleb nodded. "Yeah, you told me you was headed for England."

"And I went, by God."

"You're a man of your word, John."

"I try to be."

Neither of them spoke for a few minutes, watching the sparks fly from the fire as Caleb stirred it. John let go a long sigh and then began again, "Well, my Uncle Martin on my mother's side—the family called him Uncle Martin Brother—

was a great big man, more than seven feet tall. I don't know if you ever heard of the Robinson Circus…"

"No, can't say I have," Caleb said.

"Uncle Martin was billed as a giant with that circus, and it was getting ready to make a trip to England. He got me a job tending the horses and other circus animals. And that was OK for a start, but not what I wanted. I could shoot and ride as well as any man on earth. So, I made up an act as a sharpshooter on horseback." He stopped talking for a moment, wiped his shirt sleeve across his mouth, and then asked, "You got any brandy 'round here?"

"No, I got a little moonshine, purty good stuff from Jason Blevins."

"I'll have a nip of that if you don't mind, Caleb."

Caleb tossed a small log onto the fire and went into the house. He returned, carrying a small mason jar. "Not much here, John, but enough to wet your whistle."

John drank from the jar and then emitted a sound of satisfaction. "Ahhh, good stuff. Nobody makes moonshine like Jason Blevins, that old renegade."

Caleb thought of mentioning that Ira was getting paid well by Jason to deliver his moonshine, but thought better of it for the moment. "I keep a little here for colds, I mix it with some strong horehound tea."

"I don't drink much of it. I prefer the apple brandy that I brew myself." John took another sip. "Anyway, I traveled around Europe with the circus for nearly three years, and I was determined to learn to speak proper English, just as I told Miss Dency Martin when she was taking care of you out in Guest Station."

"I'm proud you done that, John. My Oma learned good English, and she taught my boy, Gabriel, and me some too.

He's staying with Dency Martin now, learnin, readin, and factorin,. I guess I'll never talk no better'n I do, and I'll be just as happy."

The fire flickered. Gabriel reached behind him and drew another log close to put on the fire. "He don't know his ma is dead. I have to go to Guest Station soon to let him know. I hate to do that, but I think it's right that he should know. I shor would like to have him here with me, been thinkin' 'bout fetchin' him, but it wouldn't be fair to the boy, and not what Oma would want."

John reached and touched Caleb's arm. "You got a lot to think about, and, I guess, a lot of praying to do."

"Yes," Caleb said, "but the Lord always gits me through."

"Me too," John said.

"And I'm happy 'bout that. 'Cause He knows I wouldn't be here without you."

"We all need a friend, Caleb. I don't have many, and outside God, I count you as one of the best."

"I 'preciate that," Caleb said.

"I'm going to Gladeville tomorrow morning to check on my horses and see my wife, Mattie. I'll be there for a few days. When you go to Guest Station, stop by and get me. I will go with you. I would like to see Dency and Joe Martin again."

"They are good people," Caleb said.

"You're right, Caleb. I've traveled halfway around the world, even met Queen Victoria, and there are no better people than the Martins."

"Who's Queen Victoria?"

"The queen of England. When she saw me perform in the Robinson Circus, she wanted to meet me. My Uncle Martin arranged it, and we both went to Buckingham Palace to meet her. She spoke funny, but she was nice."

"You been everywhere, John. I bet you miss traveling, don't you?"

"I'm mighty glad to be back home in Kentucky and here in Wise County. I was born in these hills, and I will die in these hills." John stood. "I'm winding down, Caleb. You got a place for me to bed down?"

Caleb got up. John followed him into the house.

"You can sleep in Gabe's bed," Caleb said."

"If I get up early, I'll try not to wake you."

When Caleb awoke the next morning just after sunrise, the bed across the room was empty. He walked outside in time to see John's back as his horse trotted down the hill and then disappeared beneath the umbrella of forest hanging over the trail.

———

The summer and early fall were interminable for Caleb. He missed Oma and thought of her often. Long nights alone brought back memories of his first love, Polly, and how much she suffered giving birth to the baby boy who died along with her. During one of those nights, he decided to go to Guest Station to see their son and bring him back home. Gabriel had turned twelve and would soon be a young man. Caleb was missing many months he wished to share with his sons. On one chilly fall morning, he hitched Tater to a wagon and set out for South Fork.

After spending time with his mother and holding Creed, he continued to Gladeville, stopping by John Wright's place for a short visit. He found John at his barn, shoeing a horse that was one of several John had for sale.

"You ought to get yourself a real horse, Caleb, and get rid of that old bag of bones."

Caleb laughed. "No, John, I don't need a fancy saddle horse. Old Tater has done me proud since I lost my mule, Codger."

John let go of the horse's hoof and stood to shake Caleb's hand. "Where you bound, my friend?

"I'm running over to Guest Station to check on Gabe, maybe bring him home for a spell."

"I know you miss that boy of yours, but I think he's in pretty good hands with Dency Martin."

"Yeah, I know, John. I been thinking 'bout that, but it gits mighty lonesome up in that cabin by myself."

"You could come spend some time this winter with me. You'd be close enough to Guest Station to go see the boy anytime you feel like it, and you would be only an hour from your baby boy in South Fork."

"Got a cow to feed and milk, and I hep Riley when he needs it. That wife of his is puny all the time, and…:"

"Don't tell me about wives, Caleb. I got three of them, and they all got problems when I'm about, but they seem to do fine when I'm gone."

Caleb laughed heartily. As his laughter subsided, he turned serious. "You had any trace of Talt Hall?"

"Haven't seen hide nor hair of him. I hear he's keeping in Pike County, out of my territory in Letcher County, and he doesn't show his face here in Wise County. He knows I'm a deputy Marshall here now, and he doesn't want The Devil on his tail."

"I hope you git your hands on him, John. I hope soon. I

don't hold nothin' against any man except him. They can't hang him soon enough for my liking."

"Oh, I will, Caleb; one of these days, I will for certain."

Caleb climbed aboard his wagon. "You want to ride over with me?"

"Wish I could, but I've got to get this horse ready for a buyer."

"Like I said, I will get Talt Hall sooner or later. You give my regards to the Martins."

"For sure, John. They'll be glad to hear you're doing well."

———

Caleb arrived at the home of Joe and Dency Martin late that afternoon, just as Dency and Gabriel were returning from the church where she taught a dozen children. When Caleb alighted from the wagon, Gabriel ran and threw his arms around his father. "Pa," he said, "I've missed you so much, and Ma, too."

Gabriel's words touched Caleb's heart. How was he to break the news of Oma's death to her devoted son? He could not put such thoughts into words. For the moment, he would not try. "We've missed you, too, Son."

"Are you staying with us?" Gabe asked.

"No, Gabe, I came to talk with Mrs. Martin."

"Excuse me, Pa, while I take these books inside."

"You readin' them books, Gabe?"

"Yes, Pa." He placed one book under his arm and held the other upright for his father to see.

Gabriel read the title aloud, "*The Laws of England.* I might be a lawyer when I'm grown."

"I'm mighty proud," Caleb said as he struggled to keep

tears from forming in his eyes. The thought that Oma would miss the fruits of her efforts overwhelmed him, and he wiped his sleeve across his eyes to hide the tears.

Gabriel carried the two large leather-bound books, one in each hand, into the house.

"Thank you, Dency," Caleb said. "You done such good things for Gabe."

"He's done them himself, Caleb. I just showed him the way. It's all he needs. I've never seen a boy so eager to learn."

"He owes it to Oma, not to me."

"It's getting a little chilly out here. Come on into the house," Dency said.

"Not just yet, please. I need to talk with you first."

They moved onto the porch and seated themselves in rocking chairs. Caleb began talking in hushed tones.

"I wanted to see my son and speak with you folks about takin' him home with me, but seein' all he's learnin', makes me think I would be makin' a mistake. "

"He is doing so well; He may be teaching me before long."

"I miss him terrible, and I ain't told you the worst news yet."

Caleb paused, his lips contorted as he sought to find the words, which he finally spoke. "His mother has passed."

"Oma? Oh, my Lord," Dency said. "How?"

"She was shot by someone when we was on the way home from bringing Gabe to stay with you. "Course he don't know, and I got to tell him. He loved her so. It will break his heart."

"You must tell him," Dency assured him, "but I don't know if this is the right time."

"I made up my mind to tell him now. If he wants to go

home with me, he can, but if he wants to stay and learn, that's all right too. I leave it to Gabe."

Dency called for Gabriel to come to the porch. She and Joe went inside the house. Caleb pulled Gabriel close to him, standing only slightly taller than his boy. "Your mother has passed, Son."

"Passed? How Pa?" Gabriel held tightly to his father as they stood quietly sobbing. Through his tears, Gabriel asked, "What happened, Pa? Was she sick?"

"No, Son. Someone shot her four months ago, the day we brought you here. I think the shot was intended for me, but it killed your Ma."

"Are you doing all right by yourself, Pa?"

"Yes, Gabe, but it's you I'm concerned about."

"No, don't worry about me," he said. "With the Lord's help, I will get by it."

"Do you want to go home with me?"

"Yes, but I'm staying here. It's what Ma would want me to do."

Caleb pondered his son's words for a moment and then said, "You're right, Gabe. That's what she would want you to do."

Two days after Caleb arrived home, Riley came riding on his horse, calling Caleb's name. Caleb ran to the door and looked out. "What's wrong, Riley?"

"Something's happened to Uncle John."

"What do you mean?"

"Ira came to my house early this morning; said they've been looking for his father for three days. He went out to check his traps and hunt for deer last Saturday and hasn't returned."

"Where's Ira now?"

"He rode back to Letcher County to continue looking for his pa."

"Do you have any idea what happened?"

"Maybe he stumbled onto someone's still and they killed him. His horse didn't come home. Patsy is worried to death."

"Do you want me to come with you?"

"No, Caleb, just keep an eye on Dessie. I may be gone for several days. We have to look for Uncle John until we find him, alive or dead."

Riley returned three days later. "No sign of Uncle John. We think someone might have killed him for his horse, or maybe he had furs. Letcher County is lawless. We sent for Devil John Wright. We hope he'll come to help us."

"John Wright. He's a good man and ain't no devil."

"How well do you know him, Caleb?"

"He saved my life in the war."

"You know what they say in Gladeville and Lecher County? When John Wright is on your tail, the devil is after you."

"Sounds like John. I ain't ever seen a braver man. If anyone can find your uncle, my friend John can do it."

"I've asked Ira to bring his mother and Louranza to live with Dessie and me for a while. The bigger kids can make out all right in Whitesburg. I'm heading back over there now to help bring Aunt Patsy here. Her health is failing, and I don't want her having to worry about all of her brood. It will be good to have her here, and Ira will be a big help to me."

"What about his moonshine business with Jason Blevins?"

"I don't encourage it, but he's laying up good money for

his future. I hear tell he has saved over five hundred dollars already, and he just turned twenty-one. He's going to be rich one of these days if he doesn't get killed for hauling shine."

"He'd best quit bragging about his money," Caleb said. "I wouldn't want some people to know my business if I was him. It might git him killed for shor."

"He doesn't really brag, just doesn't hide what he's doing."

"All the same, we got people in these hills that'll kill you for five cents."

"I'll caution him," Riley said, "not that it'll do any good."

"All right, Riley, I'll check on Dessie this evenin'. Before I do my chores and I'll feed the livestock."

Caleb went about his own evening chores and those of Riley. After feeding the horses and milking the cows, he knocked on the back door and waited for Dessie to open it. He handed her a pail of milk. "Everythin's been fed, and I'm callin' it a day," he said.

"Do you want to come in for a spell?" Dessie asked." These quiet evenin's make a person feel mighty lonely."

Caleb stood in the doorway. "I know," he said. "With my boys gone, it's as silent as the grave without them. I could stand a little of their noise, 'specially Gabe's conversation."

She set the milk pail on the table and bid him come in with a wave of her hand.

He pondered a way to reject her invitation; after a moment, he said, "I better git to the house and put my milk in the spring for cooling. When you git yours in jars, set them on the porch and I'll take them to the spring for you 'fore dark."

"Can you fetch me some eggs from the barn?" She smiled.

Caleb noticed a tooth was missing on the left side of her

mouth, detracting from her otherwise very pretty face. "In the morning, if you don't mind. I'll gather some eggs then."

"I shor could use them this evenin'. I might bake a cake if I had some eggs."

Caleb was uneasy with Dessie's subtle overtures. He backed toward the kitchen door. "I best be going, Dessie. Like I said, I'll come fetch your milk jars when you set them on the porch."

She reached for his hand. "Please don't go, Caleb. I'm so lonesome, and I know you're lonesome too."

"I couldn't," Caleb said. "Riley's my friend. I couldn't betray him."

"I just need holdin'," she said. "Riley don't ever hold me no more."

Caleb put his arms around her and held her. "I'm sorry, Dessie, but you are the wife of my good friend. I know Riley loves you."

She was crying now as she stepped away from Caleb." Maybe, but he don't know how to show me."

"I'm sorry, Dessie." He kissed her cheek. "I'll pick up your milk when it's ready, and I'll set a few eggs on the back porch 'fore dark."

Dessie's desire for company was fulfilled a few days later when Riley returned home, bringing with him his Aunt Patsy, Louranza, and her two children, the youngest only four months old. Ira soon followed, riding his horse, Danny Boy. John and Patsy's oldest son, Enos, remained home in Whitesburg with his three young sisters and his wife, Eula.

John Mullins had vanished, and the search for him was

ended except for the efforts of Devil John Wright, who never gave up on a hunt, always getting his man dead or alive.

Devil John expanded his search for John Mullins to the Pike County line. He heard rumors that Doctor Marshall Benton Taylor was riding a horse with the markings of the one John Mullins was last known to be riding. Doctor Taylor was pastoring the Mount Mariah Methodist Church of Calvert City in Letcher County, ministering to the spiritual and medical needs of his flock. When approached by John Wright, he declared that, by almighty God, he had raised the horse from a colt.

"You know me, John. I am the same man that treated your young friend in Guest Station, and I am a man of God who does not know how to tell an untruth."

"My apologies, Doc, but I am looking for John Mullins, who disappeared with a horse having the same markings as your horse."

"My young friend, God testifies for me. This is my horse," the doctor said.

"No affront intended, but I had to make the inquiry, thinking maybe you bought the horse from someone."

"No, I got him as a young colt."

John Wright accepted Doctor Taylor's assertion but rode away doubting his veracity. He had an uneasy notion that the doctor had lost touch with reality. He no longer exhibited the astute mannerisms of the professional John met at the home of Dency and Joe Martin more than ten years earlier. Although John was almost certain that Doctor Taylor was riding the horse that belonged to John Mullins, he would not pursue the matter further. For once, Devil John did not bring in his man.

Ira made weekly trips to Letcher County and returned

with wagonloads of moonshine, which he sold to other bootleggers whose stills had been destroyed by government agents and the Wise County Sheriff. Riley would not allow moonshine on his property. So, Ira bought acreage with a small cabin already built on it near Gladeville. He hauled his liquor there, where others bought it, bottled and sold it throughout the county, especially in Pound. When the Old Regular Baptist Church members complained to Sheriff Pennington, he conducted raids that hampered Ira's business for short periods. But after a few weeks, Ira resumed his trips across the mountain and supplied Wise County with the best moonshine brewed in Letcher County, Kentucky.

While his Uncle Ira broke the law, Gabriel was preparing to be a lawyer, sworn to uphold the laws of the county of Wise, the Commonwealth of Virginia, and the United States of America. At fourteen, he spent fall and winter studying with Dency Martin and apprenticing under Doctor Daniel Hollyfield, learning the art of medicine and surgery. The year he turned fifteen, he clerked for an attorney, Jerome Oxford, in Guest Station for three months and studied the law journals and books in Mr. Oxford's extensive library. He told his father that he would decide what profession he might follow, but in the meantime, he would learn all he could about law and medicine. Although Caleb desired to have Gabriel and Creed at home with him, he was determined to carry out Oma's dreams for Gabriel and was proud of his son's thirst for learning. He credited Polly for Gabe's innate intelligence and Oma for the encouragement she gave him. He thanked the Lord for two wonderful women in his life and the sons they bore him.

Caleb made frequent weekend trips to South Fork to spend time with Creed, who was growing "like a weed," as

Ginny always said. When he was five, Caleb brought him home to Bold Camp, and Gabriel came home to live with his father. He brought with him a barrel of books with subjects on medicine, law, and history, given to him by Dency Martin, Doctor Holyfield, and Jerome Oxford. He continued his studies daily and frequently read aloud to Caleb and Creed.

Gabriel had dreams of attending The College of William and Mary, but knew he could never afford to attend. Dency inquired with Roanoke College in Salem, Virginia, about the possibility of finding a benefactor who would sponsor Gabriel. They waited for a response to their request as the new year of 1882 approached. Their hopes diminished as summer passed, and Gabriel reached his sixteenth birthday. Still undaunted, he continued his studies at home, reminding himself that Abraham Lincoln became a lawyer and president of the United States with almost no formal education. Gabriel believed that the same opportunities awaited him.

Harvesting was completed in late September. Apples and potatoes, plenty for the coming winter, were banked, and more than two acres of corn shocks stood in the field, drying, to be used as fodder for Tater and the old Jersey cow. Gabriel had worked the summer, alongside Caleb, while Creed spent most of the days in the care of his grandmother, Patsy, and Dessie.

At the end of a busy day, Caleb and Gabriel stood, looking across the cornfield at their handiwork.

"Another summer come and gone," Caleb said. I don't know what I would have done without your hep, Son. Not much left to do now but cut kindlin' wood and dig up enough coal for winter."

"If you don't mind, Pa, I want to take a trip over to Guest Station to visit with Miss Dency, see if she has heard anything from Roanoke College. She's getting up in age now, Mr. Martin, too."

"Shor, Son, and we'll stop and visit a spell with Ginny and Uncle Eli, maybe stop by John Wright's place since we'll be passing right by."

"If the weather is good, maybe we can go day after tomorrow."

"That sounds good, Gabe."

"You know, Pa, this has been a satisfying day. I think I'm going to build a little fire outside and enjoy the rest of the evening before heading to bed."

"While you build the fire, I'll go to fetch Creed from Riley's."

Before long, the dried chestnut logs were ablaze, and red and orange flames reached upward as darkness approached. Caleb, Gabriel and Creed sat close to the fire, eating biscuits Patsy had baked, covered with honey. When the food was eaten, Gabriel stood and took Creed's hand. "Time for you to go to bed, little brother."

Caleb stood too. "Might be time for all of us to turn in. You go on, Gabe, and I will be in as soon as this fahr dies down."

Gabriel turned the cover up to Creed's chin. "Go to sleep, brother. I'll turn in when pa does."

As he stood, he heard rifle fire, first one shot, then another. He wondered what his father might be shooting at. When he saw Caleb's rifle standing against the corner, he realized his father did not have a gun with him. Gabriel ran for the door. As he stepped outside, he saw his father writhing on the ground.

"Pa! Pa!"

Gabriel knelt quickly and held his father's head on his

knees. He screamed into the night, "Riley, Riley, Riley, Pa's ben shot."

He heard only the gurgling sounds of his father as he took his last breaths and the sounds of a horse and rider crashing through the brush into the distance.

Gabriel was on his own with a young brother to care for. He buried his father on the hill above his house. The grave was dug between those of Polly and Oma in accordance with his father's wishes. Uncle Mack Cantrell, from the Old Regular Baptist Church of Gladeville, preached a ten-minute sermon filled with fire and brimstone and hell and damnation, assuring Gabriel that the man who shot his father would surely face the wrath of God but providing little comfort to the forlorn boy of sixteen.

A mournful crowd of friends and loved ones, singing *Wayfaring Stranger,* accompanied the wood casket up the hill. Ginny, silently weeping, was too distraught to make the trek and sat in a rocker on the porch. She held Creed on her lap, close to her breast. Gabriel, tall and straight, walked bravely up the hill, leading the procession.

As the afternoon sun slipped behind ominous rainclouds, the men hurriedly shoveled dirt over the wood coffin of Caleb Wilkens, age thirty-seven, finishing moments before the clouds above them burst, sending everyone scurrying for shelter. Gabriel was relieved when the ordeal was over, and he and his little brother were left alone listening to the downpour hammering on the shingles of their two-room log home. The past two days had crushed his spirits, leaving him searching for the will to survive, wondering how he would provide for himself and Creed. The rains continued for the next two days.

The events of the day reminded him that his mother died at the age of twenty-seven, of consumption and childbirth. He was only four then and did not comprehend the concept of life and death. He thought of the baby brother, Martin, stillborn and buried alongside his mother in a casket his father built. And he remembered Violet, who died a year earlier than Polly, from an unknown malady. He thought of Oma and how much he owed her for her encouragement and recognition of his desire and ability to learn. How different his life would be now without all those he loved.

Gabriel had been told over and over by the few mourners who came to view his mother at the funeral that she was "better off" or in a "better place" having gone to Heaven to be with Jesus. Even so, at four, he could not understand why two men nailed the coffin shut with his mother inside it. He was bewildered as his father led him away from the grave and down the hill.

He's better off. He's gone to a better place. These thoughts crossed Gabriel's mind. But he knew, just as he did not understand death at the age of four, that Creed would not understand the death of his father now. How could anyone be better off in a hole in the ground, covered with dirt? Those words, "He's better off," or "He's gone to a better place," were inadequate and untrue.

"You understand Pa's not coming back, don't you, Creed?"

"Where's he gone?"

"He's dead."

"Dead?"

"Yes, Creed. We won't ever see him again."

Creed's eyes widened and filled with tears. "Will we see him in heaven?"

"If we get there, we will."

"I'll get there," Creed nodded his head.

Gabriel placed his hand on the boy's cheek. "I'll bet you will."

"Who'll take care of us, Gabe?"

"I will, just like Pa did." His bravado belied his doubts.

A single oil lamp provided dim light and helped reduce the dampness brought on by a porous roof that allowed the rain to seep between the shingles. A bucket sat on the kitchen table, catching the trickle of water, which would be used along with the rainwater collected in barrels beneath the eaves of the house outside. A fireplace that burned coal dug from a bank two hundred yards up the hillside sat idle, not having had a fire lit for more than a week. The cast-iron cooking pot sat along the hearth. Nothing had been prepared in it for several days since his father had killed one of the hens that ranged in the yard near the house. The fireplace provided the only heat available in winter but added to the swelter in the summer, so it was used sparingly except in winter. When a coal fire did burn in it, the dampness was hardly noticeable. Now, late September was bringing cool evenings, and Gabriel would need to gather kindling wood and dig coal for colder weather, which would soon follow. He vowed to himself that if he could care for Creed, he would buy a real cookstove when he could afford it. A stove would provide more heat in winter, and the coal would burn more slowly than it would on the fireplace.

He recalled how many times he and his father had climbed up on the roof, attempting to repair the places that allowed the rain to get through. "It's hard to trace the rain from shingle to shingle," his father had said many times. "There ain't no way to tell where it's comin' from."

Each time it rained, he and Gabriel were back on the ladder, climbing to the roof and nailing down the culprit shingle. "This time for sure."

Gabriel smiled. "I'll fix it when the rain stops, Pa, I promise."

"You talking to me, Gabe?" Creed looked up at Gabriel from the rough-hewn floor where he was rolling around six marbles, the ones Caleb brought back from Antietam when he escaped, along with John Wesley Wright, from the Yankee company with which they were forced to serve after being captured at the Battle of Pound Gap. The marbles held a special place in Gabriel's heart, the only present he could recall receiving from his father. Someday, he would give them to Creed, but not until he was old enough to appreciate their true value.

"No, Creed, just talking."

"Who you talking to?"

"Myself," he said. "I'm talking to myself."

As the light of day waned and Creed was asleep in the bed he always shared with his older brother, the enormity of his new responsibilities fell hard on Gabriel's mind. For the moment, there was food aplenty, chickens for eggs and eating, mason jars filled with green beans and cabbage, and potatoes and apples banked for the winter, and other vegetables grown on their rocky piece of land. Gabriel could hunt for game as well as any man, so getting meat would not be a problem for the time being. The old milk cow, way past her prime, for most of the year, still gave enough milk to meet their needs. His little brother would need clothes since he was growing out of the trousers he wore every day. Perhaps

Gabriel could plow or dig coal for his few neighbors, to earn some money, but most of them were as poor as his own father. These considerations were on Gabriel's mind, and so was the idea of vengeance. Hatred for the man who shot his father pushed the concerns for survival aside for the moment. He had no idea who might have wanted his father dead, but he knew that such murders occurred often in that part of Appalachia without consequences. If the killer was to be punished, Gabriel would have to do it, and he doubted that he could ever kill another person. As Creed slept peacefully, Gabriel vowed to his father that he would find the man who killed him and bring him to justice before the law, no matter how long it might take or how much it may put his own life at risk.

PART 2

PRELUDE TO TRAGEDY

1

PUTTING THE PIECES TOGETHER

After two days, the rain subsided, finally stopping altogether as the noonday sun beamed down on the roof of the Wilkens cabin. Gabriel brought a ladder from the shed and leaned it against the edge of the roof.

"Can I climb up there with you, Gabe?" Creed asked.

"No, brother. You stand here at the bottom of the ladder in case I fall." Gabriel laughed. "I might not be as handy at this work as Pa was."

He climbed up and then surveyed the roof shingles in the area where he suspected that rain might be seeping through. After several minutes, he climbed back down the ladder.

"You fix it already?" Creed asked.

"No, but I see where the rain is probably coming through."

"Where?"

"Around the chimney and running down to some of the warped shingles."

"How are you going to fix it, Gabe?"

"I'm going to mix some chinking to put around the roof. If

it doesn't rain for a few days, the material will dry, and we won't have any more leaks for a while." He waited several seconds before saying, "I hope."

Creed laughed. "Me too, Gabe."

"I'll need to replace a few shingles, too, then we ought to be fine."

That afternoon, they walked up the hill and stood alongside the newly covered grave of their father, Caleb. Gabriel bowed his head and prayed silently for Polly, the mother he barely remembered, for his father, and for Oma, the woman to whom he owed his desire to learn. "I need to get Pa a stone and carve Oma's stone as well. Pa just couldn't bring himself to put her name and date of death on that slab."

"Why didn't Pa do it?"

"He just couldn't. Creed. Someday you'll understand."

As Gabriel and Creed neared the cabin door, a rider burst up the trail and dismounted.

"Get inside, Creed," Gabriel ordered as he ushered him through the open door.

"You Gabriel?" the rider asked.

"Yes, and who might you be?"

"John Wright."

"Yes, Sir, now I remember you from Whitesburg."

"Is it true?"

"What?" Creed responded.

"Is your Pa dead?"

"Yes, Sir," Gabriel said. "I'm afraid it is true. Shot down not more than twenty feet from where you stand, Mr. Wright."

John turned his face against the saddle of his horse. His big shoulders shook as he grieved silently.

Gabriel walked over to him and placed his arm on John's

shoulder. "He talked often of you, Mr. Wright, and dearly loved you as a friend."

"And I never loved any man so much," Devil John said. "Whoever killed him will feel my wrath when I find him."

"Vengeance is mine, sayeth the Lord. The man will have to answer to God one day," Gabriel said.

"He will answer to me first." By then, John had regained his composure. He tied the reins of his horse to the porch railing.

"He's buried up the hill there." Gabriel pointed to a massive oak that loomed above the knoll on which the graves lay.

Twenty minutes later, John Wright came down from the graveyard. Gabriel and Creed stood on the porch. "If you hear anything, get word to me, Gabriel."

"Yes, Sir. I will," Gabriel assured him.

"And don't go anyplace unarmed," John said as he turned his horse down the trail. Gabriel and Creed didn't speak as they listened to the horse's hoof beats fade into the distance.

With the fall season on his doorstep, Gabriel prepared for cold weather. Up the hill, a few hundred yards away, were several downed chestnut trees, cut by his father a year earlier to clear an area for planting. The wood was easy to chop and made excellent kindling. Gabriel stripped the branches of the falling timber. He hitched Tater to two logs at a time and hauled them close to the cabin, where he sawed and split the wood into the appropriate size for the fireplace. After gathering enough wood to last until spring, he dug coal from the bank above the water spring and loaded Tater's sled. He had only a few matches, which his father had hoarded and set on the fireplace mantle. By banking his fires, he would be able to keep a fire going during cold weather and use those fires to cook for himself and his little brother.

He was determined to keep his studies of medicine and law in motion despite his father's death and his devotion to Creed. By leaving him in the care of Louranza and Dessie during the days, Gabriel was able to ride to Gladeville each morning to study under the tutelage of Dr. Hollyfield. He returned each evening and spent two hours teaching reading and factoring to Creed. During the months of harsh winter weather, when snow covered the ground most of the time, he remained home with Creed. They spent their days before a blazing fire, studying from the same books Oma had provided Gabriel. By spring, Creed was reading almost as well as his big brother.

John Wright appointed himself as the guardian of the two Wilkens boys. Two days before Christmas, he rode into the yard of their cabin. Two hound dogs that had been recently acquired by Riley set up an unfamiliar cacophony, heralding his arrival.

Gabriel hurried to the door and opened it just as John was preparing to knock.

"It's good to see you, Mr. Wright."

"I'm here to check on you boys and see if you need anything before you get snowbound."

"That's mighty thoughtful of you," Gabriel said

"It's the least I can do on behalf of your Pa. I'm on my way to Whitesburg to bring two new horses back to Gladeville. I am going to call on the Red Fox while I'm there."

"Red Fox?"

"Marshall Taylor. I understand that's what he calls himself

now. And I heard tell he's big buddies with Talt Hall. I think the doc has gone mad, preaching all over Letcher and Pike Counties, claiming he is Jesus Christ. Says he can cure people without medicine."

"He saved my Pa's life, didn't he?"

"Yes, when your pa and I came back from the war, but he gave him medicine. Something has happened to the doctor's mind, I think."

"That's sad to know," Gabriel allowed. "I'll always be grateful to him for saving Pa."

"It's sad, alright, but it's dangerous when he's teamed up with a scoundrel like Hall."

"What are you going to do about it?"

"Not much I can do, but maybe the doc will lead me to Talt Hall. He knows I'm looking for him, but he gets away every time I draw near. For all his bragging, you might think he would want to face me."

"I've heard Pa say no one can beat you in a gunfight. Maybe Mr. Hall knows that, too."

"That's because God is on my side, young man. You remember that. Always keep the Lord on your side, and you will always win."

"Why didn't Pa win? He kept the Lord on his side."

"There's no explaining, Son. The Lord works in mysterious ways. Not many people will agree that I am on the side of the Lord, but He knows I am."

As John walked away, Gabriel noticed he walked with a stiff limp. "What happened to your leg, Mr. Wright? You didn't limp the last time we saw you."

John took the reins in hand and sprang onto the saddle. "When I was here last, someone took a shot at me and pierced the flesh in my thigh. Took me two months to heal, but I'm good except for a little limp. I suspect I owe that to Talt Hall, but you never know. I've brought in a lot of bad men and killed a few when they resisted. I got many enemies who want to do me in; could be any of them."

He backed his horse away from the porch, turned, and headed down the trail. Gabriel called after him, "You take care of yourself, Mr. Wright, and God bless you."

John lifted his beat-up hat and waved it but never looked back. The hounds' barking escorted the horse and rider past the Riley home onto the Bold Camp road.

Ira's moonshine business was flourishing, but came with threats of arrest by Sheriff Pennington and various deputies of Wise County. He kept them at bay by providing free shine to most of them and paying the sheriff for protection. At the sheriff's recommendation, Ira rented a small building in downtown Gladeville and posted a sign that read, 'Mullins Mercantile.' It served as a legitimate way to make a small profit while he flourished, selling Kentucky moonshine, which he stored in his cabin outside the city. The store carried farm implements and various household items such as washboards, pots, pans, and crockery. At the height of his business, Ira saved twenty dollars or more each month and gained a reputation as a successful businessman in Wise County.

During the next year, Ira and Louranza had their third child, a boy they named Anderson. Ira's mercantile business grew, giving him thoughts of abandoning bootlegging altogether. He might have done so if not for the bad news he would receive from his brother, Enos, in Kentucky the next time he visited there. Ira also learned that Marshall Benton Taylor, the Red Fox, had gotten himself appointed as a U.S. Revenue Officer and had vowed to close down Ira and all the others hauling whiskey across the state line through Pound Gap.

Ira loaded his wagon with canned goods and salted pork and departed for the homestead in Whitesburg. He planned to make a final haul of moonshine back to Wise County but learned that the revenuers had closed down Jason Blevins by destroying his whiskey still and the cistern for collecting water. In exchange for revealing where the still was hidden, in a secret room below his house, Blevins was spared an arrest. The actions by the feds had dried up the largest source of moonshine in Lecher and Wise counties.

Jason's competitors were happy to see him go out of business, and they expanded their production of corn liquor to meet demands in Letcher and Pike Counties in Kentucky and Wise and Scott Counties in Virginia. Led by Taylor, who knew the area well, revenuers searched in the vicinity of mountain streams, destroying one illegal moonshine operation after another. As supplies dwindled, prices increased much above those Ira was charging for the whiskey manufactured by Jason Blevins. By brewing his own shine, he could now save at least forty dollars each month, which would get him close to this goal of two thousand dollars by the time he was thirty years old. Such savings would make Ira one of the wealthiest men in Wise County. By his reckoning, he could quit the moonshine business by his thirty-fifth birthday and make a good living selling mercantile. With the protection of Sheriff Pennington and his deputies, Ira was able to continue his moonshine business on his way to amassing a small fortune. His opportunities dwindled two years later when Sheriff Pennington was defeated by John Miller, who upheld the letter of the law to the best of his abilities.

As Ira and Louranza expanded their family to five children. Ira continued to haul moonshine from Kentucky in a wagon loaded with hay. Gabriel farmed the land left to him and Creed by their father. In the evenings and on days when the weather did not allow outside work, he tutored his brother in the subjects taught to him by Dency Martin. In doing so, he furthered his own knowledge of law and medicine. Four years after his father was murdered, when Gabriel was twenty, he sold his cabin and land to Ira for $250 and opened a law office in Pound. He and Creed lived in a back room of the office. Out back, there was a shed for his horse, Tater, and a buggy for transportation. *Ruby's Rest Awhile* tavern was three buildings up the muddy street on the banks of Pound River, a place that lent the potential for trouble or triumph to Gabriel's fledgling law business at the foot of Pine Mountain, four miles from Pound Gap.

The business of revenuer brought Dr. Taylor to Pound and Gladeville frequently. He gradually acquired a reputation as a changed man, a shrewd and cunning genius. While pursuing moonshiners who were making a living the only way they knew, he salved his conscience by administering his brand of holistic medicine. He readily accepted the reputation of being a seer, a student of a Swedish religious fanatic by the name of Swedenborg. He claimed to have the ability to communicate with spirits and angels. On weekdays, he preyed on moonshiners, and, if he could gather a congregation, he prayed with them on Sunday. He preached hypnotic sermons, which lured people to hear his messages. Wherever he rode through the mountain and valley trails, he carried a Bible in his saddlebags. He also carried a variety of herbs that he used as medicines. The people who listened to his sermons believed he was a good medical doctor. When he traveled, he was always armed with a rifle and revolver and wore an ammunition belt for his friends and enemies to see. He also carried a long spyglass, which he used to spot moonshiners as they prepared to climb the Kentucky side of the mountain on their way to Virginia. The person Doc Taylor wanted in his sights, most of all, was Ira Mullins, who regularly crossed through Pound Gap with moonshine hidden in his hay wagon.

Ira became more cautious when he learned that Bad Talt Hall had been appointed as a U.S. Marshal for the eastern district of Kentucky and was arresting moonshiners. Ira's trips to and from Whitesburg grew less frequent. He always had an armed man riding ahead of his wagon and one bringing up the rear.

John Wright had no love for moonshiners, but he had a score to settle with his former friend, Talt Hall. When he caught up with him on the main street in Whitesburg, Talt denied that he ever took a shot at John or at Caleb Wilkens.

"You think I've gone crazy, John? I know you too well to pick a fight. We been friends a long time before now."

"How about Caleb Wilkens? Were you friends with him?"

"I had nothing against the man and was sorry to hear about his being killed. We worked together one summer on Riley Mullins' place. He was a nice feller."

"The best," John said,

Talt relished his role as a marshal and felt safe walking the streets of Whitesburg. He was aware of John's reputation and knew better than to engage The Devil in a gunfight. Thus, the two men tolerated each other, neither daring to turn his back on the other. John promised himself and Gabriel Wilkens that if he ever had proof of Talt's guilt, he would make sure Talt was dead, regardless of his status as a government agent.

Not long after his encounter with Talt, John Wright was appointed as a U.S. Marshal in the western district of Virginia. He continued his husbandry business and acquired additional land in Kentucky and Virginia's counties of Wise and Scott. On each trip to Whitesburg to bring back horses for sale in Virginia, he stopped at Gabriel's law office in Pound to visit with Caleb's sons. Each time, he expressed to Gabriel his enduring affection for Caleb and vowed that he would bring to justice, dead or alive, the man who killed his father. Unlike Talt Hall, John Wright had never shot a man in his back, but he vowed that if he ever learned with certainty that Talt was Caleb's killer, he would gun him down just as Talt had done to the boys' father.

The uneasy tolerance of these men for each other created a tenuous situation in 1890 when Gabriel was twenty-three and Creed was fifteen. As the nation moved forward with modernization, new inventions and the availability of newly invented farm implements, including reapers and thrashers, improved people's lives; life in the hills of southwestern Virginia and southeastern Kentucky, however, remained much as it had since the end of the Civil War. A notable exception was the installation of a railroad brought in by Norfolk and Southern Railway, investors, hoping to exploit the coal and minerals of the area. The railway ran from Norton to Guest Station, and then to Bristol, and connected with a mainline, which opened the region to destinations across the country. But internecine animosities still lingered, and the residents of that area still scratched out a living from the dirt or sold moonshine to stay alive. Lawlessness prevailed, especially in Letcher County, spilling across the mountain into Wise County. Renegades and lawmen alike were feared by the people of the mountains. Opportunities frequently arose for the services of an erudite young lawyer who was gradually gaining a reputation as a wise counselor and legal practitioner in matters of real estate, property rights, and criminal justice before the courts in Wise County. Gabriel Wilkens was about to make himself known in the hills of southwestern Virginia.

2
____

DESPERATE MEN

The reasons Thomas Talton Hall turned out to be one of the most dangerous desperados in Appalachia are not mysterious. He grew up amidst famine, crime, and corruption in Eastern Kentucky, fifteen miles from Whitesburg. At an early age, he witnessed unprovoked killings and wanton bloodshed.

His family home was a one-room log cabin near a mountain stream called Troublesome Creek. It was a location that supplied ample water for his father's moonshining enterprise and set the scene for gun battles defending his father's illegal activities. He witnessed his father's handiwork with a Winchester rifle and Colt revolver and saw his first man murdered at the hands of Bad Dave Hall. He grew up surrounded by budding outlaws, many of whom died at early ages by facing more fierce men who did not fear for their own lives or give a damn about the life of someone else. With these influences, Talt Hall was destined to become one of Kentucky's most notorious killers.

When the Civil War was raging from 1861 until 1865,

terror reigned through the hills and valleys of Eastern Kentucky. The people in the area were about evenly divided in their support for the North and South. Talt joined the Confederate army and acquitted himself well, proving to be a fearless and deadly fighter for the Southern cause.

While Talt was fighting in Northern Virginia, bands of desperate men evading conscription rampaged through the mountains, attacking remote cabins and raping women whose husbands, sons, and brothers were off to War. Small skirmishes between the North and South, not noted in the history of the War, took place in the mountains surrounding the home of Talt Hall. When the War ended, he returned to his home and settled in Troublesome Creek. He was filled with bitterness because of Lee's surrender and vowed to kill any man who fought for the North.

In the mountains, the turmoil of the War did not end with the surrender of the South, especially in the remote hills of Virginia and Kentucky, which were subjected to a reign of terror. Murders occurred daily, and Talt Hall eagerly joined in the bloodletting. By the time he was appointed as a U.S. Marshal, he was alleged to have killed at least one hundred men. He had been arrested for eight murders and found not guilty by juries of his peers, comprised mostly of killers like himself. Even his kinfolk did not escape the fury of his weapons; he killed at least six of his in-laws and cousins.

Talton learned about winning gunfights from his father, Bad Dave Hall, who killed many men. Known for his accuracy, Talt never bluffed and always hit his target. A friend noted that while Talt's guns were not impressive in appearance, they were dead-center when fired.

He became a lawman with the help of his relatives because of his boldness and prowess with a gun and his service in the Confederate army. They sent word to Letcher County Sheriff Hassel Stamper that it might be good for his own health if he appointed Talt as a deputy, which he did. Talt's five years as a deputy helped him polish his reputation and eventually be selected for the position of U.S. Marshal for the Eastern District of Kentucky. His extensive family, all members heavily armed, traveled with Talt wherever he went, shielded by his status as a law enforcement officer. They all considered themselves lawmen and not subjected to the same laws they ostensibly upheld. Such was the state of law enforcement in Letcher County, Kentucky, as the twentieth century drew closer.

Stories about Marshall Benton Taylor, also known as "Doc Taylor" and "The Red Fox," are manifold: true, exaggerated, or fabricated. The stories of his activities are still told throughout the mountain empire, which sits astride the Kentucky-Virginia border at Pound Gap. Many folks of the mountains still know, and are eager to tell, how their great-great-great-grandmother, when young, would send for Dr. Taylor and how he would cure her without giving any medicine at all.

One of the stories tells of how the red-headed, red-bearded mystic sat for a while beside a patient, carrying on conversations unrelated to any ailment of which the person complained. He cautioned his patient not to allow her mind to wander, but to concentrate on him only. Then he rose from his chair and left the room. Outside, he lifted his eyes to the heavens and meditated. After the session with Doc Taylor, the health of his patient was restored. This and similar accounts made the self-taught doctor legendary throughout the hills and valleys of southern Appalachia.

Like most doctors of his day, Marshall Taylor had no medical degree. He acquired his knowledge of human illnesses and medicine by studying under the tutelage of Dr. D. B. Hollyfield, a relative and noted physician in Wise County. With his keen mind, Doc Taylor learned how to treat fevers and common illnesses. He was always willing to go when called to a home where someone was suffering from an unknown malady.

He was born into a modestly well-to-do family for its time and was encouraged to educate himself, attending school occasionally when the opportunity availed itself. He was inspired by Dr. Hollyfield and, in the early days of his practice, adopted the renowned doctor's methods of diagnosing and treating illnesses. His studies under Dr. Hollyfield were interrupted briefly when the Civil War started in 1861. He immediately joined the 64th Virginia Mounted Cavalry but returned home after three months, vowing that he would never fire a gun at another man in violation of God's laws.

"I have seen enough killing in just two months to last me a lifetime," he said.

After returning home, he resumed his professional duties as a doctor, treating patients widely scattered throughout the mountainous regions of Virginia and Kentucky. He set up his office in the city of Gladeville, Virginia, and gained a reputation for his medical prowess. That was the reason Joseph Martin traveled from Guest Station to Gladeville when John Wesley Wright staggered from the woods carrying Caleb Wilkens on his back. Caleb's admiration for Doc Taylor remained steadfast until Caleb's death twenty years later.

However, Doc Taylor's ideas of doctoring evolved during those twenty years. He took up preaching at a small Methodist Church as a fervent believer of every word in the Bible. An apparent metamorphosis occurred in his thinking. In due course, and as his religious fervor grew more intense, he began preaching to a Swedenborg faith congregation. Then, he developed his concepts of holistic medical treatment, performing more as a mystic than a medical doctor.

Two years before Gabriel Wilkens began practicing law in Wise County, Doc Taylor returned to Gladeville. He ingratiated himself with the new sheriff, John Miller, and manipulated an appointment as a deputy U.S. Marshal, acting principally as a revenue officer. He made numerous arrests in Scott, Lee, and Wise counties, sending the Virginia moonshiners into hiding. Then he turned his attention to the accelerated moonshine traffic coming from Letcher County, Kentucky. He set up a lookout point on a gigantic overhanging rock, giving a full view of Little Elkhorn Creek and the traffic coming up the Kentucky side of the mountain. He knew most of the Kentucky moonshiners and had informers who would tell him when one of them would be making a trip across the mountain. With his five-foot telescope, he was able to see the Elkhorn road. After spotting his prey, he waited on the Virginia side of the mountain alongside the wagon trail. After the moonshiners passed into Virginia's authority, he arrested them.

Doctor Taylor was still loved and praised by many, but feared and hated as a revenue officer by those who saw an insidious side to The Red Fox; he never passed up an opportunity for continual stalking of moonshiners and peddlers of the intoxicating mountain dew. Soon, the bootleggers began planning his death. Rumors abounded that one of these was Ira Mullins.

Ira Mullins, the son of John Mullins and the nephew of the elder Riley Mullins, was determined to break free from the poverty into which he was born. He was just a boy when Doc Taylor and Talt Hall were making names for themselves, both good and bad. The time Ira spent with his prosperous uncle whetted his appetite for a life better than that of his father and mother. He was resolute in his ambition to become wealthy by the standards of that day, ultimately becoming the most successful moonshiner in Letcher County, Kentucky, serving a clientele that extended into the three closest counties in Virginia. At the height of Ira's success, Doc Taylor and Talt Hall served as revenue officers, and Ira Mullins was considered the biggest prize viewed through the sights of their rifles. Without the protection of former sheriff Pennington, Ira gambled dangerously with each load of whiskey he carried across the state line into Virginia. A conflict was inevitable.

3
____

STAYING ALIVE

Gabriel Wilkens received the sad news of the death of Daniel Bartley Hollyfield, his benefactor and the wisest man Gabriel knew. He was humbled when he received word from Dr. Hollyfield's daughter, Grace, that the great man's entire library and medical equipment were left to Gabriel. He always appreciated the encouragement he received from Dr. Hollyfield, and now he felt a duty to live up to the expectations the doctor had in him, which the doctor often expressed. It seemed to Gabriel that he was losing the great people in his life. His father and Oma were gone, and now Dr. Hollyfield. He realized others he loved and owed gratitude were getting older and might pass without him ever expressing his appreciation for their faith and encouragement. He thought of all he owed to Dency and Joe Martin.

Gabriel and Creed drove to Guest Station the day after the funeral. He was determined to express his appreciation to Dency Martin, who had nurtured his intellect and encouraged him to pursue his dreams. Long days and many nights, burning the midnight oil provided a good life for him and Creed, not that he was by any means wealthy, but at least he was staying alive. The little office on high ground, overlooking the river, was fast becoming a popular place for people who needed the legal services of a bright young lawyer. If not for Dency Martin and Dr. Hollyfield, he might be following Tater through a field, holding onto a plow and hoping for a good growing season.

Gabrial drove his wagon through Gladeville and stopped at Ira's Mercantile store. He bought two bars of Colgate bathing soap, a bottle of Pond Lily Toilet Water, and five yards of floral cotton material, the latest products carried at the mercantile, gifts he thought Dency would appreciate. The trip onward to Guest Station took two hours. Gabriel and Creed arrived early that afternoon.

Dency, now almost sixty years old, was teaching twenty students at a new one-room schoolhouse, recently built by the citizens of Guest Station. Joe Martin, thin and worn, greeted Gabriel as he climbed down from his wagon. Creed followed as the two men shook hands.

"What a great surprise," Joe said. "You will make Dency's day."

"It's good to see you, Mr. Martin."

"And this is Creed?"

"Yes, my companion, student, and most of all, my brother."

Joe reached for Creed's hand. "It's good to meet you, young man."

He turned to Gabriel. "What brings you all the way over here?"

"I think it's about time I paid my respects. You and Dency have done so much for me."

"I guess you know where she is; she'll be teachin' 'til the day the Lord calls her away, I guess."

"How are you doing, Mr. Martin?"

"Joe, please. I'm doin' ok, got some lumbago and arthritis, but it ain't stopped me yet."

"Are you still doing everything around here by yourself?"

"No, I got a young feller, name Joshua Crumb, helps me two or three days a week. He'll go full time when plantin' starts."

"How old is he?"

"'Bout twenty-one, got a wife, but Dency talked him into goin' to school to learn to read and write. He's down at the schoolhouse now."

"She never gives up, does she?"

"Not likely," Joe said.

Gabriel and Creed followed Joe into the house. Gabriel carried a brown paper poke, which he set on the kitchen table. "That's for Dency, just a little gift for her."

"She'll be surprised and delighted," Joe replied. "Can you spend the night with us?"

"No, I have appointments tomorrow. We have to get started back this evening."

"In that case, I better go to the schoolhouse and get Dency. She'll want to visit with you for a while." He turned for the door. "You boys wait here and I'll git back shortly."

"Why don't I go get her. No use you hitching up a wagon."

The ride to the school took twenty minutes. Dency sent her students home an hour early and returned home with Joe, Gabriel, and Creed.

Caleb pointed to the poke on the table. "That's for you, Miss Dency."

"You shouldn't have spent all that money," she said when she saw the contents. She held up the cloth and let it unfold. Tears filled her eyes. It will make a beautiful dress." She walked around the table and hugged Gabriel and Creed. "You've made me cry, Gabrial."

"It isn't much for the person I owe so much to."

She wiped her eyes with her palms. "Are you hungry?"

"No, we ate some biscuits and sausage on our way here."

"It's a long ride back to Bold Camp. Are you sure you won't eat?"

"No, Miss Dency. We'll eat when we get home."

"By the way," Joe said, "we got the news all the way over here in Guest Station that revenue officers destroyed Jason Blevins's moonshine operation, the biggest in the state of Kentucky." He laughed. "We get all the important news out here."

"Then I guess you know it has run the price of shine sky high," Gabriel said. "I'm not complaining, though. Half my legal work is spent negotiating fines and jail time for the poor souls still trying to make a living at it. The problem is that I don't get paid much of the time."

They were still standing around the table when Joe pulled a chair out and offered it to Dency. "Let's sit and talk a while. At least you boys can have some tea or coffee with us. You know, coffee is almost affordable these days."

When they were seated, Gabriel asked. "Have you heard that Doctor Hollyfield passed away?"

"No. When?" Dency half whispered the question as if she found the news hard to accept.

"Three days ago. The funeral was yesterday. I expect his obituary will be in the Abingdon Dispatch tomorrow."

"What a great man. He will surely be missed here in Wise County."

"I owe him so much," Gabriel said. "Without you and him, I don't know what I would be doing today."

"You would be doing well, Gabriel, with or without our help. You have it in you."

"I just want to live up to your expectations, yours, Dr. Hollyfield's, and Oma's."

"You will," she said. "I'm certain of it, and your father would be happy to see that you deserve the name he gave you, Gabriel."

The news was out that The Red Fox was hell-bent on stopping bootlegging in Wise County. His professed belief that drinking was an abomination to God was given as the reason for his extreme assault on moonshiners of the county. A mysterious fire, asserted to have been set by Marshall Taylor, destroyed the cabin where Ira Mullins stored his illicit contraband. This allegation deepened Ira's hatred for and fear of the man hiding behind the badge of a U.S. Marshal.

Ira vowed to get even with the Red Fox, and his determination to do away with Marshall Taylor became more intense when Ira learned that his Mercantile business was in the gunsight of Taylor. Rumors abounded that the mercantile would be the next target of arson if Ira continued to sell moonshine. Ira decided to relocate his base of operations. That summer, Ira sold the mercantile to the owner of a competing general store in Gladeville for $1,000. Afterward, he continued his moonshine trade by hiding himself and his whiskey in a jolt wagon filled with hay. A driver in the wagon hauled the hay and whiskey across the mountain to Bold Camp. From there, the moonshine was distributed throughout Wise and surrounding counties.

Ira's prominence as a businessman gave him considerable influence with local politicians and city officials and enabled him to continue his illicit moonshine sales. This influence shielded him from overt actions against him by revenue men and was a source of gnawing resentment by Doc Taylor.

The Red Fox made it known to his friends that he would be gunning for Ira Mullins if he ever brought another load of moonshine into Wise County. He referred to Ira's manner of dress because he always wore a white shirt, black vest, and tie when he ran the mercantile. "I'll rid Virginia of the scourge of that little dandy if he breaks the law again."

For Ira, bootlegging had been a way of life since he was fifteen, and he was not about to stop because a preacher-man threatened his life. He lay low for the remainder of the summer. In September, he drove his wagon to Whitesburg, loaded it with moonshine, and lay down in the wagon. After covering the wagon with hay, the driver crossed the mountain at Pound Gap and made his way to Gladeville without encountering The Red Fox. When the coast was clear, Ira stood in the wagon. Just then, Marshal Taylor and three deputies came riding toward Ira with rifles aimed at him. He reached for his own rifle and fired in the direction of the riders. A shot from the rifle of the Red Fox or one of his deputies pierced Ira's side. He fell back into the hay, unable to move. The driver slapped the horse with his reins and headed the wagon toward Pound. He crossed Indian Creek Mountain and didn't stop until he pulled in front of the law office of Gabriel Wilkens. His screams brought Gabriel outside, where he looked at the wounded man.

"I'm not a doctor, Gabriel said, "but I'll do all I can."

He and the driver carried the immobile but semiconscious man into the office and laid him on a thick pallet that Creed made.

Gabriel stripped away Ira's shirt and examined the wound to his side. He. noted that the blood was oozing from the wound, but not in spurts, indicating that an artery had not been pierced. He applied a cloth pad against the wound and pressed until the blood stopped flowing. By then, Ira was in and out of consciousness. In a moment of lucidity, Ira said, "I can't move my legs and arms."

Gabriel recognized the symptoms of paralysis, probably from a bullet that was still in his spine. He whispered to Creed and the driver. "We can only hope for a recovery, but I doubt it. I wouldn't dare to try to remove the bullet, and I don't know of a doctor in our county who would do it. Maybe when he's better, we can take him to Bristol, Tennessee. There's a civilian hospital with two surgeons. Right now, he's too weak to make the trip. It's almost a hundred miles from here."

"You're right," the driver said. "I drove there once fer Mr. Ira, and I was wore out when I got there. I tried drivin' in the dark, but went off trail a dozen times. And you never know who may be roamin' in them woods."

Gabriel checked Ira's wound. "The exterior bleeding has stopped. If he isn't bleeding internally, he might survive."

He crushed two feverfew flowers for pain and mixed them in water. He held Ira's head in his lap and held the cup to his lips. He remembered that small amounts of opium and morphine were in the medicines left to him by Dr. Hollyfield. Gabriel had heard stories of morphine addiction in many Civil War veterans and was reluctant to inject it into Ira.

Instead, he mixed a small amount of opium with whiskey and forced Ira to drink.

The driver asked, "What are we goin' to do fer him, Mr. Wilkins?"

"We can't move him for a couple of days. I'll make him as comfortable as possible. You drive to Bold Camp and let Riley and Louranza know what has happened. If they want to see him, they should come soon."

The next morning, Ira was awake and not in terrible pain except for the wound on his side. Gabriel assumed that no internal organs were damaged by the gunshot and that the bullet was almost certainly lodged in Ira's spine. He described his uncle's condition in a short note he prepared to send by telegraph to the physicians in Bristol. When Riley and Louranza arrived at his office, he gave the note to Riley and asked him to ride to the telegraph office in Gladeville. "As the note says, a response is urgent. You should get an answer from the surgeon right away."

Riley returned that afternoon with a response the telegraph operator had written. It read:

Dr. Wilkens, your diagnosis appears correct. We will need to see the patient to confirm. Bring him to Bristol when he can travel. Give small amounts of opium if pain indicates need. Good luck

The enormity of a doctor's responsibilities overwhelmed Gabriel. He felt humbled by the title "doctor" as signified in the telegram from the physician in Bristol. However, he recognized his limitations in meeting the medical needs of the people of Pound and Wise County. Although he was likely better qualified than many, due to his studies under Dr. Hollyfield, he did not present himself as a doctor. Confronted with the task of caring for a critically injured man, he made a decision that would benefit the people of the hills for years to come. He would send Creed to the hospital in Bristol to study under physicians Dr. James Wallace and Dr. Joseph Fillmore, both of whom had refined their medical skills under D.B. Hollyfield during the War. When Creed was ready, Gabriel planned to send him to the College of William and Mary. One day, there would be a Dr. Wilkens from Pound, Virginia, who would rightfully deserve the title.

After a week of lying in Gabriel's office, Ira was taken home to Bold Camp. Movement had returned to his right arm, but he was unable to move either of his legs. Unwilling to travel to Bristol for medical treatment, he convalesced for two months, not venturing from his cabin. His hatred for the Red Fox intensified as Ira lay in bed, unable to move without assistance from Louranza or his eldest son, John Harrison. He vowed to get even with "that sonsabitch" and sent word to Talt Hall that he would pay $300 to any man who would kill Marshall Benton Taylor. Talt refused the offer, sending word back to Ira that the Red Fox was a good friend and federal police officer, and he did not savor the idea of having the feds after him.

"If he wants the Red Fox kilt, he can let that grown boy of his do it," he told Ira's messenger.

Talt made a trip from Whitesburg to inform Taylor that Ira had hired a hitman to kill him. Taylor responded by offering a similar sum of money to anyone who "delivered Ira's head to him on a platter."

One afternoon, when Louranza and John Harrison went to the store, Ira heard a noise at his bedroom window. Unable to get up from bed, he called out, "Who's there?"

A pistol shot rang out, followed by another. Ira's revolver lay by his pillow. He picked it up with his one good hand and fired at the window. He waited for a sound but heard nothing. When Louranza and John Harrison returned shortly afterward, she found two bullets lodged in Ira's mattress. He was unaware that a fire was smoldering inside his mattress and could have burned to death if his wife and son hadn't returned home when they did.

Ira got word to Devil John Wright that Doc Taylor had tried to assassinate him. He believed the Devil would avenge him since he was Caleb's brother-in-law.

"Leaving me as a helpless cripple ain't enough for that bastard. He wants me dead."

John Wright informed Ira that he would track down Doc Taylor to see if he was connected to the attempt on his life. The Red Fox asserted he was with a dedicated church member in Pike County, Kentucky, as she was facing complications with her pregnancy. Devil John visited the woman's mother to verify the Doc's story. She told him that Doc Taylor had spent much of the month at her home, caring for her pregnant daughter.

Ira doubted that her story was true when he learned from the woman's husband that he had caught the Red Fox and his wife, Mary, in a compromising situation. Ira believed it was just another example of the irrational religious fervor of the Doc's followers.

Ira had accumulated a significant sum of money, which was always carried by Louranza during their travels. She kept at least $5,000 in a sash worn around her waist to ensure its safety, as leaving the money in their cabin was deemed unsafe. The rumors surrounding Ira's wealth made him a potential target for any renegade who might be in the vicinity when Ira's wagon traversed the mountain. Consequently, he determined that it was no longer prudent to transport moonshine across the mountain. The hostility between him and the authorities in Wise County led Ira to relocate back to Letcher County, close to Enos and his immediate family. To preserve his life, he realized that he must permanently abandon the moonshine trade. Moreover, with sufficient funds to sustain a comfortable lifestyle, he decided to open another mercantile in Letcher County.

GATHERING OF GUNS

John Wright resided in Wise County, where he acquired a thousand acres of land through claims prepared for him by Gabriel Wilkens. He also owned property in Kentucky and visited there frequently to spend time with his three wives, who lived in Letcher and Pike County. In Virginia, he had two wives, one in Wise County and another in Lee County, together having seven children. His Kentucky families included six children. With his considerable wealth, he was able to support all of them. As his reputation as a gunfighter increased, so did his family size

Although Doc Taylor considered himself a doctor and devout Christian, his practices became associated with witch-doctoring and spiritual healing. He began dressing all in black and carrying at least five guns and his massive telescope with him wherever he travelled. He held seances at his house, claiming to be able to talk to the dead. Instead of relying on medical treatments prescribed by doctors of his day, his eccentricities included healing with herbal remedies and incantations. Some believed he had special physical powers and could transcend time and space, and they relied on him for his healing abilities. Others feared him and questioned his sanity. The community's concerns and fears of a crazy man armed to the teeth caused officials to remove him from his position as U.S. Marshal. Doc Taylor blamed his demise on Ira Mullins, and he vowed revenge. An uneasiness fell over the city of Gladeville and Wise County with the expectation of violence between supporters of Ira Mullins and those of the Red Fox.

John Wright also had both supporters and adversaries. He never wavered in his support for his friends, and Gabriel Wilkens, now a successful attorney, was a friend to whom he felt a special obligation to protect. Each time he passed through Pound, he visited Gabriel. Although he was always grateful to Doc Taylor for his treatment of Caleb, rumors of Doc's apparent departure from reality and hatred for Ira Mullins caused John concern for Gabriel's safety.

"Doc Taylor knows you saved Ira after he was shot," John said, "and he may hold that against you. They say the old man has lost his mind. No kin of Ira's are safe from Doc Taylor."

"I'm careful, but I don't carry a weapon. I could never kill anyone."

"You might if your life depended on it, Gabriel, and it very well may."

"I have Pa's rifle here. Maybe I'll start carrying it with me when I travel to South Fork or Gladeville. But I'm not expecting trouble from Doc Taylor."

"I hope you're right, but if you ever do, you get word to me."

After Ira was paralyzed, Riley Mullins armed himself. He sent word to the Red Fox to remain in Kentucky, where he was living then, if he wanted to stay alive. Having survived three years of War, Riley declared that he did not fear any man, not even Satan, and he had no fear of Doc Taylor.

One day, Riley lost a wheel off his wagon as he drove toward Pound from Bold camp, and it rolled into the woods. He got off the wagon and walked downhill to retrieve the wheel. Doc Taylor suddenly appeared beside him, silently taking every step with Riley. He had a stoic expression and never spoke. Disturbed by Taylor's silent presence, Riley hurried toward the wheel, picked it up, and rolled it back to his wagon. Taylor stayed alongside without uttering a sound. Riley hoisted the axle with one hand and slipped on the wheel. He looked over his shoulder to see Doc Taylor walking apace toward Pound. As Riley watched after him, Doc Taylor vanished.

After securing the wheel, Riley continued toward the Gap, but he was unable to get the encounter with the Red Fox off his mind. In a moment of contemplation, he attributed the incident to his imagination, but he still felt uneasy. He continued his trip to The Pound. Later, he reached into his pocket for a twist of tobacco. And felt something he did not recognize. He pulled out a small piece of hard candy with a written note attached that read: "Beware, Riley Mullins, the Red Fox is watching you." Riley had never feared another man, but he decided then that Doc Taylor was no ordinary man. He lashed his horse and drove as fast as possible back toward Bold Camp, turning on a road leading to the home of his friend, Jeremiah Poindexter. He remained there overnight before returning home. His concerns for the safety of his cousin, Ira, heightened. He was happy to have two hound dogs that barked incessantly whenever anyone approached his or Ira's property.

Creed was studying under two physicians in Bristol, Tennessee, and kept in touch with his older brother through a letter sent monthly to Gabriel Wilkens, Esq., General Delivery, Pound, Virginia. Gabriel did not claim any formal education in law since he had never attended law school. Like other men practicing law in the area, he gained his knowledge by studying books provided by Oma and under the guidance of Dr. Hollyfield. Despite this, he appreciated Creed's respect for him and hoped to one day address Creed as Doctor Wilkens. More importantly, he was glad that Creed was far from the dangers that many near Pound Gap faced daily.

When Ira Mullins was paralyzed by a gunshot wound, Talt Hall seized an opportunity to replace him in the moonshine trade. He began transporting it from Letcher County to Virginia. The source of this illegal trade was soon discovered, and Hall was dismissed as a marshal. He expanded his activity and moved to Gladeville to better distribute unstamped whiskey in Wise County, leading to conflicts with local law enforcement.

Not long after settling in Gladeville, Talt became involved with Mary Salyer, a married woman and wife of the Deputy Chief of Police of Norton. Her husband, Frank, was killed a few months later. Although circumstantial evidence pointed to Talt Hall, he was not arrested immediately for the crime that everyone was sure he committed. When Chief of Police Enos Hylton finally hunted Talt down to question him, Talt shot him without warning. Devil John Wright was called in by the Sheriff of Wise County to help with the hunt for Hall, who had fled back to Kentucky. John Wright found him hiding in a cabin in Rockhouse Creek, Kentucky, and brought him back to Gladeville for trial in Wise County Court. Always proud of the number of men he had killed, Talt confessed to the murder of Enos Hylton, Chief of Police of Norton, a town five miles from Gladeville.

As Talt's trial day approached, he had a dispute with his attorney. He beseeched John Wright, who was responsible for Talt's arrest, to find a lawyer who would defend him. John rode to Pound and met with Gabriel Wilkens.

"No," Gabriel said. "He probably killed my father. Why would I defend him?"

"Because you're a fair man, Gabriel Wilkens. Just like your Pa."

"I don't care what happens to Talt Hall. He deserves to hang, if not for the killing of Enos Hylton, then for all the others."

"I have no love for Talt Hall," John said, "but the man was once my friend and he deserves representation in court."

"I don't want to represent a man with no redeeming qualities."

"You're the only attorney I know who might be willing."

"Is he guilty, John?"

"Guilty as hell but needs a lawyer."

"I would need help from a more experienced lawyer to aid with court procedures. I've never practiced law in a criminal trial."

"I know you can do it, Gabriel. Your Pa would want you to."

"I will have to think and pray about it."

"I need an answer today; I might not get back this way for a month."

"I don't want to do it."

"But will you?"

"Go back and tell him I will represent him, but I will not defend him. I cannot tell the court he is innocent when there is overwhelming evidence and the man has confessed. If he wants me with those conditions, I will do it."

"That's fair enough, Gabriel. I'll tell him."

A cold winter wind blew through the Virginia mountains when Talt Hall's trial began at the courthouse in Gladeville. One hundred men and boys armed with Winchester rifles surrounded the courthouse. In the contiguous woods, dozens of Talt's supporters, equally armed, watched as court officials, witnesses, and the curious arrived each day. The judge and prosecuting attorneys, as well as the curious, carried their weapons, some concealed, some intentionally obvious, giving warning to Talt's potential rescuers.

On January 26, 1892, a young lawyer stood before Judge H. A. W. Skeen and heard his client pronounce his innocence, knowing the plea to be false. When it came time for Gabriel's opening statement, he began: "My client once confessed to the crime of murder. He now withdraws that confession and enters a plea of innocence. I leave it to the court and this jury to decide which version of my client's claims is true. The defence is ready to proceed, Your Honor."

The trial lasted five days. Sixteen jurists were selected. Talt was allowed to peremptorily discharge four of them, leaving a jury of twelve. The Prosecution presented the testimony of three deputies and twelve bystanders. Their eyewitness accounts left no doubt as to the guilt of a wanton killer. Bad Talt Hall had escaped hanging for murder eight times in the tainted trials held in Kentucky. Because of the overwhelming evidence, regardless of his new claims of innocence and self-defence, he was not likely to escape the gallows in Wise County, Virginia.

The first witness, like most of them, observed an altercation from a distance. A tall man and a much shorter one were in a heated discussion with the Chief of Police and two deputies. The tall man pulled his pistol from his belt and fired into Hylton's stomach. He fell writhing on the ground. After a moment, he got to his feet, staggered toward the shooter, who fired again. Hylton fell to the ground. The two men ran toward their horses, which were tied to a rail in front of the barbershop. The appearance of the shooter was that of Talt Hall. The two deputies who testified stated that their guns were holstered, and they did not have time to protect Hylton or arrest the man they positively identified as Talt Hall.

The defense offered no witnesses except the defendant himself, who swore he was in Letcher County, Kentucky, when the murder of Enos Hylton occurred. The man who was with Hall at the time of the killing returned to his home in Tennessee and could not be found to witness for the accused. Talt told the court that Doc Taylor could vouch for his time in Kentucky, but he was battling a serious illness, probably lung fever, and had to remain in Letcher County. Like many other sworn statements by Talt Hall, this allegation proved untrue. Doc Taylor returned to Gladeville two days after the trial to visit the jailed man. He offered to pray for Talt's soul, but Talt informed him that he could pray for himself if he ever thought he needed it.

In final argument for the defense, Gabriel said only that the facts before the court spoke for themselves, and the jury's verdict must speak truth to those facts. "If you believe Talt Hall is innocent as he testified, your verdict must be one of "not guilty."

Talt Hall was convicted on January 30th, and he was sentenced to be hanged by the neck until dead. He was destined to become the first man to be hanged in Wise County, Virginia, unless his unsavory associates saved him from the gallows. The sentence was to be carried out on September 2, 1892. The seven months between sentencing and execution would allow time for automatic appeals to the Virginia Supreme Court.

After sentencing, Talt calmly promised that he would seek a new trial and would be proven innocent. As the date approached for his hanging, word was spread throughout Wise County that Talt's friends from Kentucky were poised to break into the jail and rescue him and that seventy-five men were hiding in the woods, ready to charge the jailhouse, rescue him, and take him back to Kentucky.

The city of Gladeville was awash with concerns that Talt Hall might be lynched by members of Enos Hylton's police force or rescued by Talt's supporters from Kentucky. Devil John Wright, who was now a Deputy U.S. Marshal for the southwestern section of Virginia, was appointed by Judge Skeen to accompany Talt to Lynchburg, Virginia for safekeeping. John handcuffed himself to Talt, who was shackled and subdued. Talt was aware of John's prowess with a gun and his willingness to use it when necessary. Bad John

Wright always got his man, and he was determined to safely deliver him to Lynchburg for safekeeping until his hanging in September. He would deliver Talt to the authorities there, dead or alive.

5

TENUOUS TIME

The trial of Talt Hall ended, and Devil John Wright took him to Lynchburg for safekeeping, disarming the powder keg that appeared about to blow in Wise County. The sale of moonshine decreased, especially after Ira Mullins' mercantile, a front for illicit whiskey, closed, and Talt Hall was out of business. Though locals felt safer, they were now cautious of wealthy northern strangers seeking iron, oil, and coal rights in the area. Land was bought near Big Stone Gap, Norton, and Clintwood in Dickenson County, and along the Holston River near Kingsport, Tennessee. The community welcomed the investors with a wary eye, hoping they would bring job opportunities with them. The incursion into the mountains brought financiers, businessmen, engineers, and a few tradesmen, but not many opportunities for local men, who were considered inferior by the Northerners. This environment fomented discontent for many people in Wise County, but not for the business boom in the little town of Pound.

Doc Taylor took umbrage at the Northerners' incursion

into his mountain home. On two occasions, he formed a posse to harass and intimidate the newcomers who were invading the mountain, surveying land, and drilling to sample for Coal and oil. These foreigners to the hills would soon learn they were courting danger, and some of them would pay the price with their lives.

While Talt Hall was safely incarcerated in a heavily guarded jail in Lynchburg, Gabriel Wilkens worked with a more experienced attorney, William Gray, to file an appeal on behalf of Talt. The basis for the appeal was Gabriel's relative lack of experience in courtroom procedures, resulting in an inadequate defense of the condemned man. The Virginia Supreme Court took only three weeks to consider the case before affirming the conviction and sentencing by the Wise County Court, agreeing that Talt Hall should hang on September 2, 1892.

The city of Pound had long been the stopping-off place for travelers going over the mountain through Pound Gap. With some moonshine still making its way from Kentucky, Pound became more of the center of "association" than the larger towns of Gladeville, Norton, and Guest Station, which was in the process of changing its name to Coburn. *Ruby's Rest Awhile* was joined by two other taverns, *Mary's Place* and *The Jerky.* All three places were considered dens of iniquity by the local Old Regular Baptist Church. Workers from Big Stone Gap, Gladeville, and Norton came to the taverns by the wagonload on Friday nights, following payday. Conflicts between the Kentuckians who crossed the mountain for entertainment and the "outsiders" soon surfaced. A northerner from Pennsylvania, Charles Cook, accused of spending too much time pursuing Estelle Roper, a hostess in *Mary's Place,* was shot to death by Talt's eldest son, Floyd, who was sweet on Estelle. Floyd and his gang crossed Pine Mountain and disappeared into the Kentucky woods. Two other Northerners died on the muddy street of Pound, but their killers were never identified or arrested.

This incident led the Old Regular Baptists to call for the closure of these three entities. Gabriel Wilkens presented their demands to the town council. Instead of closing them, he petitioned to regulate the taverns' hours and ban the sale of unstamped whiskey. His efforts angered moonshiners in Kentucky, and some even claimed his Uncle Ira would be glad if someone killed him. However, Ira praised Gabriel's legal skills and did not act on these allegations.

"If I ever need a lawyer," Ira told a friend, "my nephew, Gabriel Wilkens, is a good one. Made it on his own." Then he added, "With the help of my dear sister, Oma."

Moonshine continued to come through Pound Gap, often delivered by Ira's handyman, as Ira no longer sold it himself. The sheriff of Wise County, focused on more pressing issues, such as investigating killings and hunting assassins from Kentucky, did not strictly enforce bans on illegal whiskey. So, business at Pound's three watering holes continued almost unabated despite the court order to cease and desist.

While Gabriel gained experience and built his reputation as an attorney, Creed remained in Bristol, studying under two reputable doctors. Gabriel contacted William and Mary College about enrolling his younger brother in medical school. He discovered that Creed needed to complete two years of apprenticeship under practicing doctors to be eligible for admission to the William and Mary medical program.

In early April, persistent rain raised the Pound River to near-flood levels. Muddy roads halted most horse-and-buggy travel. By the end of the week, the river had reached its highest level ever, prompting many residents to evacuate. Gabriel's office, on a higher elevation, remained safe from flooding.

From his back porch, he saw the wooden bridge upstream collapse and float away in pieces. Shortly after, *The Jerky* and *Mary's Place* drifted by. He expected *Ruby's Rest Awhile* to follow, but it didn't. The next day, he discovered it had been destroyed beyond repair after being flooded and dislodged from its foundation. Members of the Old Regular Baptist Church believed God's storm achieved what the court could not, but Ruby, not an adherent to their religious doctrine, stated that she would build a new tavern that neither hell nor high water would destroy or dislodge. A few months later, a new *Ruby's Rest Awhile* was as busy as ever, catering to the wanton renegades who passed through Pound on their way to somewhere. *Mary's Place* and *The Jerky* did not reopen.

After the storm, Gabriel purchased an acre of land in Pound Bottom and built a three-bedroom home while keeping his office by Pound River in the town's business section. Although the city was not incorporated then, officials were elected, and council meetings were held wherein residents requested street improvements. Gabriel led a group petitioning for street repairs and gas streetlights, which were approved. Streets in the business district were covered with stones from Pine Mountain, and six gas streetlights were installed. The Abingdon Dispatch credited Gabriel Wilkens for his efforts when the project was completed six months later and held up the little town of Pound as an example of what citizens could accomplish by their participation in local government.

The city of Pound continued to grow. A new grocery store, operated by Henry Mullins, a distant relative of Ira's, was opened in March. A ladies' benevolent organization opened a small library, stocked with used books. A grade school opened in the Old Regular Baptist Church with more than a dozen students attending.

While Pound flourished, a tenuous peace hovered over the cities of Gladeville and Norton, whose citizens still talked of the murder of Police Chief Hylton and the trial of Talt Hall. In his absence, as he awaited his hanging in protective custody in Lynchburg, people anticipated news of his escape and return to Letcher County. No one in Wise County would truly feel safe until the most notorious killer in the region was dropped ten feet at the end of a rope.

Rumors abounded that his brothers in crime, numbering nearly a hundred, had amassed near the jail in Lynchburg and were prepared to rescue Hall. Citizens feared that if that happened, he would return to Gladeville and wreak revenge on the judge, the prosecuting attorney, and the members of the jury who convicted him. Adding to their concerns was the fact that Doc Taylor had returned to Gladeville and was practicing a brand of medicine akin to witchcraft. He still had his followers, but most of the people who knew him when he was younger believed the old man had gone mad.

The Red Fox had lost much of his credibility as a doctor, but still held sway over many who followed his religious practices. He was sought by people, mostly women, seeking to communicate with their deceased loved ones. His mesmerizing seances captivated these women, who saw him as a trusted disciple of Jesus Christ, and some even thought he was the Second Coming. His faithful followers defended his eccentricities and attributed rumors of his illicit and illegal behavior to infidels who were bound for hell. They believed that Doc Taylor was a healer of mind, body, and soul and would never do harm to anyone.

The residents of Gladeville and Wise County anxiously awaited Talt Hall's return for his hanging. Kentucky renegades threatened to rescue him while an old feud was reigniting in Letcher County. The Adams and Mullins clans had long harbored animosity. In the fall of 1891, Jason Mullins was shot dead while stacking corn fodder, and Henry Adams was blamed but never charged. This escalated the tension between the clans.

In March, two of Henry Adams's sons fell ill with typhoid fever, and one died. Henry accused Wilson Mullins of poisoning his well and vowed revenge against "every Mullins" in Kentucky. This tense situation persisted as April 1892 approached.

6

A FATAL TRIP

A fair wind blew that Friday evening of May 13, 1892, bringing with it the first hint of an approaching summer. Ira Mullins and his family had settled into a new cabin home a few miles from the town center of Whitesburg, Kentucky. Ira had acquired enough wealth to allow him and his family to live a comfortable if not affluent lifestyle, which had not been gained without great sacrifice. He was a cripple, unable to walk, resulting from a gunfight that he attributed to Doc Marshall Benton Taylor. Ira was not flamboyant, but he did not attempt to hide the fact that he lived well, and Louranza had confided in a few friends that she always carried a large sum of money in a sash around her waist. That morning, she carefully placed $1,600 into a small purse attached to the sash. It was the proceeds from the sale of land by Ira the previous day.

Ira had moved his family from Bold Camp in the fall of 1891, but still had many belongings left in the cabin that was once owned by Caleb and Gabriel Wilkens. That Friday evening, with the help of a hired hand, John Chapell, he began preparing for a trip over Pine Mountain to bring a wagonload of goods back to Whitesburg.

At about 10 a.m. the following morning, Saturday, Ira's party departed Whitesburg. John Harrison Mullins, aged 14, and a friend, Greenberry Harris, walked along behind the wagon. Riding ahead was John's uncle, Wilson Mullins, the husband of Ira's sister, Jane. John Harrison's mother, Loranza, and his father, Ira, rode in a wagon with a young cousin, Amanda Mullins. John Chapell was driving the wagon. Jane followed the group on horseback.

Beginning the previous evening, Wilson had attempted to convince his daughter, Amanda, to remain in Whitesburg with her maternal grandmother. Mandy, as she was called, insisted on making the trip. Her father convinced her to remain behind by promising to buy her something good to eat. Shortly after getting underway, they stopped at a small store, and he purchased a can of store-bought peaches for his nine-year-old daughter. It was only a short distance to the home of her grandmother, and she agreed to walk there alone. She would never see her father alive again.

The party made several stops along the way, giving those on foot an opportunity to rest. Everyone was in a convivial mood, including Ira, who sat up on a special feather-filled mattress Louranza made for his travel. John, at fourteen, and Greenberry took short jaunts through the woods, rejoining the entourage. The sun shimmered through the oaks that were just filling with leaves and the evergreen pines that covered the mountains.

"Let's stop for a few minutes when we reach the Gap and rest the team," Ira said, referring to the two horses pulling the wagon.

"Sounds good," Wilson responded over his shoulder.

"And I need a lady's break," Louranza said. "There's a private spot near the Red Fox Trail. Let's wait 'til we git there."

"Alright, Louranza." Wilson turned to see that Ira concurred.

Ira nodded.

Wilson slapped the reins lightly across the backs of the horses, emphasizing that they would continue into Virginia before stopping to rest the team.

The party crossed Pound Gap at about 1 p.m. and started down the Virginia side of the mountain. The beginning of the Red Fox Trail lay just ahead, off to the right. On the left-hand side of the trail was a massive stack of huge rocks, moved there to clear the trail for wagons. Tree limbs had been cut and laid across an opening between the rocks. The leaves had wilted, indicating that they had been placed there a few days earlier. A barrage of rifle shots rang out from behind the rocks, and the horses pulling the wagon fell to the ground. Next, Wilson Mullins, who rode ahead, plummeted to the ground as he reached for the rifle that he was carrying on the side of his saddle.

Before anyone could take cover, more shots rang out. A shot to the heart of Greenberry Haris felled him. Two more shots found their mark as he lay on the ground. Young John's horse was tethered to the back of the wagon. It panicked and broke loose, running back through the Gap and down the Kentucky side of the mountain. John took shelter behind a large oak tree. When he saw three shooters rise from behind the rock formation, he ran wildly down the Virginia side of the mountain, not stopping until he reached Pound.

Louranza looked up to see John Chapell keel over from a gunshot to the head. She jumped to the ground and crawled under the wagon. Seven rifle bullets riddled her body.   By then, Ira attempted to roll over but was unable to move. He was struck in the heart and then mutilated with eight gunshot wounds to his head.

Jane Mullins, petrified, unable to move, sat on her horse while death rained around her. She was astounded by what was happening. She appeared frozen, making no attempt to escape, and her horse did not panic and run away. When the shooting stopped, not a sound could be heard, and then from under the wagon, Louranza begged," Someone, someone…"

Jame got down from her horse and knelt over Louranza, who whispered, "They've killed me." She stretched out her arms toward Jane before letting them fall lifelessly to her sides.

Jame crawled over to Wilson and attempted to turn over his body, but quickly realized her efforts were useless.

Three men stood behind the rocks. They wore hats, and their faces, except for their chins, were covered with black bandannas. One shouted profanity at Jane.

"You stupid woman, you had better git goin' if you don't want to end up kilt like the rest of them."

She screamed, "For the Lord's sake, boys. Don't shoot anymore. Let me stay with them until somebody comes and finds us?"

One of the men yelled back, "Goddamn you, woman, you better git movin' if you don't want to end up like the rest of them." A rifle shot into the air emphasized his warning.

She mounted her horse and kicked its flanks; it started galloping, and she headed toward Pound Gap and the Kentucky side of the mountain. Four hours later, she and her horse were still wandering through the woods near Elkhorn Creek without direction.

A half hour after the shooting, an incoherent young man burst through the door of Gabriel Wilkens' office.

"They're dead." He bellowed. "They're all dead."

Gabriel ran to the boy and held him up as he gasped for breath.

"Who's dead, John?"

"Ma and Pa and Uncle Wilson, all of them, and Greenberry too, I guess." He spoke between gasps for air. "I need to git word to Jemima Harris and let her know what's happened to Greenberry."

"I'll go with you," Gabriel said. They set out on foot to find Greenberry's mother. When they arrived at Jemima's house, John fell, sobbing into her arms. Between gasps, he told her a horror story about an ambush on the mountain near Pound Gap. Jemima broke down, wailing as Gabriel embraced her, attempting to ease her grief.

When John regained his composure, he continued his tale in horrifying detail. "I seen Uncle Harrison and Greenberry fall, the horses, too. I begin to run as soon as I seen what was happenin'."

"We have to get up there," Gabriel said, "and see if we can help any of them." He noted that one of John's suspenders was slashed. He looked closely at it. "My God, John, your suspender has been shot."

John inspected his suspenders, then looked at his trouser legs, which had several bullet holes in them. "God Almighty," he exclaimed, "they almost got me too."

Gabriel asked, "Did you recognize any of the shooters?"

"I didn't have time to look," he said. I just run down the mountain as fast as I could. I must've run nearly a mile when the shootin' stopped, but I kept on runnin' 'cause I thought they might come after me."

"I've got to git up there and check on my baby," Jemima Harris said. "Will you come with me, Mr. Wilkens?"

"You know I will, Miss Jemima. Do you want me to get my buggy ready?"

"No," she said. "I need to go now. Will you walk with me?"

"You go on ahead, and I will catch up with you. I must get word to the sheriff in Gladeville."

Jemima Harris immediately started out for Pound Gap. She went to the house of Floyd Branham and asked his wife, Elizabeth, her closest friend, to go with them to the top of the mountain. The three-mile walk up the mountain was made in forty minutes.

Jemima prayed out loud with almost every step she took. "The Lord giveth, and the Lord taketh away. I pray to Him that my son is still alive. "When she arrived on the scene, one look at her Greenberry, sprawled on the trail, told her God had allowed her son to die in a horrible way. She bowed her head and gave thanks, in the manner of Job, for sharing Greenberry with her for fifteen years. Minutes later, Gabriel arrived at the site of the murders.

Robert Mullins, a distant relative, happened to be walking up Pine Mountain on his way to Letcher County. His home was three miles down the Virginia side of the mountain. At the same time, Arnold Bentley, who owned the store where Wilson Mullins had purchased canned peaches earlier that day, arrived from the opposite direction. The scene was reminiscent of the sites at Antietam and Gettysburg, where both men had served during the Civil War. The time was 2:30 in the afternoon, four and a half hours since Ira and his party left Whitesburg, and a little more than an hour since the shooting from the hill began.

Arnold Bentley was a magistrate. He and Robert Mullins took control of the tragic scene, attempting to comprehend what had taken place. The ground was covered with blood. A mother, weeping uncontrollably, knelt over a deceased boy as another woman attempted to console her. Four bodies surrounded the wagon, which was still hitched to two dead horses.

Gabriel had arrived moments before the two men. He related John Harrison's account to them. Magistrate Bentley climbed up on the wagon and saw the mutilated body of Ira Mullins, a man he had known well but barely recognized now. Ira had received eight shots to his face and head. The magistrate removed his hat and stood for a moment, uttering a prayer. Hay had been raked and stacked to one side of the wagon as the killers apparently searched for moonshine, which they had expected to find.

Gabriel helped Jemima to her feet and led her away from the bloody body of her son. He found a clearing close by, where travelers frequently stopped on their trip across the mountain. She and Elizabeth Branham watched as Gabriel, Robert Mullins, and Magistrate Bentley examined each of the bodies.

The wagon had been riddled with bullets. Louranza Mullins lay under it with gunshot wounds to her chest. Her apron and dress were over her head, covering her face. The sash, which she always wore, containing a large amount of money, had been removed from around her waist. It was apparent to Gabriel that too many people had known of her practice of carrying the money for safekeeping.

Handyman, John Chapell, the driver of the team of horses, had fallen in a heap near the horses. Apparently, the wagon continued rolling for a short distance after the horses fell, dumping his body when the wagon stopped. He had been shot six times, making it obvious that the rapid shots came from an automatic rifle. He was a black man with a wife and a family of six children.

The body of Greenberry Harris was behind the wagon, having been shot in the head twice and through the heart. Some of the bullets he received were undoubtedly intended for John Harrison, the son of Ira. If John had not sought shelter and then run immediately, his body would have been alongside his good friend, Greenberry.

Wilson Mullins, riding ahead of the pack, had received one shot through his heart. His horse, one of the few living things to survive the massacre, was nowhere to be seen. It was found with a bloodstained saddle, roaming the woods on Southfork the next day.

Arnold Bentley noticed Jane was missing from the party. Elizabeth Branham hadn't mentioned her, and both Jane and her horse were gone. They searched the mountain near the crime scene but found no trace of either. The possibility that Jane was kidnapped and being held by the killers was voiced by Bentley, or that she might have betrayed her brother by planning the ambush of his party. In the fog of confusion and horror, anything was possible.

The alarm spread quickly, and many people climbed the mountain up the oft-traveled trail and arrived within an hour. Arnold Bentley and Robert Mullins asked each newcomer about Jane, but no one had seen her. There was no evidence that an injured person had left the road.

Three hours later, Jane emerged from the woods above Little Elkhorn Creek. "They're all dead," she screamed to everybody she saw. "They're all dead but me."

A man walking along the main road grasped the horse's bridle and held on until it stopped. "Who's dead?"

"Ira; Ira, my brother. Everyone, everyone has been shot.'

"Where?" the man asked.

"The top of the mountain," she whispered as she leaned to one side in her saddle.

The man caught her as she fell and eased her to the ground.

"My poor brother," she moaned. "What will we all do without Ira?" Her eyes closed as she rested on the ground, sobbing.

PART 3

THE RECKONING

1

____

CONFUSION REIGNS

A crowd assembled around Jane as she lay on the ground, moaning and speaking incoherently about the murder of her family members. A woman from within the group of over a dozen individuals assisted her in sitting up and provided her with water. "Tell us if you can," the woman said. "What has happened to your brother?"

Jane appeared confused but managed to say, "We were ambushed by Cal Fleming and two other men."

"How do you know it was 'Cal?'"

"His face was covered, but I recognized his voice."

"Are you sure?"

"No," she said, "I need to go home and tell my family what's happened."

On the mountain, a crowd was gathering. The sheriff of Wise County had been notified of the killings but had not yet arrived on the scene. Arnold Bentley, as magistrate, was overseeing the investigation. He and Robert Mullins examined the area behind the rocks where the killers had hidden. They discovered a black bandana worn by one of the assassins. Lying beneath some branches, hidden by pine knots and leaves, they found shell casings, all the same: 44-75 black powder shells.

Bentley knew of two guns of that caliber; one belonged to Henry Adams, who had feuded with Wilson Mullins and accused him of poisoning his well. The other belonged to James Potter. Potter, a church-going Baptist, had voiced his disdain for the lifestyle of Ira Mullins and his family. Bentley did not state his opinions regarding ownership of the murder weapons until he was able to make his investigation known to the sheriff, who would have jurisdiction of the case.

Bentley finished examining all the bodies and noting their mortal wounds. The wounds were large, like the shots a Winchester rifle would make. By then, John Harrison had returned to the mountain and was giving his version of the events of that afternoon.

"We didn't have no warnin'. They just commenced shootin'. The horses fell first, and then Wilson. That's when me and Greenberry started to run, but he fell down right then, bleedin' from his head."

"Did you recognize any of the shooters?" Bentley asked.

"I didn't git a chance. Bullets was flyin' all around me. I just run like the dickens; scared to death, I was."

After answering the magistrate's questions, John climbed onto the wagon and sat near his father's body. Tears flowed down his cheeks as he then climbed down and knelt beside his mother.

It was after six p.m. when Jane, Enos, and two other men of the Mullins clan arrived on the mountain. Gabriel had walked back to Pound and returned with his wagon to haul the dead to Wilson and Jane's home near Elkhorn Creek, where they would be washed and dressed for burial. The men began loading the bodies onto Gabriel's wagon. They were ready to commence the dreaded trip down the mountain before dark set in, but Magistrate Bentley wanted Jane's version of events before they left the scene of the killings.

One of the first things that he questioned her on as part of his investigation was where she had been and why no one had encountered her on the road. Jane said she had wandered through the woods, afraid the killers might come after her. At one time, she tied her horse to a small tree and hid in a thicket, not daring to venture back onto the trail. When asked if she had any idea who might have done the shooting, Jane told Bentley she couldn't be certain because she never saw their faces. One voice she heard might have been that of Cal Fleming, she said, but she couldn't be certain. Another voice sounded like Hanen Fleming when he cursed her and ordered her to leave the scene. And she might have gotten a glimpse of the beard of one of the killers, which she thought might have been Doc Taylor. The beard was red, streaked with grey, and the man dressed like Doc Taylor. Jane once spent a weekend at the home of Taylor and his wife and was very familiar with his appearance. Since the doctor was known to be a ladies' man, some people thought there might be more to her story than she revealed. Jane originally stated that she didn't see anyone at all, but got on her horse and rode down the mountain as fast as possible. This story did not account for her not being seen by anyone for more than four hours. Then, the magistrate advised her not to say any more about the identity of the killers until she could be protected by officers of the law.

After hauling the bodies to Jane's home and placing them on the porch, Gabriel and neighbors built a large fire and fed it with damp leaves so the smoke would keep flies away from the dead. The next morning, he drove to a sawmill and bought lumber. Several men and women came to pay their condolences to Jane and to help build caskets for the dead. There was room for two wooden caskets inside the house; the other three remained on the porch. During the overnight wake, volunteers dug five graves in Murdered Man's Cemetery in Camden, Kentucky, near Little Elkhorn Creek.

Hundreds gathered for the burial on the mountainside. They came from Letcher and Pike Counties, in Kentucky, and Wise County, Virginia. They included relatives and friends, who mourned, Ira's enemies who silently gloated, and the inquisitive who came to confirm the inconceivable news of the murder of five people. Murder was not an unusual occurrence in Letcher and Wise Counties, but mass murder shocked the sensibilities of all who lived in those counties. It sent fear throughout the mountains and valleys of southeastern Kentucky and southwestern Virginia.

A few days after the funeral, Jane Mullins, accompanied by Gabriel Wilkens, rode to Gladeville so that Jane could give her version of the massacre to Sheriff John Miller. In the safety of the courthouse, she spoke more freely of what she witnessed during and after the killing. She no longer doubted that the three killers were Cal and Henan Fleming and Doc Taylor, all of whom she knew well. The sheriff advised her never to travel alone and to make certain that whoever accompanied her was well-armed and a good marksman.

Gabriel readily admitted that he was not such a man but was prepared to offer whatever legal assistance Jane and her family might need throughout the coming ordeal. Before leaving Gladeville, Gabriel drove to John Wright's place and requested that he ride back with them to Pine Gap. They felt safe enough riding alone to Jane's home in Elkhorn Creek. John agreed to go with them and did not head back to Gladeville until Jane reached her home safely.

People in the mountains began to talk, if only in whispers, about the crime. Doors that had always been left open were shut and locked. Rumors of the killings spread quickly across the states of Kentucky and Virginia. Folks were willing to accept the possible participation of Cal and Hanen Fleming who wished to be perceived as dangerous and daring as Talt Hall, then languishing in a Lynchburg jail, waiting to be returned to Gladeville for his hanging, but it was inconceivable that a man of God such as Marshall Benton Taylor could be involved in such an insidious act of violence.

Doc Taylor had cured their ills, saved their souls, and preached their funerals. It was nothing less than heresy to accuse such an upright man of mass murder. But those few who had come to believe The Red Fox had departed from reality, accepted the accusations without much skepticism. They believed the old man was "off his rocker," and might be perfectly capable of such an act, especially if his victims were known to be carrying a large sum of money.

And there were people who thought that Ira got what he deserved. For years, he had flaunted the law and gained considerable wealth by doing so. The "little dandy" had created many enemies, and any one of them might have participated in his killing. As for those who perished along with him, they were unfortunate enough to keep bad company. They simply paid for "being in the wrong place at the wrong time," or "keeping company with the devil." Others eased their conscience for such horrendous utterings by proffering the saying, "When you lie down with dogs, you get fleas." Not everyone was unhappy that Ira Mullins, his wife, brother-in-law, and two unrelated people lost their lives at Killing Rock that day.

The mystery might have gone unresolved if the Fleming brothers had not begun to brag about their participation in Ira's murder. At first, people accepted what they were hearing from the Flemings as mostly braggadocio, and they might not have given it any credibility if the Flemings and Doc Taylor were not now keeping constant company. After the slaying, they no longer travelled alone, but the three of them were always together and heavily armed. Random suspicions of the trio congealed, and Doc Taylor and the Flemings became the prime suspects.

2
____

KILLERS AMONG US

After Jane's report to Sheriff Miller, a warrant was issued for the arrest of the suspected killers, and word was sent out that it might be best for their well-being if they turned themselves in willingly. However, Doc Taylor and the Fleming brothers were avoiding the enforcement of the warrant by staying in Kentucky, outside the sheriff's jurisdiction. The Fleming brothers, relishing their new notoriety, flamboyantly talked of how they had murdered Ira Mullins and his wife. But Doc Taylor denied any participation in the killings. He sent word back to the sheriff that he was too busy curing the ill and doing God's work to answer false accusations.

And his followers had no doubt he was telling the truth. After all, he had never failed to cure them when they were sick. To them, he was a prophet, and like Jesus, he was persecuted for his good works. The faithful attributed the allegations against him to the northerners who had invaded the mountains. Doc had warned them that the foreigners were there to steal the mineral rights on their property. They were building railroads and bringing the heavy equipment they would need to haul away the riches of the mountains. According to the doctor, they were to blame for his removal as a Deputy Marshall and the dismissal of other local men from city and county government positions. He claimed that the reasons for his problems were simple; the northern invaders wanted him out of the way. But he assured his followers that he would be with them always, even after his death, whenever that came to be.

On Sundays, the Red Fox preached the Lord's word; on other days, he brandished a 44-75 Winchester rifle. Across one shoulder, he carried a shiny belt of cartridges and, on each hip, a huge pistol. He took random walks through the woods that lasted for hours, during which he said he meditated and talked with his brother, Jesus Christ. He thought no one else was worthy enough to experience such fellowship with Christ or to follow his path. He wore moccasins backward on his feet with the heels facing forward to conceal his direction of travel.

As summer neared and Sheriff Miller became less tolerant of Doc Taylor's aberrant behavior, he devised a plan to capture the Red Fox and Fleming Brothers. He was determined to bring the suspects to Gladeville for questioning. He sent for the only man in Wise County that he trusted to hunt down Doc and the Flemings. Devil John Wright, still a U.S. Marshal for the western section of Virginia, accepted the assignment and set out for Letcher County. When he arrived, he learned that the Fleming brothers had left Kentucky, probably headed for Memphis, Tennessee. And Doc Taylor's followers were keeping his whereabouts to themselves.

About the same time, the sheriff received word that Talt Hall had escaped from jail in Lynchburg and was probably on his way back to the Kentucky mountains and safety. Sheriff Miller called off the hunt for Doc and the Flemings temporarily while they concentrated on the most dangerous man who ever hailed from the hills. John Wright was given the assignment to hunt down Talt and bring him back to Gladeville to await execution.

The Devil staked out Talt's home near Whitesburg for three weeks, waiting for Talt to come to him. On a Saturday night, early in June, he heard a horse nicker, apparently tired from being ridden hard. John kept silent as he crept to the corner of Talt's home. A rider dismounted and hitched his horse to a post.

"Where you headed, Talt?" John stepped out of the dark and politely asked.

Talt's hand reached for the gun he was carrying in his belt.

"I wouldn't do that if I was you, Talt."

Talt's hands went up into the air. "You sonsabitch, John. I let you git the draw on me, didn't I?"

"No doubt," John said, "and I'm mighty glad of it."

"What do you want with me?"

"I'm taking you to the gallows, Talt, as bad as I hate to do it."

"We was friends once, John. Don't that mean anything to you?"

"And I'm still your friend. I'm just doing my job. You can't go around killing people, especially lawmen. You know that."

"I've never killed nobody without good reason."

"But the judge didn't believe you, did he?"

"I can't rightly say he did, John."

"OK, mount up, Talt. We got to get back to Gladeville before daybreak."

"Can we wait 'til morning"? I'm awful tired to travel over that mountain tonight and I ain't seen my wife in three months."

"I'm afraid not. I can't afford for that son of yours to shoot me in the back."

"Can I just say something to my wife before we go?"

"Yes, but we'll do it out here where I can keep my eye on you."

Talt called his wife, Manda, by her familiar name. After a minute or two, he called again, louder. "Rinda, Hey Rinda. It's me, Talt."

They waited for a short time. Talt cupped his hands to his mouth, prepared to call his wife again. Just then, the door opened, and a petite woman in her nightgown broke through the door and ran toward her husband. John reached for her arm, keeping his gun levelled at Talt. "Sorry, Rinda; you got a weapon on you?"

Manda was jolted to a standstill. "No. Course not."

She wrenched her arm angrily from John's grasp. What's goin' on, Talt? Why ain't I heard nothin' from you all this time?"

"I was coming home to you, Rinda, but John here's got to take me into Gladeville for hanging."

Rinda began crying and rushed by Devil John. She threw her arms around Talt. John Wright held his gun, now aimed at both of them. He said nothing as she held onto her husband and sobbed. They stood, holding each other, knowing they were sharing their last goodbyes.

John cleared his throat. "It's time to go, Talt. We've got a long ride to Gladeville."

"I know," he responded, removing his wife's hands from his waist.

John held his gun steadily on Talt and held onto his horse's reins. "You better take yourself a leak cause you're going to be on your horse for the next three hours."

John waited while Talt turned away from his wife and relieved himself. John anticipated that Talt might break and run at any minute. His pistol was cocked and ready to fire if that happened, and he was confident his prisoner did not wish to die at the hand of Devil John Wright.

As Manda wailed, Talt reached his hands toward John, who tied them together with a rope from his saddlebag. Then he tied each of Talt's legs to his stirrups. He fastened a rope to Talt's saddle horn and led it to his own horse.

"You lead the way." He told Talt. "I'm going to keep you ten feet in front of me with my gun at the ready."

Talt kicked his horse in the flank, and they set out for Elkhorn at the foot of Pine Mountain. Halfway up the mountain, clouds moved across the moon, and the visibility was limited to a few feet. Three hours passed before they reached Pound Gap. "We're stopping for a while," John said as he brought his horse to a halt.

"Can I get off this horse?" Talt asked, "My rump is killing me."

"Yeah," John said. "We're just going to stay here 'til daybreak."

John untied Talt's feet and allowed him to slip to the ground. "You ought to get yourself a nap, Talt?"

"That sounds good to me, John. How about you?"

"Not me," John replied. "No rest for the wicked, they say. I have to keep my eye on you, Talt, and my gun at the ready."

"I ain't about to test you, John. I hope you know that. I've done some wild things, but I'm not that damned crazy."

"Just the same, I won't be taking the risk. Go ahead and get a little sleep. He patted the handle of the pistol, rising from the holster on his hip.

Talt sat with his back against a pine, and John Wright sat across from him, fifteen feet away. The early morning forest was silent except for the occasional snorting of the two horses and sounds of crickets and tree frogs. John watched as Talt closed his eyes, apparently sleeping. When the first shreds of light appeared through the trees, Talt stretched and yawned.

"You know, John. I should have made a break for it earlier this morning. I opened my eyes, and I swear, by damned, you was sleeping. I could've up and run. But I must be tired of running. They're going to hang me one of these days. So, I just might as well git it over with."

"You would be a dead man right now if you had tried anything. I haven't slept in two days, and I wasn't sleeping this morning. You know what they say, Talt; Devil John always gets his man."

"Just the same, John, I'm still here, and you still got that gun looking at me. I ain't going anyplace but Gladeville—anytime you're ready."

They continued down the mountainside toward Pound. Two hundred feet from the Gap, they passed by Killing Rock. John spoke. "I guess you heard about the Doc killing Ira and his wife, didn't you?"

"Yeah, I heard, and they can't blame that on me."

"Or me," John said.

"I've done some bad things, but I ain't ever killed a woman or child." He paused, as if recounting his past deeds. "I ain't killed nearly as many men as people say."

"How many do you think, Talt?"

"To tell you the truth, I don't really know. I never kept count. But I would say twenty or so, but nowhere near a hundred, like I mentioned once, just to shut down talk about me. "

"Did you kill Hylton?"

"I did, and I regret that. But he was feeling his oats with his deputy badge and all, and I think he was itching for a fight with me."

"Did he draw on you?"

"No, but I kind of thought he might, so I shot first."

"But they testified you shot him twice."

"I guess I did John, but after the first shot, I had to make sure he wasn't going to testify against me."

"How about the others?"

"You know I been on trial eight times and was proved innocent every time."

"Were you innocent?"

"Some say I was. I say I was."

"Were you?"

"The law said I was, and that's what matters."

The sun was rising in the sky as they reached the bottom of the mountain and turned toward Pound. With the horses and both men nearing exhaustion, their pace slowed considerably. It was nearing nine a.m. when John brought his horse to a halt in front of Gabriel's office. He untied Talt's feet and helped him to the ground. John knocked on the door, then opened it. He motioned for Talt to enter ahead of him.

Gabriel looked up from his desk to see Talt Hall with his

hands bound together and a tether leading to his captor. "Who do you have here, John?"

"I have your client; just caught up with him in Letcher County."

"Well, Talt, the last I heard you were ensconced in a Lynchburg jail."

"His buddies broke him out, and he hightailed it home only to find me waiting for him," John said. "That right, Talt?"

Talt spoke. "I ain't saying. You boys mind if I sit for a little spell? I'm about wore out."

"For a minute or two," John said, "then we got to get going." He laughed as he turned to Gabriel. "Are you still representing this scoundrel?"

"No," Gabriel replied. "I think he fired me, and maybe with good reason. I didn't fight very hard for my client."

"Wouldn't have done any good, Mr. Wilkins," Talt said. "They had me dead to rights. No use for you to dirty your hands defending me."

"I did what my conscience dictated and what the law required."

"And I appreciate it," Talt said.

"Maybe I could have done more if you hadn't shot my pa."

Talt stood. "I swear by God Almighty; I didn't do that. I swear. I ain't ever denied killing a man if I did it."

John Wright interjected. "I expect that's true, Gabe."

"Tell me, Mr. Hall," Gabriel said, "If you didn't do it, who did?"

"Tell you the truth, Mr. Wilkens. "As God is my witness, it wasn't me."

"Who then?"

"It wasn't me, for sure."

Gabriel stood and pounded his fist on the desk. "Damn you, Talt Hall. Who was it that shot Caleb Wilkens?"

"I heard tell it was The Red Fox."

3

____

ATONEMENT

With Talt Hall in a cell at the Gladeville jail, the sheriff and Devil John Wright turned their attention back to tracking down the suspected killers of Ira Mullins. The Flemings were previously rumored to be in Memphis, Tennessee, but the latest news of them came from Bluefield, West Virginia, about one hundred miles away. That information came by way of hearsay from Henry Adams in Letcher County. Henry was one of the first men to be suspected of taking part in the murder because of his feud with Wilson Mullins, and he was eager to divert accusations from himself.

Devil John was not to be outdone nor outsmarted by two ignorant desperadoes. He contacted Ira's older brother, Enos, to keep his eyes and ears open for any information on Cal and Henan Fleming. Before long, Enos got word back to John that the brothers made infrequent forays into Letcher County, remaining for a day or two. Enos heard that the brothers often met with Doc Taylor, who was holding the money they took from Louranza's sash. The story was that the doctor was letting the money out, a little at a time, so Cal and Henan wouldn't go on a spending binge and confirm the suspicions that the three of them killed Lourenza and stole her money.

John Wright wanted very much to catch the Flemings, and he kept Enos and other informers on the lookout for news of them. But his focus was on catching The Red Fox, who was being protected by his ardent followers. While John stalked the hills of Letcher County, waiting for The Red Fox to make a mistake, Talt Hall found the need to rinse his soul for his sins. He could hear the sounds of hammering from outside, where jailer, Charles Renfro, was constructing a gallows for the first ever legal hanging in Wise County. The banging of the hammers made him think he would hear them through eternity unless he confessed his sins and sought redemption.

Talt was a proud man, and confessing of his sins was unexpected by those who knew him best. But facing the fires of hell led him to ask that Brother Mack Cantrell visit him in Gladeville to hear a "deathbed" confession. When Brother Mack arrived, he was accompanied by Gabriel Wilkens. He had his well-worn Bible in one hand and another Bible in the other, which he carried to the jail for Talt.

"Why did you bring this lawyer with you, Brother Mack?" Talt asked through the cell bars.

"Young man," the preacher replied, "I've heard of your duplicity, and I want a respected witness of our time together, and Gabriel is the most respected young man in this county."

"But, preacher, I want to talk about redemption, not make a statement for the public."

"Well, Talt, I want to save souls. If your story will keep others on the path of righteousness, you and I both will have done a service to God."

"But you can't publish anything I tell you."

Gabriel said, "We promise that. I am here for you and Brother Mack. Whatever you say will remain between the three of us if that is what you want." Talt began to talk.

"I guess I've done more killing than any man alive; I mean, outside of killing in the War. I think I must have been fifteen when I shot Joe Webb for something I don't even remember. It bothered me for a while, but then when Frank Blevins started hanging after Mandy, I shot him, too. I think I was eighteen then. I went off to the war right after that, and I was told, I was a good soldier.

"When I came home after the war, the Home Guard that had been formed in my absence to protect the wives and children of soldiers came after me. I didn't understand why, with all the stealing and horse thieving that was going on in Floyd County, where I was living. I didn't want no trouble, so I went to live in Texas and stayed there for three years. I returned to Letcher County because I wanted to marry Mandy, but the Home Guard wouldn't let me be.

"I know you remember how it was in all the counties of Kentucky after the war. There was plenty of friends and enemies left over. I guess I was like most men, expecting each day might be my last. I had plenty of enemies and was always armed and watching for somebody who might want to kill me.

"The first man I killed after the war was Henry Maggard in Lecher County in 1866. We had a political disagreement, and he decided to draw on me. Of course, I won that fight, but was arrested for murder. I stood trial and was acquitted.

"There have been lots of killings blamed on me that I never done. Even in the war, I got blamed for killing a man in the home guard that was killed by David Garret. That was one of the reasons I left my home and went to Texas. The whole time I was gone, my friends and family thought I was dead. I was never able to enjoy the harmony of a happy home because I was on constant guard for my life because of the lies that were kept in circulation about me."

Talt stopped talking for a moment and then raised his head to speak out loud, talking to the jailer. "Hey Charlie, can I git a glass of water here. My throat is parched dry from talking."

Charles Renfro appeared at the cage with a bucket. He slipped the handle of a dipper through the bars and allowed Talt to drink and said, "If you'll hand me your mason jar, I'll fill it for you."

Afterward, he offered the dipper to Brother Mack, who accepted it and drank. Gabriel declined his offer and thanked him for the courtesy.

The jailer went away and returned momentarily with a mason jar filled with water.

Brother Mack said to Talt, "Do you want to rest now or continue talking?"

"I've got some more for you, Brother Mack, before you pray with me, just let me relieve myself."

Talt pulled a chamber pot from under the cot. He turned his back to Gabriel and the preacher. After a long sigh, he sat back down in his chair and resumed his story.

"I was a United States Marshal in 1878. Back then, I did a lot of work in Floyd County, where moonshiners ran wilder than even those in Letcher County. I went after them like I was supposed to, and in doing so, I run upon nineteen of them in a bunch. They came after me, guns on fire. There was a young deputy with me, and we stood our ground. There was lots of shooting, and a moonshiner by the name of Henry Triplett was shot dead and several more wounded. Rumor was that I shot Triplett in the back. So, I went to Prestonsburg, Kentucky, and turned myself in. Because I was a United States police officer, I was acquitted. But my reputation as a killer widened, and it was said that I always got my man one way or another.

"I know I've done some bad things and have a reputation for being a ruthless killer. But anyone who really knows me well will tell you I am a kind man. When I was a U.S. Marshal, I always treated my prisoners with kindness. I remember once when I went to arrest a moonshiner in Floyd County; his wife hid her face in her apron and wept. One of his little children held onto his leg and begged him not to leave them. I couldn't stand to see that little girl cry. 'Please, Papa, don't leave us.' So, I told the man, 'I'm going on ahead. You meet me down the trail.' That way the children wouldn't have to see me arrest their daddy.

"Another time, when I was still a marshal, Dr. Johnson came to my house and called me to come outside. He told me that the man who killed Sheriff Caudell of Floyd County was holed up at a certain place and facing off with some men who were afraid to go in and git him. I accepted the challenge and got together four or five deputies to go up to a big hill in the woods. When I got there, I gave him a chance to give up, but he told me to go to hell. He took a shot at Bill Bates, one of the men with me, and would have killed him if not for me. I ordered him once again to give up, but he came out, guns blazing, and I took him out. I was charged with the man's murder but was acquitted again."

Talt sat back in his chair and wiped his arm across his mouth. "I bet you're gittin' tired of my palaver, Brother Mack, but I feel the need to talk about these things as long as you will listen."

"Me and Mr. Wilkens came for that purpose. We're hoping you won't hide anything from us. You know you can't hide it from God."

"I know," he said. "And I got a idea that Mr. Wilkins thinks I might confess to killing his pa, but, like I told him before, I swear before God as a man who fears hell and damnation, I never ever took a shot at Gabriel Wilkens, and I don't know for sure who did. Some say it was The Red Fox, but you will have to ask him about that if you ever git the chance."

Brother Mack stood and stretched, and then sat back down. "We'll stay with you for one more hour, then we got to get headed back toward Pound before dark sets in."

Talt scooted his chair closer to the bars and began talking in a quiet voice.

"I was blamed for killing a man by the name of Higgins in Hindman, Kentucky, five or six years ago, but I didn't have any part in his killing. He was ambushed by Dick Vance and Abraham Hall. My brother's son was to be a witness against them. So, they paid Gibb Jones to kill my nephew to keep him from testifying. I stood up against them, and they hired Caleb Jones to come after me. He was a notorious man who had killed at least fifteen men in Kentucky.

"Not long after this, I got the news that Jones and his men was in the woods looking for me. I wasn't out for a fight with Jones, so I didn't do anything about it. The next morning, me and George Johnson started through the woods for John Wright's place in a different direction to avoid a fight. A mile or two into the woods, Jones and his men started firing on us. We took shelter behind some large oaks. Thinking that Jones probably had as many as twelve men with him, we wasn't in a hurry to engage them. But Johnson and me both got off shots and each one of us killed a man. I guess Johnson thought things were gittin' too hot for him cause he and his men hightailed it to a safe distance away. There was an old house nearby, and we run over there. Our horses took off, and we was stranded for sure. Jones and his men stayed out of our sight but kept firing toward us. We made a break for it, running right through their line. One of his men stepped out of hiding and fired at me. I killed him dead. Jones shot me in the hand, the first time I had ever been shot. And I never forgot about it over time. That encounter made me and Jones bitter enemies, and that was bound to come to a head one day.

"Later, I got a warrant signed for Jones' arrest and went up to a little stream called Cade Creek. I closed in on his gang with a posse of six men and told them to surrender. They commenced firing, and I was badly wounded. One man by the name of Abe Little was killed immediately, shot by my man, W.J. Bates. Jones and the rest of his men got away.

"The enmity between me and Jones continued even after he sent word that he wanted peace. I sent back word that although he and his men had wounded me grievously, I would not hold it against him. But soon, I learned Jones was spreading lies on me, telling H.A. Hall that I was improper with his handsome wife. I say before my Almighty God that I never wronged her or her husband. She was a gracious lady, kind to me, one who always gave me good advice. I said that she was mighty pretty, and I would surely love to kiss her, but that was all. These lies set me at odds with Hall for a long time.

"As decent men, you might wonder how I became such a killer. When you are born into it, killing just becomes a way of living."

'"The men that I lived around all my life believed it was an honor to kill another man. The reason I have lived this long is that I learned at an early age to be aware of my surroundings and to keep my eyes open when I was associating with dangerous men. I was determined to be as ruthless as any man when I had to fight. I always tried to be more ready than my enemies and to get off the first shot when I was threatened. More important, I had to make the first shot count.

"My 'Blue Grass State' has not been what Almighty God intended for the past ten or fifteen years. I regret that I was one of its worst desecrators, and I am resolved to make atonement in some way or another if I am able. Instead of cultivating the rich bottoms and fertile valleys given to us, we used the fields as battlegrounds. The men that God gave to us for companionship, we made into bitter enemies. God's seventh commandment, Thou shalt not kill, was violated over and over, and I was one of the biggest offenders..."

Gabriel broke in. "You sound like a reasonable man. And if you had directed your life in a different direction, you might be revered by the ones you will leave behind. They will suffer the stigma of your hanging. I believe your loved ones should hear the words you have just spoken here today."

"And I regret my life, Mr. Wilkens, believe me. The way I figure, though, is that I have done the best I knew how. My ma was a Godly woman, but you and the world know of my pa's reputation. And I followed in his footsteps."

Brother Mack reached through the bars and touched Talt's hand. "I know you have done some awful things, but God doesn't choose. If you repent and accept my Lord, Jesus Christ as your savior, you will go to the gallows cleansed as white as snow."

"Is it enough to be sorry for what you've done?"

"That is called repentance, Talt. You must ask Jesus to enter into your heart and never intentionally sin again."

"Give me a little time, preacher."

"You have until the second day in September."

"Talt's eyes moistened, but he kept his head held high. "This is not an easy thing for a proud man to do, preacher, but I'm willing to try."

"You begin by humbling yourself before man and God," Brother Mack said. "Would you like for me to pray with you?"

"I guess I don't know how to pray," Talt said.

"You begin by asking God to help you and telling him that you are sorry for your sinful life. Tell him you want Jesus Christ as your savior. That is all. Your sins will be forgiven, and you can start anew."

Talt pushed his chair aside and fell to his knees. He clasped his hands under his chin and began reciting the Lord's prayer.

Brother Mack reached his arm through the bars and gently touched Talt's shoulder. "That was a fine prayer, brother Talt."

"Will you be with me when they hang me, preacher?"

"If I can be of comfort, I will go with you to the gallows,"

"And you, Mr. Wilkens, will you represent me again?"

"You know, Talt, there is no way I can claim your innocence."

"I'm not claiming that I'm innocent. I once did, but God knows I killed Enos Hylton just because I wanted to. He was kind of itching for a fight, but I could have walked away without shedding his blood. I'm sorry for his wife and children, but I can't bring the man back. I'll hang for it, and I can't do more."

"I'll be here too," Gabriel said. "All these years, I thought you shot my pa, but no longer. I'm glad I came with Brother Mack to see you today."

"May the words of the twenty-third Psalm be of comfort to you." Brother Mack opened the Bible, with a page marker at the words of David, which the preacher had underlined: *'Yea though I walk through the valley of the shadow of death'…"*

4
____

THE GALLOWS

As the execution day of Talt Hall approached, Wise County Sheriff Miller hunted for the Red Fox. The sheriff organized a posse of twenty-two men and spread them out through the woods from Gladeville to Pound Gap. Legally, they could go to the top of the mountain and look down the side toward Elkhorn, but they had no authority to go further. While the posse combed the hills on the Virginia side, Devil John Wright gathered information from his neighbors and lifelong friends in and around Whitesburg. Eventually, he got word that The Red Fox was staying at the home of Basil and Mildred Redding, close to the Floyd County line. John took two men with him and closed in on the Redding home.

Devil John had his friends and informants but so did Doc Taylor. When John arrived at the little cabin and raised a ruckus demanding that the doctor give himself up, no one exited the house. After a few minutes with no response from inside, John fired two shots into the air. The front door was cracked open, and someone waved a white cloth through the opening.

John called out, "Come on out Doc, we won't kill you."

Basil Redding emerged carrying a white handkerchief. "The doctor ain't here."

"Where is he?" John demanded.

"I don't know; he left here during the night, maybe heading for West Virginia, where he said the Fleming boys are."

"You better not be lying, Basil. If I find out you are, I'm coming back for you."

John and his men headed toward Pound Gap.

In the darkness of the early morning, Doc Taylor had returned to his home in Norton and hid in the attic of his son Sylvan's home. Sylvan was a respected surveyor and businessman in Norton, and no one suspected he would harbor the doctor, who was accused of horrendous murders. Earlier, he told authorities his father wanted to give himself up and face a trial to prove his innocence. Instead, he advised him to go to Florida and hide out. However, by then, authorities became suspicious that Doc Taylor may be hiding in his son's home, and they began to survey it constantly.

Not a person to be outdone, Doc Taylor devised a new plan for evading the law. He would head north while authorities thought he might be going to Florida. In the darkness of night, Sylvan hauled him to the trainyard and secreted him aboard a freight car, where he hid among the freight. The train took a full day to arrive at the station in Bluefield. A company detective, making his rounds aboard the train, discovered Doc Taylor and arrested him. He was turned over to authorities, where he was placed in custody.

John Wright was given the job of traveling to Bluefield to return the prisoner for trial.

The Red Fox was taken to the Wise County jail and placed in a cell adjacent to that of Talt Hall. At the sight of him, Doc Taylor reached through the bars to shake Talt's hand. Talt slapped it away. "Do you reckon I would shake the hand of someone who would shoot a man in the back or shoot a dead man's eyes out the way you done Ira Mullins? And I never killed women or children. I done a lot of bad, but you done worse. You better get down on your knees, prayin' to God for mercy on your bloody soul. You're goin' to burn in hell for what you done."

"May the Good Lord forgive you for damning a innocent man. I heard tell you killed a hundred men, and yet you fault me."

"No matter, I ain't never killed women and children the way you done."

"How much longer before they stretch your neck, Talt?"

"Too soon, I guess, but it won't be nothing I don't deserve."

"That's enough, boys," Jailer Renfro said. "I don't want to hear no more."

"Just one more thing, Talt. I will never go to the gallows because, unlike you, I'm a innocent man."

Talt replied, "I am man enough to admit my guilt. I've repented, and I'll be looking down from my home in Heaven when you swing from the end of that rope."

As September 2, 1892, grew closer, Talt heard the resumption of hammering down below the jail cell where he would meet his doom. He assumed that the jailer was making the final changes to the new gallows. The county of Wise had never hung a man, and Talt was destined to be the first. He had frightful thoughts about the sturdiness of the gallows being built by the jailer because Renfro stated that he had never built a gallows and apologized to Talt for his morbid task. He was unsure how to go about it and had decided on the design for his menacing device after visiting the jail in Floyd County, Kentucky, to get an idea for its construction. Talt prayed for Renfro's competence and hoped his death would be quick and painless, but it was not to be.

Talt appeared to accept the verdict of the court and his impending death with grace, but a band of outlaws from Kentucky was making plans to storm the jail and rescue him. Many people who had heard of Talt's apparent conversion doubted his sincerity and assumed it was a ploy to escape the gallows and divert attention from his potential rescuers.

To counter the threat emanating from Kentucky, the vigilantes from Big Stone Gap recruited young men, itching to be heroes, to join the Home Guard with Sheriff Miller to protect the jail and see that Talt's hanging was carried out peacefully. The volunteer force had increased to one hundred men. Josh Bullitt, head of the vigilantes, came from Big Stone Gap and drilled the men every day. Several volunteers stood guard while the others drilled and checked their weapons and ammunition.

In the city of Pound, progress was still being made to recover from the effects of the devastating floods that dislodged *Mary's Place* and *The Jerky* from their foundations. But the oldest city of Wise County still harbored scoundrels from the sister states of Kentucky and Virginia, and those from other states who were passing through Pound Gap for adventure or to escape capture for crimes in other states. Despite efforts by upright citizens such as Gabriel Wilkens, new flop houses and places of ill repute had sprung up, providing haven to the unwanted and unwashed. Amongst these men were outlaws who had grown up with Talt or served with him during the war or as deputies when he was a U.S. Marshal. The certainty of his guilt did not matter to them. A dozen or more of these reprobates pledged their support to renegades in Kentucky who were planning to rescue Talt on the day of reckoning.

News of the impending hanging had spread for six months to the far reaches of Kentucky and Virginia. As the day drew near, potential spectators from the counties of Scott, Lee, Dickenson, and Buchanan in Virginia and Floyd, Pike, Harlan, and Knott counties, in addition to Letcher County in Kentucky, set out for the site of the hanging in Gladeville. There had never been a state-sanctioned hanging in Virginia, and the citizens of the sister states were eager to witness it. Not only would they experience a memorable event, but they would see their homes made safer after the noose was placed around Talt's neck and the trap door opened. The horror of seeing a man hanging by his neck never occurred to them. They were prepared only for entertainment or satisfaction, giving no thought that, before their eyes, life would be ebbing from the man dangling from the end of a rope. It was not an appropriate sight for children. But much like the first Civil War Battle of Bull Run, where the crowd gathered, ready to celebrate a victory, families, the old, the young, the in-between, came to be part of history. They gathered in nervous or gleeful anticipation outside the courthouse where the hanging would take place.

The crowd was continuing to grow, newcomers joining

hundreds who had waited for hours. Finally, the sheriff appeared at an open window on the second story. Alongside him was attorney Gabriel Wilkens. The two men were talking, but their words could not be heard by the crowd below. The crowd fell quiet, hoping to catch a word or two of their conversation,

Faces of the young men of the Home Guard and gun muzzles were visible at the portholes and windows of the courthouse. The guardsmen outside stiffened their lines, bracing for a possible hostile surge from the thickening crowd.

"What time is it?" a strong voice called from the onlookers.

Another man responded, "Eleven forty-five. Almost time for a hangin'."

Chatter from the crowd subsided, preceding a low rumble of murmurs as a tall, dark man appeared in the window, standing next to the sheriff and Gabriel Wilkens.

"It's him," someone shouted, "It's Bad Talt Hall."

"He don't look so bad now," someone else said.

"He's goin' to confess," the same man said. "I heard that his lawyer wants him to confess for all of us to hear." He pointed to Brother Mack Cantrell, who had been singing hymns with Talt. "That preacher right up there told him he ought to confess, and I hear tell that Talt Hall wants to confess."

The only possible source of such rumors must have come from the jailer Charles Renfro, who overheard Talt's earlier testaments to Brother Mack and Gabriel. Renfro was a simple man who meant no one harm but sometimes spoke with innocent indiscretion.

How much more Talt might reveal, only Talt knew. His

friends credited him with more than nineteen killings, while those who wanted to see him hang put the number at not less than thirty. There to witness his end, looking at him were three widows of innocent men he had murdered and children he had orphaned. Another spectator was a little woman in black, the widow of Enos Hylton, whom Talt had shot dead a year earlier.

Talt moved closer to the window. His lips moved.

"Shh," moved across the crowd. "Listen."

He said nothing but grasped the sides of the window frame for support. The sheriff brought him a chair, and he sat. His lips moved again, but no sound was emitted.

An utter silence fell over the crowd as they watched the man sitting before the upstairs window. He said something to the sheriff. Someone standing near the courthouse said he had asked if he might give his sister a message. Talt's words were repeated again and again from the front of the gathering to the back.

The Judge, who had presided over the trial was present as a member of the Home Guard. He denied Talt's plea to deliver a message to his sister. Tears welled in the judge's eyes when Talt requested that a handkerchief be tied around his throat to hide the red marks the rope would make. He took a white handkerchief from his pocket and pressed it into Gabriel's hand. Gabriel tied it about Talt's neck. The many eyes of the crowd were on the window where the big man sat looking beyond them, perhaps skyward. The spectators wondered if he was praying or forming his thoughts, ready to confess to killing his uncle, Henry Maggard, his brothers-in-law, Henry Monk, and Mack Hall. He had been cunning enough to escape punishment until now. Perhaps today, as he was about to face his maker, he would confess to these crimes and more. He could clear up many unsolved cases if he would. He did not admit to any crimes but got up from the chair. He stood straight and tall, and with a firm step, headed toward the stairway that would lead him to the grounds below and waiting gallows.

Talt ascended the steps to the gallows platform and stood next to Sheriff Miller and jailer Charles Renfro. A third man tied Talt's hands behind his back and placed the noose over his head, carefully locating the hangman's knot at its lethal spot. Next, he slipped a black hood over Talt's head. The two beams holding the trapdoor were knocked loose. The trapdoor sank with a jolt and then settled an inch lower. The crowd gasped, but Talt stood stiff as an oak as the trapdoor settled on the short rope, which had to be cut to spring the trapdoor and send the prisoner crashing through the opening. The suspense was palpable as the sheriff raised the hatchet above his head and cried in a loud voice, "May God have mercy on this poor man's soul!" He struck the rope with a hatchet, and the black-capped body shot down with a sudden jolt. A loud grunt shot from under the black hood. The sheriff ran down the gallows steps and disappeared into the courthouse, tears streaming from his eyes. The hooded body jerked and twitched like a dying chicken before settling in silence.

After five minutes, a doctor approached the victim and checked his wrist for a pulse. A medical attendant came close, and the doctor whispered to him. "Still has a pulse." Five minutes again elapsed before the doctor determined Talt was still alive but growing weaker. Eight minutes later, he ordered that the rope be cut, and the body was allowed to fall onto the ground. The doctor placed a stethoscope on Talt's chest and then lifted the black hood from his face. He was heard to whisper to the attendant, "He choked to death. His neck isn't broken."

The doctor stood and announced, "This man is dead."

Talt's sister came forward to claim the body. We're taking him back to Letcher County for burial."

"Where?" a curious onlooker asked.

"In John Wright's family cemetery." She stated. "That's what my brother requested."

"Why there?" He asked.

"Because they were once friends," she said.

The county of Wise let out a deep sigh of relief after Talt Hall's body was taken away on a wagon, heading for Letcher County, Kentucky, for preparation and burial. There would be mourners at the deceased man's graveside, but none from Norton or Gladeville. With Talt gone from their midst and The Red Fox behind bars, they could breathe easier. Two days later, Talt Hall was laid to rest in the John Wright family cemetery despite criticism from some of John's friends and family. "A man must keep his word," John said. "The man is gone, and whatever he was —good and bad —is gone with him. He can never harm anyone again. So, let the man rest in peace."

5
____

A DOUBTFUL OUTCOME

Gabriel's law practice was thriving. His excellent penmanship enabled him to prepare outstanding documents; however, due to an increasing workload, he required a clerk to assist with case research and general office duties. After interviewing several young men who were only marginally qualified, without finding anyone with the potential for a future in law practice, he advertised in the *Coalfield Progress*, a local weekly newspaper published in Norton. After the second week, a young woman named Cindy Sturgill applied. She had attended school for ten years and would have pursued further education, but formal grade levels were not established at that time. Her experience included two years of clerical work for her uncle, H.A.W. Skeen, the judge who had sentenced Talt Hall to death. Gabriel hired her in October, and she moved to live with her aunt in Pound. By Christmas, they had fallen in love.

Cindy was an avid reader of *Harper's Weekly*. A company by the name of *Wykoff, Seamans, and Benedict* advertised a

Remington typewriter for $15 plus shipping. Neither Gabriel nor Cindy knew how it worked, but both realized the advantages they would have if Gabriel bought one. The strange-looking contraption arrived before Christmas, and she typed the first official letter on it two weeks later.

Rail passenger service began between Norton and Coburn, opening the far western county of Wise to the more developed northern and eastern counties. Creed came home for two weeks and returned at the end of January 1893 to complete another year of apprenticeship under the doctors in Bristol. Letters of introduction and recommendation from the doctors there would be necessary as part of an application to The College of William and Mary for medical study.

When Gabriel told Creed goodbye at the passenger platform in Norton, He and his younger brother embraced and shook hands. "I'll come to Bristol soon to meet with Doctors Wallace and Fillmore before we apply to William and Mary. Get me an appointment with them if you can."

"I've already spoken with Dr. Wallace about attending William and Mary. He thinks I won't have a problem being accepted if we have funds for tuition available."

"I'll take care of that," Gabriel said. "Stick by the doctors and learn everything you can."

"I will, brother."

"Write often," Gabriel said, "and send me a telegram if you need anything."

Gabriel returned to his office, thinking about Shakespeare's words: parting is such sweet sorrow. He missed his little brother, who was growing into a man in his absence. He was happy to see Cindy, busy at her typewriter, and he thought about how fortunate he was, unlike many acquaintances, to have such wonderful people in his life. His thoughts then wandered to the tragedy that occurred the previous May at Pound Gap, taking the life of his Uncle Ira and so many others.

As if she could read Gabriel's mind, Cindy handed him a copy of *The Roanoke Times*, opened to the second page where an article concerning the Pound Gap massacre appeared. The article stated that Doc Taylor, the Fleming Brothers, and Henry Adams, a resident of Elkhorn, Kentucky, would be the subject of a grand jury investigation. Henry Adams allegedly owned one of the guns used in the Pound Gap massacre, but there was no evidence that he was present during the killing. An indictment was issued for the four men in June, and Circuit Judge Colt Williams was assigned to preside over the case.

County Prosecutor Robert Bruce determined that there was insufficient evidence to try Henry Adams, and the charges against him were dropped. Cal and Henan Fleming were still on the run while Dr. Marshall Benton Taylor was confined to the Wise County jail to await his trial, which was scheduled to commence September 5th, just over a year since the hanging of Talt Hall.

A reward of $700 was offered for the capture of the Flemings, and several bounty hunters set out for Bluefield, West Virginia, to capture the fugitives. They returned to Gladeville empty-handed after learning that the Flemings were no longer in Bluefield.

Complicating the Commonwealth's charges against Doc

Taylor was the uncertainty of the testimony of Jane Mullins, the only eyewitness. Her story had changed since the massacre. However, John Harrison, Ira's son and Jane's brother, had been questioned several times, but his version of events remained unchanged. He ran for his life and never looked back. From the start, he stated that he never heard any of the killers speak and never saw them. His only damning testimony would confirm Jane's account that the victims were given no warning before the shooting started.

The trial commenced on September 5th as scheduled by the appeals court. There were twenty-three witnesses for the prosecution, with the most important one expected to be Jane Mullins. She was the only survivor who saw the killers and heard them speak. The court still held her in protective custody, fearing for her life. The defense called fifteen witnesses, of which only two were cross-examined. Gabriel attended the trial every day to gain experience by observing the proceedings.

The first witness to take the stand for the Commonwealth of Virginia was John Harrison Mullins, now fifteen. His testimony was that the shooting began suddenly before he or anyone else realized what was happening. When he saw his best friend, Greenberry Harris, fall, he ran for his life, not having any idea who was doing the shooting. His testimony was not challenged by the defense.

Next was the direct testimony of Jane Mullins, whose version of the massacre had evolved since her original statements. She was no longer doubtful of the killers' identities, stating that she recognized the voices of the three shooters and was familiar with the physical appearance of Dr. Taylor.

On cross-examination, the principal defense attorney

hammered Jane about the four-hour period following the murders.

"Missus Mullins, may I call you Jane?"

"Everyone does," she said.

"Well, Jane, tell us again what happened right after the shooting. I mean, you were gone for more than four hours before anyone saw you. Where were you all that time?"

"I'm not sure," she said, "I was confused and afraid. I think I hid for a while."

"Knowing your brother may be dying, you hid?"

"Maybe. I knew there was nothin' I could do to help him. They was all dead, before I rode off."

"How did you know they were dead?"

"They was all bleedin', and I knowed Wilson and Louranza and all of them was dead."

"Why didn't you go for help right away?"

"I don't know," she said. "I was confused and scared and not thinkin' right."

"Alright," the attorney said, "Let's turn to something else that is puzzling to me."

Jane sat quiet, waiting for the next question.

"If you were confused and scared, how sure are you that Dr. Taylor was one of the shooters?"

"I'm positive," she responded.

"How could you identify him if the killers were wearing covers over their faces?"

"I recognized the way he dressed, and I saw his beard."

"Jane, I have a record of your original statement to Sheriff Miller. You said you didn't know who the shooters were, didn't you?"

"Yes," she said.

"Why did you say that, and why have you changed your story?"

She didn't answer right away but paused for a moment to reflect on what she had told officials, her family, and acquaintances after recovering from the horror of that day. She always intended to tell the truth, but memories of the massacre were often too horrific to contemplate. Immediately after the killings, she had been too shocked to think clearly, and in the days ahead, she added details that she recalled.

"We're waiting for an answer," the attorney said. "Why has your story changed?"

"Because I was scared," she said. "I was afraid Dr. Taylor and Cal and Henan would come after me."

"Are you scared now?"

Jane thought for a minute and looked at the prosecutor, who nodded for her to answer. "Yes, I'm scared, but the judge is protectin' me. I'm tellin' you what I saw and heard that day. It was Cal and Henan and Dr. Taylor behind the rocks."

"How did you recognize Cal and Henan Fleming?"

"Their voices, I know their voices," she testified.

The defense attorney conferred with an associate, then turned back to Jane. "Missus Mullins, I know all this has been traumatic for you, but you have to admit that your testimony now is not the same as your earlier statements, don't you?"

"Maybe," she said. "But I know who killed Ira, and I told the truth about that."

"I don't think you have, and if that is indeed the case...," The lawyer paused. "If that is a fact, Jane, then you have given false testimony in this case, haven't you?"

"No,' she said, her voice quivering.

"Both statements cannot be true, can they, Jane?"

"I guess not," she said, "but there's a reason."

"Then that makes you a liar, doesn't it?"

"I didn't lie."

"Yes, you did, and that makes you a liar whose testimony cannot be believed by this jury. Do you know what perjury is?"

"No," she answered.

"This witness has committed perjury." The attorney waved his arm in the direction of the twelve men sitting in judgment.

"I object," the prosecutor interjected.

"Overruled," Judge Williams ordered.

"I'm through with this witness, your honor," the attorney said to Judge Williams.

The judge said to Jane, "You may step down, Mrs. Mullins."

Nineteen additional witnesses for the Commonwealth of Virginia were called to the stand over the course of three days. Most of the testimony repeated the events of May 14, 1892, and consisted largely of monotonous hearsay. Even so, it captured the attention of news reporters from far and wide. Just when a conviction of Dr. Taylor appeared doubtful, Robert Mullins, one of the first to arrive at the site at Pound Gap, took the stand.

The routine questions regarding name, domicile, occupation, and so on were asked of the witness, as well as how he had come upon the scene of the massacre. Robert Mullins testified that he lived in Kentucky, a few miles from the murder scene, and that it was by coincidence that he arrived shortly after the killings occurred. He recounted that he was on his way to The Pound on business when he and Magistrate Bentley, coming from the Virginia side of the mountain, happened upon the site of the murders.

The prosecutor asked, "How long after the killings did you arrive?"

"Maybe a half hour or thereabouts," he answered.

"Will you describe what you saw when you first arrived?"

Robert Mullins testified, "It was a terrible sight. Five people were dead, and blood was all around the bodies."

The prosecutor then asked the witness, "Did you recognize the dead?"

"Yes," he said. "I knew Ira Mullins and his wife, Louranza, and Wilson Mullins. I found out later that the dead driver was John Chappell, a darkie, and the fifth was Greenberry Haris, whose mother lives in Pound."

"Tell us what you did next, Mr. Mullins."

"Me and Magistrate Bentley examined the wounds that we could see."

"And would you describe those wounds?"

"Yes, Sir," he testified. "Of course, we didn't want to violate Mrs. Mullins, but we checked the wounds of her husband and the others. Most of them appeared as rifle shots because they made large holes in the dead. We saw some wounds that appeared to come from revolvers, too, but you know we couldn't be sure."

The prosecutor spent the next hour taking Robert Mullins through the account of his arrival at the scene until he and Mr. Bentley finished their examination. The witness described where, on each body, the wounds were located and where the bodies were found relative to the wagon and the rocks where the killers had lain in wait.

To emphasize the cruelty performed by the killers, the

prosecutor asked the witness to describe the condition of the horses.

"They was still hitched to the wagon, layin' dead, shot fifty times, I would guess."

"Now, Mr. Mullins, did you and Magistrate Bentley determine where the shots came from?"

"Yes, Sir," he responded." There wasn't any doubt. If you've been through Pound Gap, you must've seen that stack of big rocks beside the trail. They was moved there to clear it for wagons. That's where the shots come from, no doubt about it."

The prosecutor followed that question with another. "About how far from these rocks were the wagon and bodies of the dead?"

"I would say twenty feet or so. There was a little path between the road and the big rocks, but we didn't see no tracks."

"Is there anything else you can tell us about the rocks?"

"Yes, Sir. Some tree branches had been cut and placed across the openings between the rocks to hide the killers."

"And did you examine the area behind the rocks?"

"Yes, sir, we did."

"Tell us what you found."

The witness testified, "Well, sir, there was some brush and pine knots heaped up behind the rocks, which was curious to us. We raked away the pine knots and found some spent shells; looked like they were rifle shells."

"And did you later determine what kind of shells they were?"

"Yes, Sir, we did. They turned out to be 44-75 caliber Winchester rifle shells."

And the prosecutor quickly followed up the answer from Robert Mullins.

Was there anything peculiar about the shells?"

"I wouldn't say peculiar, except that they was rim fired."

"And for the members of the jury who might not know, will you explain it for us?"

Robert Mullins began his testimony, which had obviously been rehearsed with the prosecution's assistance many times. "Well, sir, not that I'm any expert, but I know that the Remington rifle has a plunger that hits the rim of the shell casing when the gun fires. Some guns have firing pins that hit the center of the shell, but not the gun used to kill Ira Mullins."

"Do you know anyone who owns a rifle like that?"

"Yes, sir, I do, Henry Adams and Doctor Marshall Benton Taylor."

"Are you certain about that, Mr. Mullins?"

"Yes, I am. Dead certain."

"How do you know that kind of gun was owned by Doctor Taylor?"

"Cause he always carried it with him, 'specially since Ira Mullins was killed. He carried two pearl-handled Colt 45 pistols, too. I think most everybody knew that."

The prosecutor turned to the jury and then back to his witness. "Tell us, Mr. Mullins, was the rifle carried by Marshall Benton Taylor rim-fired or center-fired?"

The air left the room in silence for several seconds after Robert Mullins' response. "I couldn't rightly say; I just know that the shells we found at the murder scene was rim-fired."

Magistrate Arnold Bentley was called as the Commonwealth's next witness. He confirmed the testimony of Robert Mullins and added details about the condition of the victims. He testified that many of their wounds appeared to come from a rifle.

Next, the prosecution called Vince Gardner, a gunsmith and weapons expert, to the stand. After having him sworn in, Prosecutor Bruce held up a Winchester rifle for the judge's inspection and requested that it be designated as Exhibit 32 for the prosecution. Next, he entered two Colt 45 pistols into evidence. He began by asking questions that validated Mr. Gardner's education and experience, providing evidence of his qualifications as a small arms expert. He then proceeded to ask specific questions related to the guns that had just been entered as evidence.

"Mr. Gardner, I am handing you this Winchester rifle, Exhibit 32."

Mr. Gardner accepted it, put an empty cartridge into the chamber and pulled the trigger. He then ejected the shell, picked it up, and held it out for the prosecuting attorney to see.

"Mr. Gardner, are you currently in business as a gunsmith?"

"Yes,"

"Where is your business located?"

"In Kingsport, Tennessee, for the past twenty-two years."

The prosecutor stepped aside to allow the jury members to see what would happen next. "Mr. Gardner, that gun you are holding, can you describe it for us?"

"Yes, indeed. It is a Winchester 44-75 repeating rifle manufactured in 1873."

"Is the year of manufacture important in this case?"

"I would say so," replied Vince Gardner. It is important because the rifles, like this one, that were manufactured from 1873 to 1877, were all rim-firing guns. The first center-fired Winchester rifle of this model was made in 1878."

"Now, Mr. Gardner, you just demonstrated the firing of the Winchester Rifle, identified as that of the defendant, didn't you?"

"Yes, Sir," the witness responded.

"And for what purpose did you activate the firing mechanism of that gun?"

"If you will look at the empty shell I just gave you, you will see the plunger struck the shell casing near the center."

"But, Mr. Gardner, how is that possible if the 1873 Winchester rifle you have in your hands is a rim-firing gun?"

"There is only one answer," the witness said. "The gun has been modified to strike in the center of the shell."

A rumble came over the courtroom, and the judge brought the court back to order.

The defense attorney asked for a recess.

"Without objection," the judge said, "we will recess for thirty minutes."

After the recess, the prosecutor informed the judge that his evidence was concluded. The defense presented its witnesses, most of whom testified as to the fine character of Dr. Marshall Benton Taylor. One after the other, they recounted his good deeds, how he had cured their illnesses, befriended them, and saved their souls. They testified that the man they knew as Doc could never commit such a heinous crime. After a day and a half of such testimony, the defense attorney informed Judge Williams that he had no more evidence to present. After the summations and final arguments, the case went to the twelve-member jury the next day.

After four hours of deliberation, the jury requested a summary of the testimony from the gunsmith, Vince Gardner.

Outside the courthouse, a crowd gathered, waiting for the jury verdict, but it did not come right away. Instead, three members of the jury requested that they be allowed to inspect Dr. Taylor's rifle. The judge ordered that this request be granted.

All three jurors were experienced in handling, cleaning, and firing guns and were familiar with the Winchester rifle. They dismantled it, piece by piece, and inspected the parts. While it was disassembled, the other nine members were asked to examine each part.   When the jurors attempted to assemble the rifle, some parts did not readily fit. The jury concluded that the gun had been tampered with and reported this fact to the prosecuting attorney. By order of the court, the men signed an affidavit swearing that, while in the custody of Doc Taylor, the gun's firing mechanism had been altered to strike the center instead of the rim. Because the shells found at the death scene were rim-fired, the modifications to the rifle had to occur after the massacre.

The next day, Doctor Taylor was found guilty by the jury, and a sentence was passed.

"I sentence you to be hanged by the neck until dead," Judge Williams ordered. "May God have mercy on your soul."

A date of October 27, 1893, was set for his execution.

During the next forty-five days, leading to the execution date, the doctor's wife, Nancy, visited him every day. For most of their marriage, he had treated her with indifference and, on many occasions, cruelly. But, facing imminent death, Dr. Taylor expressed his love for her and elicited her promise to carry out his wishes after death.

"I will rise up again on the third date. Keep watch over my body at home to see that it is not desecrated. Find comfort in knowing that, like my brother, Jesus Christ, I will be with you after I sleep for a short time. "

The doctor requested that Nancy make him a white linen suit to be worn at the execution. "And make me a white hood so that black will not touch my countenance during my unjust hanging. Strew white handkerchiefs in my pathway so that my feet do not touch the earth on my way to the gallows."

Faithful as always, Nancy promised to carry out his wishes.

On October 27, 1893, the Red Fox appeared before the same upstairs window where, just one year earlier, his nemesis and one-time cohort, Talt Hall, had stood. The time was 10:00 a.m., two hours before his appointment with the gallows. He was dressed from head to toe in white linen, a suit his wife made. In his hands, he clutched a large, leather-bound Bible, the one he had carried in his saddlebag wherever he traveled. He was dressed in a white suit for preaching his own funeral, and as he announced, the sermon would be taken from the book of Revelations.

Outside, the mid-morning temperature had not reached sixty degrees, harboring a chill in the air for the spectators, many of whom were ill-prepared for the cool of the morning. Before the window, the jailer had placed a small table for the doctor's use in celebrating his final sacrament. Next to the table, Nancy Taylor stood, dressed in mourning black with a sunbonnet drawn close to her face. The Bible had been placed on the table along with a few pieces of bread. Doc Taylor called down to the crowd, "Will any of you break bread with me?"

It is probable that the people in the crowd did not comprehend what was taking place as the pathetic condemned man lifted the bread and asked the crowd to come forward to share in his final sacrament. They held fast, staring up at the window. His wife, who had been ill-treated and deserted by him for many years, timidly turned her face, filled with love and pity, toward him for a moment. Then, with childlike hesitancy, her hands trembling, she reached for the bread. The act of communion completed, she left his side, descended the stairs, and mixed into the crowd outside the window.

The sermon that followed drew on the words attributed to Jesus from the Book of Revelations. He denounced his "persecutors" and swore his innocence before God Almighty. Like Jesus, he was betrayed by those he trusted and sentenced to death as a scapegoat. And like Jesus, he would suffer the hanging even though he could call upon his Father in Heaven to pluck him from the midst of his enemies. His few sins were forgiven, and he was prepared, in all manner, to face a temporary death. Like his brother, Jesus, he would rise on the third day to walk among his flock before being lifted into Heaven to dwell at the right hand of God. "For me," he said, "death has no sting. I go to the gallows knowing I am purified and sanctified."

He turned his back to the window and disappeared into the interior of the courthouse.

Moments later, he reappeared at the foot of the scaffold steps. He stood blinking, attempting to adjust to the bright sunlight. He looked up at the gallows, as if inspecting it for its sturdiness, and apparently concluded that it would do the job for which it was constructed. The little woman in black had placed a white handkerchief on each step, leading to the scaffold platform. She had made a white hood, which she handed to the jailer. It was to be drawn over his face at the last moment before placing the noose around his neck.

He climbed the steps briskly, turned his back to the sheriff, and allowed his hands to be tied behind him with a white handkerchief. He then requested the privilege of reading a passage of scripture and offering a prayer. He dropped to his knees and prayed in a subdued voice that only those standing over him could hear.

Sheriff Miller slipped the white hood over the doctor's head and placed the noose about his neck. The sheriff, a religious man, whispered something to the condemned man and then backed away, holding an axe in his hand. He ordered the timber supporting the platform from underneath be knocked away. The trapdoor on which Doc Taylor stood sank an inch or more, giving the impression that the moment of execution had occurred. The doctor, thinking his end had come, sank to the floor. The sheriff waited until the doomed man could straighten up. Once the doctor stood erect, the sheriff struck a resounding blow with the axe, severing the rope that held the trapdoor. The doctor plunged through the opening in a mass of white. whirling around and around

"May God have mercy on your poor soul," The sheriff hurried down the gallows steps, ran to the corner of the courthouse, and vomited.

The rope, holding the victim by his neck, twisted tight

and then unwound over and over, which kept the struggling man whirling. After the body came to a stop, it was left to hang for 19 minutes before being lowered to the ground in a heap of white.

Dr. H.M. Miles and a medical assistant examined the body. "This man is dead," he pronounced. "Who will claim the body?"

A sad little lady in black stepped forward. "He is my husband. I am taking him home."

6

———

PENANCE

Faithful to the end, Nancy Booth Taylor watched over the body of her dead husband for three days as he had requested. She, along with many other mourners, believed that the doctor would rise again, and they prayed in unison for his resurrection. On the third day, the stone that weighed heavily on their hearts was rolled away, and all hopes vanished. He did not rise. The wood casket holding his body was carried up a hill above the courthouse and buried there in an unmarked grave without ceremony. Only a few mourners offered prayers over the grave, among them was a small pale lady dressed in black who remained steadfast in support of her husband long after dirt was shoveled over him.

The day following the hanging, Jane Mullins was released from protective custody because the sheriff believed that the Flemings would not voluntarily return to the Pine Mountain communities since they were still wanted men. A reward of $700 remained in effect for the return of one or both of the brothers to Wise County for trial. A week later, Jane married Isaac Belcher of Camden, near Elkhorn. The hasty marriage took her remaining family, as well as her friends, by surprise. Some people suspected that their romance may have preceded the death of her husband, Wilson Mullins.

Her reason for marrying Isaac was simply stated. "He will keep Cal and Henan from killing me."

After the hanging of Doc Taylor, word was received by Wise County authorities that the fugitive brothers were working at a logging job at Boggs in Webster County, West Virginia. There was no shortage of men in need of money who sought to pursue the brothers. "Big" Ed Hall, "Gooseneck" John Branham, and A. J. "Doc" Swindall, who had previously gone to Bluefield with a 22-man posse, had not given up the hunt. In January 1894, Big Ed gathered a new posse and boarded a train in Norton, bound for Bluefield. From Bluefield, they would go on foot to the little town of Boggs, where they expected to find the unsuspecting Fleming brothers. When they arrived in Bluefield, Devil John Wright was waiting. He knew where to find Cal and Henan, and he planned to arrest them, with or without the help of Big Ed's posse.

A cold wind was blowing, and the threat of snow hung in the air when John Wright and the posse from Wise County set out for the little town of Boggs. No one in the posse anticipated that Saturday, January 24, 1894, would be the last day on earth for the fearless bounty hunters, Big Ed Hall and Gooseneck Branham.

The previous evening, Devil John sent a man ahead to confirm that the brothers were still at the logging camp. The man returned around midnight and verified that Cal and

Henan were there; they always went to the Boggs post office on Saturdays to collect their mail. The post office was in a small general store, one of about half a dozen buildings on the main street of Boggs. The posse arrived in the town, twenty miles away, just before dawn. The members of the posse huddled together at the edge of the woods, trying to stay warm in the cold. They had a view of the general store, and when it opened for business, John, Big Ed, and Gooseneck surveyed the inside of the store, purchased some soda crackers, and returned to wait with the posse until Cal and Henan arrived.

From their vantage, the posse watched as the fugitives rode into town. It was nearing 10 a.m. when the brothers approached the post office and dismounted. They appeared to have trouble hitching their horses, making a terrible commotion, cursing their steeds as they secured their reins. John, Big Ed, and Gooseneck conferred for a moment, agreeing that the two men were, indeed, the desperadoes they had come to arrest. With their guns at the ready, they watched, poised to descend on the small building, which was now teeming with customers. After the brothers entered and the door closed behind them, the posse rushed across the street and into the small store, which was filled with loggers and townspeople. John and Big Ed were the first to enter the store; they ordered the outlaws to drop their guns and surrender. The spectators, too astonished at first to move, sensed the danger and ran for the door. By then, five more members of the posse had entered the store.

Cal Fleming was standing at the post office window, opening a letter with Henan standing near him. Cal clutched the letter in one hand and drew his gun with the other. He and Henan ran to the back of the store and began firing their weapons. The posse opened fire. Black smoke filled the air, making it difficult for either party to see their targets.

Big Ed Hall was the first member of the posse to fall, hit in the head by a bullet from the gun of Cal Fleming. John Wright dropped to his knees; he aimed his gun directly at Cal and fired. Cal sank to the floor, dead. Henan fired wildly, fatally wounding two more members of the posse. When the firing stopped, Cal Fleming lay dead on the floor a few feet from the body of Big Ed Hall. Henan Fleming sat in a heap, bleeding severely from multiple wounds, his gun still pointed in the direction of the posse.

John Wright moved closer to Henan, his gun leveled squarely at the injured man's face. "Damn you, Henan; you have killed three good men. Give up now, or you will join your brother in hell."

Henan let his gun fall from his hand onto his lap and then slide onto the floor.

The letter that Cal was reading lay next to his body. John picked the bloody letter up, unfolded it, and read:

> *Brothers. I am fine. I hope you are fine too. Got your letter, and I will take care of the business here. I will let you know when she is gone so you both can come home soon. Ma is fine too and misses you.*
>
> *Love,*
>
> *Orb*

'Orb' was the nickname of Arbin, the youngest boy of the Fleming clan. Like his brothers, he had proven to be a renegade, skirting the law for crimes he was accused of committing, including murder and robbery. While Henan recuperated from his wounds and awaited trial for the Pound Gap Massacre, Orb schemed to save his brother from the gallows.

Jane Mullins and her new husband, Isaac Belcher, lived in a small cabin in Camden, Kentucky, near Little Elkhorn Creek. Not far away, up a steep hill, was the Potter Family Graveyard, recently renamed Murdered Man's Cemetery because the overwhelming number of grave markers commemorated the death of men who were murdered in or near Letcher County. Among those interred there now, brought low by killers, included a woman, Louranza Mullins, and a fifteen-year-old boy, Greenberry Harris. Jane visited the grave of her brother often and prayed for his soul.

She wrapped herself in a heavy Mackinaw coat that her husband wore when he hunted for deer. She pulled her bonnet close to her face and tightened the strap against her chin. For a few moments after stepping outside into the cold, she considered turning back and foregoing the trip up the hill until the weather eased. Since she had not visited Ira's grave in almost a week, she trekked up the hill anyway, leaving footprints in the three-inch snow. At the top, she found Ira's crude grave marker, wiped it clean of snow, and bent to say a prayer for her brother. From the nearby brush, the eyes of a killer watched her every move. She shivered in the cold as she turned to walk down the hill. A shot rang out, striking her in the back of her head. She fell beside her brother's grave.

A story in the *Roanoke Times* the next day told of another tragic murder in lawless Letcher County, Kentucky. A survivor of the Killing Rock Massacre had been assassinated only two hundred yards from her home. The article stated that authorities were seeking their prime suspect, Arbin "Orb" Fleming, younger brother of the notorious Cal and Henan Fleming, suspects in the murder of Ira Mullins and his family. Authorities believed Arbin had fled Kentucky and was probably hiding in West Virginia.

A few days earlier, the same newspaper had recounted the horror that occurred nine months earlier at Pound Gap. It reported that Henan Fleming was making a rapid recovery and would soon stand trial for the massacre. Henan had confessed to his part in the crime, and the commonwealth attorney anticipated that a conviction was certain.

However, the death of Jane Mullins raised new doubts about the prospect of convicting Henan Fleming. To the surprise of everyone, Arbin Fleming boldly rode into Gladeville one Monday morning and met with Henan's attorney. He persuaded the attorney to seek to have his brother's confession thrown out. Henan then rescinded his admission of guilt, claiming that posse members forced him to confess and that neither he nor Cal had any part in the massacre.

In a trial that lasted six days, the Commonwealth's attorney, confident in Henan's guilt, made a dedicated effort to prove it. However, without Mrs. Jane Mullins' positive identification, the court turned to evidence from the trial of Doc Taylor. Records of Jane Mullins' testimony were submitted in the new trial, but since she had admitted to perjury in that trial, her testimony in Henan's trial was deemed ineffective. The court found him "not guilty" and dismissed all charges.

After being set free, Henan returned to West Virginia, where he became a law officer and lived the life of a model citizen thereafter. Arbin continued his murderous ways and eventually was killed by a sheriff in Floyd County, Kentucky. In celebration, The *Roanoke Times* carried the headline: *The End of a Murderous Era.*

But the people of the mountains had reason to doubt this proclamation.

7

PEACE O'ER THESE MOUNTAINS

An uneasy peace settled over the hills and valleys of that remote part of the Appalachians. The worst of the Kentucky killers were either dead or on the run from authorities. Illicit bootlegging through Pine Gap had dwindled to a trickle, and the people on both sides of the mountain breathed more easily. All liquor, including stamped whiskey, was illegal in Letcher County, and the county was kept "dry" by the votes of Baptists and moonshiners. Men who toiled all week long and needed Saturday night respites could still find legal whiskey and more at *The Jerky* or *Ruby's Rest Awhile* in Pound. The towns of Gladeville, Norton, and Pound continued to grow, while those on the Kentucky side of the mountain appeared doomed to atrophy. But that was about to change.

Engineers, geologists, and speculators who had previously descended on Big Stone Gap and Wise County, Virginia, shifted their attention to Letcher County, Kentucky. The discovery of massive reservoirs of coal beneath Pine Mountain and the surrounding hills of that county drew them there. Powerful financial magnates from the coal and steel industries in Pennsylvania and Ohio arrived in the area, eager to stake claims on the eight-foot-high veins of black gold, theirs for the taking. They mapped out their plans for a city and mighty industry that would become a reality in the early part of the twentieth century.

Accommodations for the invaders were scarce on the Kentucky side of the mountain; thus, most newcomers found rooms for rent in Gladeville and Norton. Before long, a Pound entrepreneur built a four-room hotel, and Jenny Maggard, who owned the old Jerky, rebuilt it at its previous location on Pound River. The little town of Pound was preparing for the boom, which was predicted for the area. Gabriel Wilkens, now the most respected young lawyer in Wise County, quickly acquired the accounts of entrepreneurs and investors seeking to obtain land rights on both sides of the mountain. John Wright introduced Gabriel to an equally ambitious and capable young lawyer, Julius Webb, in Whitesburg, which enabled them to provide legal services in both Virginia and Kentucky.

In May 1894, a letter arrived at the Pound Post Office, addressed to Master Creed Wilkens, General Delivery, Pound, Virginia. The letter came from Lyon Gardner Tyler, President of the College of William and Mary in Williamsburg, Virginia. Gabriel accepted the letter from the postmaster and contemplated its contents for the next two hours before succumbing to his curiosity. His hands trembled as he opened his brother's mail, unfolded the letter, and read the words: It gives me immense pleasure to inform you that you have been accepted by the faculty of the College of William and Mary to further your education in the field of medicine.

The next morning, Gabriel rode to Norton and fashioned a

message to send by telegraph to Creed in Bristol. It read: Hurrah, Brother! Great news. You have been accepted at William and Mary. Hurry home. We will need to visit there next month. Gabe.

The cost of attending William and Mary was beyond the reach of most families. Gabriel had saved for three years and accumulated over $20,000, which would cover one semester at a cost of $18,000. He hoped to find a job for Creed, assisting a doctor in Williamsburg, a distant relative of D.B. Hollyfield. He had corresponded with the doctor, who agreed to meet with him and Creed that summer. With Creed working part-time and Gabriel's practice expanding, they would be able to afford four semesters of study, the duration needed to be certified as a physician.

Creed returned home at the end of June, and he and Gabriel took a train to Williamsburg. While there, they visited the William and Mary campus, met with the head of the medical department, and registered Creed for the semester of study starting in September of that year. At eighteen, Creed would be one of the youngest students matriculating at the college at that time, and no other student as young as he had completed the curriculum for the study of medicine. They met with Doctor Charles Morgan, an established physician in Williamsburg, and he accepted Creed as a part-time assistant for the coming school semester.

During their return train trip, they discussed the opportunities each had for the future and how much they owed to their father and Oma. Caleb had not been an educated man, but he understood the value of a good education. His goal of ensuring that his sons' lives were easier than his own had inspired both Gabriel and Creed to succeed. They also owed much to Oma for her curious mind and desire for knowledge. Gabriel often thought of his parents and regretted never learning who was responsible for their deaths. The greatest regret of his young mind was that he had failed to solve that mystery. However, he never gave up hope of discovering the truth.

As the train lurched along the valley of the Shenandoah Mountains, Gabriel and Creed reminisced about their times as a family, living in the cabin in Bold Camp.

"I was just thinking," Gabriel said, "about the leaky roof of that little cabin and how many times Pa and I climbed on that roof to fix the leaks. Do you remember?"

"Yes," Creed replied, "and I remember holding the ladder for you while you finally fixed them."

"That was just a few days after Pa ..." Gabriel's voice fell away.

"I know," Creed said.

"We need to go up to Bold Camp and visit the graves before you go off to Williamsburg."

"Yes, we should," Creed nodded.

For a moment, they both were silent, lost in their thoughts of what their parents meant to them. Gabriel touched his brother's hand. "You know what, Creed, I just made a major decision for my life."

"And what might that be?"

"I'm going to ask Cindy to marry me."

"What if she refuses?"

She won't, "Gabriel said.

The wedding took place in Brother Mack Cantrell's church in August. Judge H. A. W. Skeen gave the bride away, and Gabriel happily accepted her at the altar. John Wright was Gabriel's best man, honoring Caleb Wilkens. Gabriel's grandmother, Ginny, Uncle Eli, and Gabriel's law partner, Julius Webb, were in attendance. Creed sat alongside Ginny, his eyes gleaming with pride in his brother. The church sisters prepared a meal, which was served on a table outside. Just as the meal ended and the wedding party was preparing to leave, a sudden shower moved over the church grounds, and everyone scurried to shelter inside.

As they stood, huddled together, Ginny said, "What a pity it had to rain."

"No, no," Brother Mack's voice rose above the chatter. "Happy is the bride that the rain falls on." He lifted his Bible above his head. "Thus, sayeth the Lord when he speaks of blessed rain. May the union of Gabriel and Cindy be forever nurtured by that blessed rainfall and plentiful sunshine that come only from God."

Gabriel hitched his new horse to the wagon. He, Cindy, and Creed climbed aboard and set out for the little cabin where he was born at the head of Bold Camp. An hour later, Gabriel brought the horse to a halt in front of young Riley Mullins' home, where he and his wife, Dessie, greeted them. After resting for a while on the front porch, Gabriel stood.

"We're just going up to the cabin to visit Pa's grave."

"I'll come with you," Riley said. "Better bring a scythe. The weeds have probably took over by now."

They all walked up the hill, past the cabin where Caleb and Creed were born, and which had been inhabited by Ira and Louranza before they were murdered at Pound Gap. "This place holds many fond memories for me," Gabriel said, "and some terrible ones as well. I wish Pa and Ma and Oma weren't buried up there where they will be forgotten one of these days."

"It won't matter," Riley said. "God knows where they are. He'll find them in the end time."

"I suppose it's fitting," Gabriel went on. "Pa loved this place, built onto that cabin with his own hands, and cleared this land. I guess it's fitting that he should be buried here."

The inscriptions on the flat stone markers were barely readable, and weeds had grown over the small mounds of dirt. After clearing the weeds and wiping clean the stones, Gabriel stepped back to view the graves.

"They need fitting markers, and that's my next project after getting Creed settled in school."

"I'll help you get them set up," Riley said. "They was good people, and they all died so young; looks like we never know who killed Caleb and Oma, my pa too."

"Probably not."

Gabriel picked up the scythe and began walking down the trail.

As September approached, Gabriel and Creed made final preparations for their trip to Williamsburg and his first term at school. While Cindy remained at Gabriel's office, he and Creed traveled to Norton and purchased new suits and other garments suitable for an aspiring doctor and a student of such a prestigious college as William and Mary. Creed was no country bumpkin, and Gabriel was determined that he would not be perceived as such on his arrival in Williamsburg.

"It won't take long for your professors to recognize your brilliance, little brother. Gabriel laughed. "But we're going to get you started on the right footing. You are a gentleman, and so you shall dress as a gentleman."

After making their purchases, Gabriel and Creed stopped at the home of John Wright in Gladeville.

John greeted them before they alighted from the wagon. "What brings you this way, Gabe?"

Gabriel motioned with his thumb in Creed's direction. "Getting this boy spruced up for medical school."

"Rightly so," John said. "Get down and stay a spell."

"No, John, we need to get back to my office. I don't like Cindy being alone there. We just wanted to allow Creed to say goodbye before he ventures off."

They spoke for a while longer, and then John said, "You know, they want me to run for sheriff of Wise County. You think I should do it?"

"Do you feel fit?"

"I always do."

"You will make a good one," Creed said.

"And you will make a good doctor, young man."

They said goodbye, and Gabriel turned his horse toward Pound. Just before leaving, he said, "I wish you would give up hunting outlaws, Mr. Wright. I hear tell you've done enough in your day."

"I can't," he replied. "It's in my blood."

Gabriel whistled at the horse, and the wagon began moving down the road. When they reached the office in Pound, they found Brother Mack Cantrell waiting inside.

"What a pleasant surprise," Gabriel said. "Is there something I can help you with, Brother Mack?"

"No," he said, "but I want to help you if I am able."

Gabriel pulled up a chair and sat facing the preacher. "I am always grateful for your advice."

"I don't have any advice for you today, but I do have something very important to tell you,"

"Yes, Sir?" Gabriel leaned forward.

"I've come to tell you I know who killed your father."

"How do you know?"

Gabriel stood as Brother Mack pulled a yellowed envelope from his inside coat pocket. He opened it and took out a folded sheet of paper. "Do you remember the letter Talt Hall gave me the day before he was hanged?"

"Yes," Gabriel said. "And I have thought of it often, wondering what it might say."

"The year has passed, and I waited all that time to open it as Talt requested." The preacher handed the unfolded letter to Gabriel. He accepted it and sat down as he began to read:

September 1, 1894

   the ones I leave behind:

I am leaving this world absolved of my many sins against mankind, except for them I speak of now.

I killed many men, maybe as many as twenty, and I confessed to my maker. I never feared any man in my lifetime, but as I come face to face with God tomorrow, my body hanging from the gallows, I will fear hell and damnation if I don't confess to my most awful crimes.

I kilt two good men without any cause, cept greed and jealousy. Almost ten years ago, I shot Mr. Riley Mullins on his back porch for a few hundred dollars. He was a good man and a generous man. Then I shot Caleb Wilkins' sweet wife on accident when I was shooting at him. And a year later, I kilt Caleb Wilkens in his own backyard cause he was favored by Riley Mullins when we worked his place. Caleb never done me no harm, but I kilt him out of revenge. I am shamed and condemned for these crimes and I regret the hurt I brought on the loved ones touched by them.

I am not asking for forgiveness by man, but I am asking that God Almighty forgive me for these and my many other sins.
   In the name of Jesus, I pray.
   Thomas Talton Hall

"May he burn in hell," Gabriel said. "Almost on his deathbed, he lied to us. Before God, he lied."

Tears filled his eyes. Cindy came to him and pressed his head to her side. "I know it hurts," she said," but it is good that you know. You don't have to wonder any longer."

Brother Mack spoke. "He may burn in hell, but not if he was truly repentant, and I believe he was. For your peace of mind, Gabriel, you must forgive him."

"Not now," Gabriel said, "and maybe never. He took my father and Oma, the woman to whom I owe everything."

The brothers spoke little on their trip across Indian Creek Mountain that warm September morning. They were lost in their thoughts as their wagon approached the train depot in Norton. The train was already at the station with a scheduled departure of 11:15 a.m. After purchasing a ticket, Gabriel and Creed sat on a bench waiting for the train to commence loading.

"Knowing that you will come back to Pound as a doctor makes me proud of you, Creed."

"I'll do my best to earn your faith in me, Gabriel. I could never have accomplished much without your support." Creed touched his brother's arm. "I'll always be grateful."

"You're my brother, Creed. I couldn't have done anything less."

As the loading platform grew crowded, conversation between the brothers ceased for a few moments. Then a thought occurred to Gabriel. He said to Creed, "We both owe so much to Oma and to Pa. They never had our opportunities, but they enabled us to have lives better than their own. We should never forget that."

Creed nodded. "I won't."

Gabriel continued. "I need to write to Dency and Joe Martin. They were so good to me, and Dency had the kind of faith in me that I have in you. I haven't told them about my marriage. Maybe Cindy and I will pay them a visit soon."

"You should," Creed said.

The conductor called, "Now boarding for Bristol and points beyond."

Creed and Gabriel each picked up a bag and walked toward the conductor.

"I love you, brother," Gabriel said. He reached into his pocket and removed a small pouch tied with a drawstring. He took Creed's hand and turned it upright. A puzzled look on the younger boy's face was replaced with a smile as Gabriel emptied six marbles onto Creed's open hand.

"Remember what I told you about these marbles right after Pa was killed?"

"Yes," Creed said. "And I will treasure them."

"Think of the hands they have passed through and all that

has happened since that boy died at Antietam. I regret that I never knew his name."

"All aboard," the conductor called out.

Creed picked up his bags and turned to board the train.

"Goodbye, brother," Caleb called to Creed as he disappeared into the passenger car.

After the train left the station, he led his horse to a water trough. He watched the train pull away from the platform and then boarded his wagon. "Get up," he said as he lightly slapped the reins against the horse's rump. It was good to know that Cindy would be waiting for him when he returned to Pound.

EPILOGUE

I was born in a three-room clapboard house on the side of a hill in Bold Camp, Pound, Virginia. My family of seven lived there until I was six, when we moved across Pine Mountain to the small coal town of Dunham, Kentucky, a section of the larger, incorporated town of Jenkins, which was founded in 1912 by the Consolidation Coal Company. Our passage from The Pound to Dunham took us across Pound Gap, within two hundred feet of the site of the bloody massacre of Ira Mullins and his family in 1892, about which I had no knowledge at that time. I did not learn of this terrible event until a few years ago when it was brought to my attention by my daughter, Jennifer. Then, I decided to research available sources to gain a deeper understanding of the people and events that led to that massacre. After learning that Ira Mullins was my third cousin once removed, I decided to pay him homage by creating a story incorporating his murder. *Death Comes O'er These Mountains* is a historical fiction account leading up to his death at the age of thirty-five.

Other historical figures in the story include John Wesley Wright (Devil John Wright/Bad John Wright), Thomas Talton Hall ('Bad Talt Hall), Marshall Benton Taylor (Doc Taylor or The Red Fox), General James Garfield, Riley Mullins, D.B. Hollyfield, and other minor characters.

I have drawn on various sources and historical records to correlate data with the actual and fictional events in this story. I am grateful to the authors of much of the source material used in this story; they are many and varied. I am thankful to Author John Fox Jr., who wrote extensively about the hill people of Southwestern Virginia and Southeastern Kentucky in his books, The *Trail of the Lonesome Pine, The Little Shepherd of Kingdom Come*, and *Blue Grass and Rhododendron*. Other source materials include the following:

-*Devil John Wright of the Cumberlands* by William T. Wright
-Appalachian History.net, *The Killing Rock Massacre of 1892*
-Hillbilly Files, *The Killing Rock Massacre*
-Public Records – *Wise County Hangings*
-*Marshall Benton Taylor* – A newspaper article by L.F. Abingdon
-*The Devil Came Down to Cumberland* by Steve Robinson
- *Killing Rock, The Oft Told Tale* – Kentucky-Tennessee Living
-*The Feudist, Thomas Talton Hall* – Kentucky, Tennessee Living

While I have relied on these and other written and oral lore from descendants of longtime residents of Southwestern Virginia and Southeastern Kentucky, I have not quoted or directly taken materials from these sources. They make for interesting reading, full of controversy and conflicting opinions, which must be sifted through to reach a confident conclusion about the true nature of the events leading to and following the massacre at Pound Gap. These sources offer a rich tapestry of the lives of the people who persevered during an era of hardship and enterprise. I recommend them to you.

Author, Lieutenant Commander Travis E Short, U.S. Navy retired, is a native of southwest Virginia, where he spent the early years of his life. He grew up in the coal mining town of Jenkins, Kentucky, in the heart of the Appalachian coalfields. There, he gained an appreciation for the struggles and hardships of everyday Americans like him and his family. At fifteen, Mr. Short moved to the city of Baltimore, Maryland where his father found work in an aircraft manufacturing plant. Travis worked at a community grocery store as a delivery boy where he encountered people of all levels of education and life experiences. He draws on these experiences and those of his younger years to bring his stories to life. He joined the U.S. Navy at age seventeen and worked his way through the ranks, retiring at age thirty-eight. Travis was trained as a radioman and served in that capacity until receiving a commission from the U.S. Navy Officer Candidate School, Newport Rhode Island. He saw much of the world while serving aboard destroyers, minesweepers, and combat support ships. He has a degree in Engineering Sciences from U.S. Navy Postgraduate School, Monterey, California. Before devoting his energies primarily to writing, Mr. Short held management positions in machinery manufacturing and shipbuilding industries, including Director of Design Engineering, President, Owner, and CEO. He was seventeen when he wrote his first murder mystery—My Gun Cries Justice, a parody of Mike Hammer stories—and later self-published it with updates in 2018 under the penname King Papa. He has five books available on Amazon.com. Travis is the father of four daughters and three sons. He has resided in Washington state, Tennessee, and Mississippi, among others, and now lives in Moss Point, Mississippi.

Find more about the author at his website at travisshort.com.

ALSO BY TRAVIS SHORT

Anna

A touching story from a autobiographical memoir written by Anna Marie Gamble, a tribute to a beautiful life of faith and courage.

Faraday Fox

An engaging story of a red fox traveling across the US, from Georgia to Washington state, meeting forest animals and facing perils along the way.

Killers Can't Hide

The hunt for the former beauty queen's killer rocked Cumbersome County. If they don't catch the former beauty queen's killer, the town is in peril. The suspects are many.

Corner of My Mind

Corners of My Mind is a collection of American short stories about ordinary people in extraordinary situations. The stories span a multitude of genres, providing pathos, humor, twists, and surprise endings.

THANK YOU FOR READING

If you enjoyed *Death Comes O'er The Mountain*, we invite you to leave a review online and share your thoughts and reactions with friends and family.

Publish Authority

www.ingramcontent.com/pod-product-compliance
Lightning Source LLC
Chambersburg PA
CBHW051437050726
47593CB00005B/1816